GOLD FEVER!

"You shore seen my brother Sam when you hit this valley . . . because he was here on this claim. He found this quartz. I was with him when he struck it!" cried Kalispel.

"Man alive! You've gone gold mad. Just you rustle along or Leavitt will run you out of Thunder River," ordered the guard, making a move to swing the rifle around.

"Hold on!" yelled Kalispel.

But Selback did not heed the warning. The rifle barrel continued to swerve. In a flash Kalispel drew and fired. The guard's head sank and, stumbling, he fell forward over his clattering rifle.

THUNDER MOUNTAIN
was originally published by
Harper & Row, Publishers, Inc.

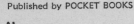

ZANE GREY

Thunder Mountain

PUBLISHED BY POCKET BOOKS NEW YORK

THUNDER MOUNTAIN

Harper & Row edition published 1935

POCKET BOOK edition published January, 1972
4th printing......................March, 1975

Standard Book Number: 671-77985-0.
This POCKET BOOK edition is published by arrangement with
Harper & Row, Publishers, Inc. Copyright, 1932, 1935, by Zane Grey,
Inc. Copyrights renewed, ©, 1960, 1963, by Romer Zane Grey,
Elizabeth Grey Grosso, Loren Zane Grey. All rights reserved. This
book, or portions thereof, may not be reproduced by any means
without permission of the original publisher: Harper & Row, Pub-
lishers, Inc., 10 East 53rd Street, New York, N.Y. 10022.
Front cover illustration by Robert Schulz.

Printed in the U.S.A.

Chapter One

A warm spring rain melted the deep snows in the Saw Tooth Range, and a flood poured down the headwaters of the Salmon River.

It washed out a colony of beavers, one of which, a crippled old female with a cub, fell behind the others and lost them. She came at length into a narrow valley where the stream meandered along a wide rocky bench wooded by stately isolated pines and fringes of willow and aspen.

The old mother beaver lingered with her cub near the mouth of an intersecting brook. In a sheltered bend under the looming mountain slope she began her labors. While the little cub played and splashed about she toiled industriously, cutting branches, carrying sticks, dragging rocks, and padding mud until she had bridged the brook and built a dam. A still pool rose behind the barrier.

One night when the afterglow of sunset loomed dull red upon the pool and the silence of the wilderness lay like a mantle upon the valley, the old beaver noticed a strange quivering ripple passing across the placid surface of her pool. There was no current coming from the brook, there was no breath of wind to disturb the dead calm. She noticed the tremors pass across the pool, she sniffed the pine-scented air, she listened with all the sensitiveness of a creature of the wild.

From high up on the looming mountain slope, from the somber purple shadow, came down a low rumble, a thunder that seemed to growl from the bowels of the great mountain.

The old mother beaver did not wait to hear that again. With her cub she abandoned the quivering pool, and taking to the main stream she left the valley.

The last remnant of the Sheepeater Indians pitched camp on the rocky bench across the stream from the abandoned beaver dam.

Outcasts from various tribes, they were fugitives and had banded together for protection, fifty-one in all, warriors, squaws, and children, under the command of Tomanmo.

While the braves put up their lodges, the weary squaws

1

unpacked meager supplies and belongings. The lame children, exhausted from continuous march, sat silent with somber eyes.

Tomanmo gazed up and down this valley to which he had been led by the Nez Percé member of his band. Long and hard had been the tramp hither, and the last miles over solid rock. The soldiers could not track them here. It was a refuge. Deer and elk as tame as cattle grazed under the pines; white goats shone on the high bluffs of the south wall; mountain sheep stood silhouetted against the sky, watching the invaders of their solitude.

"We will hide here and rest. It is well," said Tomanmo to his band, and he sent hunters out to kill fresh meat.

When the chief sat down he found himself facing the north slope of the valley. It struck him singularly, and he gazed with the falcon eyes of one used to the heights. Bare and steep, this slope, open to the south, slanted abruptly from the edge of the rocky bench some few hundred yards distant. What first attracted Tomanmo's curiosity was the fact that no game trail, not even a single track, marred the smooth surface of the incline. It sheered up a long way before its purple continuity was broken by a thin line of fir trees, pointing skyward like tufted spears. From there the color gray and the smooth surface broke to scantily timbered ledges that stepped up and up prodigiously, at last to turn white with snow on the skyline. Precipitous looming mountains were the rule in that range, and all the south slopes, where the snow did not long lie, were bare of timber. But the endless south slope of this mountain showed no solid foundation of rock, no iron ribs of red granite, no bulge of cliff sheering up out of soft earth. Tomanmo shook his lean dark head.

Presently the Nez Percé approached the chief to open a skinny fist to his gaze. He held a handful of wet gravel and sand among which glinted bright specks.

"Ughh!" he ejaculated. "Gold!"

"Bad. White man come," grunted the chief.

"Some day, long after Sheepeaters gone," assented the Nez Percé.

The solemn still day wore on. The pointed lodges of elk hide and the brush shelters, the columns of blue smoke rising upward, the active raven-haired squaws with their colored raiment flashing in the sun, the hunters dragging carcasses over the stones, the ragged hollow-cheeked children asleep on the ground—all attested to a settlement of perma-

2

nent camp. Soon pots were steaming, fragrant viands broiled over the red coals, cakes of bread baked on the hot flat stones.

At sunset the band feasted. Only Tomanmo did not share the sense of well-being after long hardship. While he ate he watched the changing colors on the steep slope, the darkening purple at the base, the merging of gray into the gold-flushed snow, high on the peaks.

Dusk fell, and then silent night, with the dark velvet sky studded by cold stars. The fires burned low, gleaming red over the haggard visages of the sleepers. But Tomanmo did not sleep. He stalked to and fro, listening as a chieftain who expected the voices of his gods. A low roar of running water permeated the silence and a sharp bay of a wolf, far up the valley, accentuated it.

Tomanmo's ears, attuned as those of the deer to the whisperings and rustlings of the wild, registered other sounds. He sought out the sleeping Nez Percé and roused him with a moccasined foot.

"Ughh!" exclaimed the brave, sitting up.

"Come," said the chief, and led him away from the circle of dying fires and sleeping savages. "Listen."

Across the bench, away from the murmur of stream and song of pine, close under the black looming slope, Tomanmo bade his scout bend keen ears to the silence.

For long there was nothing. The valley seemed dead. The mountains slept. The stars watched. Wild life lay in its coverts. Then there came a ticking of tiny pebbles down the slope, a faint silken rustle of sliding dust, a strange breath of something indefinable, silence, and then again far off, a faint crack of rolling rocks, a moan, as a subterranean monster trying to breathe in the bowels of the earth, and at last, deep and far away, a rumble as of distant thunder.

"Hear?" queried the chief, with slow gesture toward the looming bulk.

The Nez Percé's somber eyes, mirroring the stars, dilated in answer. Tomanmo was assured that his own sensitive ears had not deceived him.

"It is the voice of the Great Spirit," he said, solemnly. "Tomanmo is warned. This mountain moves. . . . When the sun shines we go."

Years later, long after Tomanmo had gone to join his forefathers, three adventuring prospectors, brothers named Emerson, toiled down into the valley from the south, and late in the day unpacked their weary burros and made camp.

"Reckon it's the place, all right," said Sam, the eldest. "Thet old Nez Percé gave me a clear hunch."

"Wal, I shore hope it ain't," replied Jake, the second brother, with a short grim laugh.

"Why?"

"Hell, man! Look around!"

Sam had been doing that avidly. The long valley, shut in by the rough red and green wall on the south, and the insurmountable and prodigious slope of talus on the north, evidently had taken his eye. But Sam was thinking of the isolation, the possibility of finding and working a gold claim without sharing it with other prospectors or being harassed by robbers. The dark caverned and notched wall on the east side, where the stream cut its way in cascades down to the valley, had a fascinating look to Sam Emerson. Those cliffs would hide gold-bearing ledges of quartz.

"Jake, I didn't befriend that poor old Injun for nothin'," replied Sam, with satisfaction. "This is the valley."

"Wal, Sam, we never seen things alike, even as kids," rejoined Jake, resignedly. "To me this is shore a hell of a hole. Gettin' out will be worse than gettin' in, an' that was a tough job."

"I'll grade out a trail," said his brother, cheerfully, "if that's all you're rarin' about."

"It ain't all. It ain't even a little," retorted Jake, nettled by the other's imperturbability. "This is a gloomy hole. The sun comes late an' leaves early. It'd be hotter'n hell in summer an' colder'n Greenland in winter. It's too far to pack in supplies. It's too lonely. Shore I know you an' our gun-packin' cowboy brother here like loneliness. But I like people. I like a barroom an' to set in a little game now an' then."

"Jake, thet last objection of yourn may soon remedy itself. You may see this valley hustlin' with miners, an' a gold-diggin's town springin' up overnight like a mushroom."

"Wal, it won't last long, I'll gamble. Look at thet slope. Five thousand feet of silt an' gravel on end, fresh as if some one was diggin' above an' slidin' everythin' down. No grass, no brush, no trees! Nary a damn rock! It's alive, Sam, thet slope is, an' some wet day it'll slide down an' obliterate this valley."

Sam was impressed, and gazed up at the sinister slope.

He had to tip his head far back to see the snow-patched summit.

"Queer-lookin', at thet," he said. "But I reckon it's been there just as long as these other mountains."

Jake turned to the youngest brother, Lee, who stood leaning on his rifle, looking about with piercing hazel eyes. He was a stalwart young man with the lithe build of a rider.

"Wal, Kalispel," drawled Jake, "you ain't often stumped for speech. Are you linin' up with Sam in favor of this ghastly hole?"

"It's great, Jake."

"Ah-huh. . . . Wal, just why? I reckoned you'd stand by me, consider'n' your weakness for horses, girls, an' such thet can't be had here."

"I like it, Sam. You know I don't care a heap about diggin' gold. Too darn hard work for a cowboy! But I love the wildness an' beauty of this valley. It's a paradise for game. I'll bet I saw a thousand head of elk today. An' deer, bear, goat, sheep—even cougars, in broad daylight! I'll hunt game while you fellows hunt gold."

"Humph! . . . Sam, what you think of Kal's shiftin' to your side?"

"All proves I was right draggin' Lee off thet bloody Montana range," replied the eldest brother, forcefully. "I feel relieved 'cause he won't be lookin' for thet hard-lipped sheriff an', for all we know, some more of them ridin' gents. . . . Rustle some firewood an' water now while I unpack."

Lee Emerson, nicknamed Kalispel by the first outfit he had ever ridden for in Montana, laughed at his loquacious brothers, and laying aside his rifle for a bucket, he made for the stream. It was a goodly body of water, dark green in color, still high and somewhat roily from melting snow. In places it was running swiftly, in others tarrying in pools formed by huge boulders. Kalispel espied a big leather-back salmon rising to break on the surface, and that sight considerably enhanced the charm of this valley which had already intrigued him. There were sure to be mountain trout, also, in this stream. Stepping out on a sand-bar, he dipped the pail and filled it with water as cold as ice. As an afterthought then, Kalispel scooped up a handful of wet sand. He saw grains of gold glistening in it.

"By thunder!" he ejaculated. "As easy as that! . . . Sam will be wild. I'll let him discover it. . . . I wonder. Minin' might beat runnin' cattle. Reckon I was sick of the range."

5

Thoughtfully he returned to camp. There seemed to be a vague portent in connection with their arrival in this wild valley. Jake came staggering in under an enormous load of dead wood. Sam had spread supplies out on a tarpaulin and was awaiting the water to mix dough.

"About a week's rations, not counting meat," he said. "If we make a strike here two of us will have to go to Salmon an' pack in grub."

"Ah-huh. An' if we don't strike it we'll starve," rejoined Jake, humorously.

Sam had no answer for that and silence fell upon the trio. Kalispel performed what camp tasks offered, and lastly unrolled his canvas and blanket in the lee of a fallen pine. Next he found a bit of soap in his bag and a towel that resembled a coal-sack. Repairing to the stream, he enjoyed a wash in the icy water. After that he sat down to wait for supper.

The valley changed every hour. Shadows were dusking the far corners. He saw a black bear amble along the lower reaches of the stream, where it turned into the dark canyon. A troop of deer had come down off the south slope. Eagles soared above the sunlit crags. The upper third of the north slope blazed with gold and the snowy summit had a rosy flush. The place had a fascination for Kalispel that he could not define in a moment. The longer he gazed the more he appreciated things not strikingly noticeable at first. On all sides the formidable walls frowned down. White and black tips of mountains peeped above the ramparts. Purple veils deepened in the notch where the valley turned to the east. He had thought at first glance that the valley headed at the eastern end, but he decided that the stream split there, one fork leaping down off the ledges, and the other turning with the narrow valley into a defile. It was a big country, just what his gaze encompassed, and incredibly rough on the heights. The gold faded up off the north slope and the whole atmosphere changed as if by magic. The steely grays and blacks stole upward out of the valley, as if now free of their arch enemy. And night was at hand.

Kalispel thought that he would find enough loneliness there even for him. Not often did he yield to the memory of the past. But he did so now. No doubt his brothers Sam and Jake had found him in the nick of time; otherwise that wild Montana range where he had gone the pace of hard cowboys would have soon seen his end. Still, he could excuse it all to himself. His serious blunders, his shooting-scrapes, his

6

deflections which, if continued, would have made him an outlaw, he could trace to circumstances for which he was not to blame. What Kalispel had longed for was a little ranch, with cattle and horses of his own, a wife to keep him straight, and a chance to realize the promise he knew he possessed. But he never could save a dollar; his several attempts to gather a herd of cattle had led to questions he could only answer with a gun; and nothing but trouble had ever come of the girls who had attracted him.

His brooding reflection was interrupted by a low rumble of thunder.

"Say! So early in spring?" he muttered, looking up in surprise. The sky was clear and cold, already showing tiny pale stars. "That was an avalanche somewheres. Strikes me these Saw Tooths might cut loose a lot that way."

He returned to camp and the blazing fire. Jake was lighting his pipe with a red ember. Sam bent his ruddy bearded face over some task.

"Did you fellows hear thunder?" asked Kalispel.

"Shore did," replied Jake. "Sam says it wasn't thunder."

"Slide somewhere, then?"

"Son, thet wasn't thunder or slide," answered Sam, looking up. "My Nez Percé friend told me we'd know the place when we came to a valley under a high white mountain-face thet talked. I reckon we've found it."

"How do you account for that rumble?" queried Kalispel, puzzled.

"Damn if I know yet. Must be earthquake."

"Nix," said Jake. "Thet was just a slide rumblin' down somewheres. These hills must be full of high bare slopes like this one. It gives me the creeps. Don't you remember some of the steep Lemhi slopes? An' thet knife canyon over on Trail Creek?"

"Wal, what's the odds one way or another—if there's gold here."

"Suits me. The spookier the better," returned Kalispel, and sought his bed.

He listened for a while, but the rumbling sound was not repeated. Then he fell asleep. When he awakened it was broad daylight with rosy flush upon the peaks. His brothers were bustling about camp. The ringing bugle of an elk brought Kalispel to a sitting posture, wide awake and thrilling.

"Kal, go out an' bust thet bull," said Jake. "The valley's alive with game. Seems different by day."

7

"Son, take a peep in thet pan," called Sam, sonorously.

Kalispel got up and pulled on his boots, then stretched his tall frame. Sam, impatient at his nonchalance, thrust the pan under his nose. Kalispel saw a thin layer of sand and gold, about half and half.

"Dog-gone! Looks like a strike," rejoined Kalispel, lazily.

"Nothin' to rave about," replied Sam, setting the pan down. "But if we can find the lode thet came from, we're rich. You'll have the ranch your heart desires, an' a thousand hosses, an' ten thousand cattle before the year is out."

"Rich!" ejaculated Kalispel, incredulously.

"We'll sell out for a million. An' damn me, I've a hunch we've struck it this time. But even if we can't find the lode there are good diggin's all up and down this bench, one way or another!"

"Sam, are you talkin' sense?"

"Kal, he's been up since daybreak, roarin' around," interposed Jake.

"If it doesn't turn out my luck to have other prospectors driftin' in here," muttered Sam, somberly. "Thet has happened before."

"What difference would it make, Sam, if we located first?" asked Kalispel.

"Wal, a lot. If we can't find the lode we can clean up a fortune off this bench—giving us time."

"Ah-huh. Sam, do you trust thet Nez Percé?" added Jake, scratching his stubbly chin.

"You bet. He'll not tell. An' let's not borrow trouble. We ought to be singin'. Come on an' eat. After thet we'll set to work. We'll move our camp out of these rocks. There's a likely sheltered spot across the stream. Kal, you fetch in some meat an' hang it up in the shade. Then you might scout around a bit. Have a look at the outlet of this valley. Jake, you stick your pan in every sand an' gravel bar along this stream. I'll take a pick an' look for the lode."

Kalispel found it impossible not to respond to Sam's forceful optimism. Sam had always been a born prospector. Always seeing the pot of gold at the foot of the rainbow! And he had always been poor. He had never made a real strike. On more than one occasion he had almost had fortune in his grasp. This time would probably end like all the others. Yet Kalispel felt himself profoundly stirred by his eldest brother's inevitableness. Kalispel did not have the gold fever in his blood. He was not given to false hopes. As a cowboy he had been the poorest gambler on the whole Montana range. But he responded to the thrill, the dream of what impetus it would give life actually to find gold.

When camp had been moved to a pretty sheltered spot, Kalispel took his rifle and made off for the widest part of the valley. At the moment he did not see any game. The spring morning was fresh, clear, cold. A film of ice gleamed on still pools; red buds showed on the willows. He remarked the absence of small game and birds. The first living creatures he espied were Sam's burros. Next he located a herd of elk fairly high on the south slope. He kept on, however, up the stream, making for the widest part of the valley. It proved to be a high bench, well wooded, and merging on a steep mountain slope where the black timber came down thickly to the level. He caught a glimpse of moving gray objects. Presently a small group of deer, does and fawns, trooped out of the brush to stand at gaze, long ears erect. As he approached them they bounded away as if on springs. Soon after that he sighted a buck, which he shot. It was too heavy to pack into camp, so he dressed it on the spot, and carried it in quarters.

While passing to and fro over the bench, taking a straight cut to camp, he spied numerous deer. The ground was cut up by tracks of hoofed game. He saw beds in the grass, and the bones of two cougar kills, one old and the other comparatively fresh. Cougar tracks showed in every patch of soft ground. Game trails led down off the south slope to the water, but he did not note that they crossed the stream. The problem of meat, which constituted the main food supply for hunters and prospectors in the mountains, appeared to be solved for an indefinite period.

This hunting job attended to, Kalispel washed his bloody hands, remarking again the icy shock of the water, and then strolled down the valley. The sun shone overhead now and lent brilliance to the many colors of slope and cliff. On one side the valley was stark and naked, on the other fringed and patched with forest, green ledges, and gray crags.

He proceeded far down around the bend to where the valley boxed in a red-walled canyon. This he could have entered, and perhaps followed for some distance, had he chosen to wade. But he did not like the idea of immersing to his neck in the melted snow water. Retracing his steps, he halted in a sunny spot with fragrant sage all around, and there he flung himself at length, as had been his wont so often on the cattle range. He liked the intimacy of the great walls. The monotonous purple reaches of the Montana ranges had palled upon him.

"Dog-gone!" soliloquized Kalispel. "I'd like to settle in this country. That cottonwood flat over on the Salmon River shore took my eye."

And he gave himself over to a daydream, fostered by Sam's ineradicable hope of the good fortune about to be.

Kalispel marked that spot. Somehow it had induced lingering hours of happy reverie, to which he had long been stranger. The place was down around the bend from the valley, where a bench of sage nestled under a great wall. The melodious murmur of the stream came up; the warm sun beat down, reflected from the cliff; a still, sweet, drowsy languor pervaded the place; the sweetness of sage was almost intoxicating; the solitude was omnipresent; and across the canyon sheered up a tremendous broken slope as many-sided as that mountain could boast. Long glistening slants of talus, rugged narrow defiles winding up, grassy benches fringed with firs, huge sections of splintered cliff hanging precariously, and patches of black lodge-pole pines stepped up endlessly to the blue sky. This wonderful mountain-side would have been fascinating to Kalispel without a sign of life. But the reward of searching, patient exercise of keen vision made hours there seem like moments. At first the vast slope had appeared bare of life; before the westering sun had turned Kalispel campward he had espied elk, bear, sheep, deer, cougar. And to see cougar in the sunlight was rare indeed.

He found camp deserted. Evidently neither Sam nor Jake had been in since morning. That augured well for this first day. Kalispel set to work at camp tasks, pausing once to laugh when he heard himself whistling. He put things in shipshape, halting only for the mixing of biscuit dough, at which he was a signal failure. But he liked to swing an ax, which art he had mastered during his boyhood along the hardwood creek bottoms of Missouri.

Meanwhile the colored lights of the valley had succumbed to waning afternoon. Kalispel began to grow anxious about his brothers. Presently Jake appeared some distance up the stream. He looked a tired man. Kalispel hallooed and waved. Jake made a weary response. Upon nearer view Jake was a sight to behold. He was the dirtiest, muddiest, wettest, raggedest object of a man Kalispel had ever seen. He carried under his arm his gold pan, and in his left hand something small and heavy wrapped in a bandana handkerchief.

"Dog-gone-it, Jake!" ejaculated Kalispel, undecided whether to laugh or whoop. Then as Jake staggered into camp, Kalispel met a wonderful look in his eyes.

"Boy, look ahere," panted Jake, and he forced the bandana into Kalispel's hands.

The contents were soft, wet, heavy, significant to the touch. Kalispel knew what it contained without being told, and suddenly he was mute. Jake fell on his knees beside his pack and began to fumble around in it.

"Whar's my weighin'-scales? . . . My Gawd!— gotta have them! . . . Ah-ha! . . . Kal, cluster around now an' pour out the gold."

Kalispel did as he was bidden, and as the tiny golden stream of grains and nuggets thudded into the scales he became aware of trembling hands and knocking heart. Three times the scales had to be emptied before all the gold could be weighed.

"Ten ounces—an' over," boomed Jake, breathing thickly. "At eighteen dollars the ounce. . . . Hundred an' eighty dollars! . . . An' as Sam ordered, I only panned one pan at each bar."

"Heavens!" ejaculated Kalispel, incredulously. He fingered the shiny nuggets, some of which were as large as peas. All were smooth and worn, due, no doubt, to the action of water and gravel. The majority of the gold was like fine sand, and it slipped from Kalispel's palm in a yellow stream. Suddenly he sat down to stare at Jake.

"Boy, we're rich! Rich! . . . Our fortunes are made. Sam hit it plumb center this time. . . . My Gawd! if mother could be alive now! We was always so poor."

"Jake, it—it's hard to—believe," replied Kalispel, choking. "But here it is. Gold! . . . An' you panned all that in a single day?"

"Boy, I could have doubled—trebled thet ten ounces. But Sam wanted me to cover all the bars. So I did. All showed yellow. But some more than others. . . . Several were lousy with gold."

"Gosh! I'm glad for Sam—an' you, Jake. . . . Reckon for myself—a little."

"Lee, you be a hell of a lot glad for yourself," replied Jake, deep-voiced and husky. "Your cattle ranch is in sight."

Suddenly Kalispel leaped up to let out such a cowboy yell as had never pealed from his lungs. "WHOOPEE!" The stentorian sound rang along the walls and beat back in hollow echo. It was answered, too, by a halloo from upstream.

11

"You hear that?" cried Kalispel.

"Shore. Thet was Sam. . . . An' there he comes."

"Gosh! Is he drunk, staggerin' along like that?"

"Boy, Sam's packin' a heavy load."

"Can't be firewood. Too small."

"Nope. . . . It's white. . . . An' shore as you're born—it's a rock."

"Rock! What'd Sam be packin' a rock for? . . . He hadn't got his pick an' crowbar, either. . . . *Jake!*"

"Boy, I reckon I'm a little weak on my pins." Jake sat down heavily.

Kalispel stared, his thoughts whirling. Sam came on sturdily, but manifestly under great physical strain. He plunged into camp to thump his heavy burden upon the ground in front of his brothers.

"Look at—thet!" he panted.

Kalispel saw a thick slab of white quartz, brilliantly veined and belted with gold. It appeared to be the most beautiful inanimate object that he had ever beheld. But he could not speak, and Jake strangled over incoherent words.

Sam wiped the sweat from his face which betrayed traces of feeling. He now appeared calm, though his eyes held a singular effulgence.

"I went straight—to the lode—like steel to a magnet," he said, in cool, slowly expelled words. "Thar's five hundred dollars—in thet chunk. . . . An' a million more—where it come from!"

Chapter Two

Excitement prevailed in the Emerson camp. Sam succumbed to some extent to the uncontained joy of his brothers. Jake declared it was a good thing that there was not any whisky in the packs. They fell over each other preparing supper and partaking of it. Jake could not decide what he wanted to do with his share. Lee had his ranch picked out, his herds, his horses, and he decided that a rich young cattleman, not bad-looking, might possibly find a wife.

Faint thunder came rumbling from the darkness.

"Ah-huh! Thar's the old-man mountain grumblin' thet we ain't got the gold yet," exclaimed Sam.

A menace seemed momentarily to hold the three in thrall. It passed, and with it the hilarity, the boyish indulgence in wild prospect.

"Listen, boys," spoke up Sam, seriously. "We've struck gold. Maybe I need to tell you thet the majority of prospectors who strike it rich never reap the profits of their discovery."

"Why'n hell not?" roared Jake, aghast, his rugged visage red in the firelight.

"It's just a fact, thet's all. Prospectors ain't business men. They're usually ignorant, heedless, improvident. They lose out somehow."

"We ain't gonna lose nothin'," declared Jake, belligerently, he who had formerly been the most pessimistic. The gold fever had inflamed his brain. Kalispel looked on silently, conscious of a sinking sensation within his breast.

"If we can sell out for a hundred thousand dollars we'd be wise to do it," said Sam, ponderingly.

"Hell no!" yelled Jake, and entreated Kalispel to side with him.

"A hundred thousand seems a lot of money, but—" muttered Kalispel, struggling with his feelings.

"Right here we form a company," went on Sam, emphatically. "Thet is, a company to work this quartz vein. Thet'll leave us free to take up placer-minin' claims on the bench. We want to pick out the three richest claims before the stampede."

"Stampede?" echoed Jake.

"Shore. They'll be a mad rush to this valley the day thet chunk of quartz is shown in Challis, Boise, or Salmon."

"I might have figgered thet," admitted Jake.

"Sam, why need anyone learn about the quartz vein?" queried Lee.

"It'll take a ten-ton stamp mill to work this mine."

"Ten-ton!" ejaculated Kalispel. "How on earth could such a mill be gotten here?"

"Packed in on mules. It can be done. It must be done. . . . An' now you see why we must sell out, or sell a half interest, at least. We have no money."

"Why not keep the quartz mine secret, while we work all this placer mine for ourselves?" asked Kalispel. "Then afterward sell out or finance the job ourselves?"

"Thet's a big idee," agreed Jake.

"It may be a good idee, but it's not good business. We want action. We'd risk everythin' to keep this quartz mine

13

a secret. Because sooner or later, while we are workin' the placers, other miners will drift in. The Bitter Root range an' the Lemhi are full of them."

"Well, let them drift," declared Kalispel. "We can take care of ourselves an' hang on to our holdin's. All the time we'll be diggin' gold while keepin' our best secret. Then, when we are forced to show our hand, all right. An' the situation will be precisely the same as it is now."

Jake agreed with Kalispel, and they argued with Sam. But he was obdurate, and at length out of deference to his superior experience and judgment they let him have his way. Whereupon they fell to discussing the other aspects of the case. Sam finally worked out a plan. He would stay in the valley, guarding the quartz mine, while working the placers along the stream. Jake and Kalispel were to trace the best trail possible out of the mountains and then make their way to Boise, where they would exhibit their quartz finding to prominent mining-men, and consider no less than a hundred thousand dollars for a half interest, the contracting parties to furnish the mill, have it packed in, and work the mine. If a good deal could not be consummated at Boise, they were to proceed to Challis and Salmon. Sam said he could stretch food supplies for a month and it would be necessary for one of the brothers, at least, to pack in before the expiration of that time. They settled all before going to bed at a late hour.

Kalispel could not sleep at once. His mind was full. It seemed that the unlucky star under which he had always ridden had marvelously brightened. And while he lay there the old mountain rumbled its faint deep thunder of warning.

On the following morning Kalispel and Jake, driving three lightly packed burros, headed up the valley on their important mission. Sam accompanied them as far as his quartz vein, which was located in an outcropping ledge of rock at the edge of the bench where it merged into the mountain. Jake, who did not like this separation, strode gloomily along without looking back. Kalispel, however, at a curve of the stream, turned to wave good-by. But Sam had already forgotten them. His red-shirted frame bent over his precious gold-bearing ledge.

Jake had been given the task of lining a trail that could be used later by a heavily-packed train of mules. Wherefore he kept to the watercourse. They found that the narrow valley did not box at all, but wound to the south, grading to a rough pass between forest-patched mountain summits. They headed the stream, and by noonday had worked to the divide from which an elk trail descended under beetling cliffs. It led to a wide valley through which ran the Middle Fork branch of the Salmon river. It was a wide, swift, shallow stream. They crossed with difficulty, finding the icy water and slippery rocks hard to contend with. They camped on the opposite bank, where a roaring fire, dry clothes, and hot food dispelled the discouragement that had attended the inception of this doubtful journey.

Next day they zigzagged up a vast mountain slope, covered with thick white grass, and picturesque for its numerous patches of black fir. Elk and deer scarcely took the trouble to move out of their path. Once on the summit of this range Jake encountered obstacles to the much-desired, easily-graded trail to the southwest. He made a false start and was compelled to return and more carefully study the baffling maze of sharp peaks and dark canyons. In the end he led around a mountain, from the higher shoulder of which, before sunset of that day, he pointed out to his brother the valley of the main Salmon, the town of Challis, the Lemhi mountains and to the south rolling, gray country that opened into the purple range.

It took three days to grade out a trail down to Challis. The brothers camped on the outskirts of the little town. After supper Jake made inquiries, and to his dismay ascertained that a stage for Boise did not leave until Saturday, and that the supplies needed must be brought from Salmon, sixty miles down the river.

Jake was a thoughtful man that night round the camp fire. Finally he unburdened himself.

"Lee, I didn't like leavin' Sam alone in thet hole. An' we can't go on to Boise, make this minin' deal, an' come back to Sam inside of a month. So here's what we'll do. I'll go on to Boise alone. . . . Don't worry. I won't lose the quartz an' I'll be shore nobody gets a hunch about it. Reckon I'll not need more'n a few dollars till I make the deal. So you can have this money. You go to Salmon an' buy three more burros, an' all the supplies you can pack on them, an' rustle back to Sam. . . . What you think of my idee?"

"It's a damn good one," replied Lee. "By the time I get to Salmon a week will be gone. It'll take a couple of days to outfit there. An' with six burros all loaded down, an' allowin' for the steep grades an' rough ground on that trail

15

ve worked out on—why Jake, even with good luck I couldn't make it back to Sam in two weeks."

"You shore couldn't. Say a month. An' then you'll beat any cowpunchin' job you ever had. . . . Wal, it's settled, an' I'm relieved."

Late afternoon of the second day, on the way down the river, Kalispel came to where the Salmon made a wide, slow bend. The several hundred acres of land inclosed by the stream in that circling constituted the ranch he had seen from a mountain-top on the way in. From that far point he had made out several groves of cottonwoods, the wide, flat, brown and green fields, the fringe of trees bordering the river, the sheltered log cabin under the lea of the hill. But at close range this ranch appeared the finest prospect he had ever encountered. The soil was fertile. He crossed several brooks on his way toward the log cabin. On each side of the river sloped up endless acreage of grazing-land. Kalispel thrilled with his resolve to own that ranch.

A settler named Olsen lived there with his small family. Lee had supper with him and talked casually.

"Been prospectin'," he explained. "Don't care for it much. But I like ranchin'. Could you use a good cowman?"

"Huh! Got more work than I can do. Couldn't pay wages, though. Fact is I'd like to sell out."

"That's interestin'. What'd you take?"

"I'd hate to have some real money shoved at me," replied the settler, tersely.

"So?—well, if I strike pay dirt I'll come back an' shove some at you."

Next day, late, Kalispel trudged footsore and weary into Salmon. He had been there several times and he liked the place. It had been a mining-town for years and had seen more than one gold boom. Even in dull times Salmon was a bustling center, being a distributing point between towns over the Montana line and those west into Idaho as far as Boise. Salmon resembled other Western mining-towns in its one long, wide, main street, but off this thoroughfare it reminded Lee of some of the hamlets back in Missouri.

He found pasture for his burros, and made a deal to secure three more, including pack-saddles. Then he repaired to the main street and a lodging-house he knew. When former acquaintances failed to recognize him, Kalispel decided that he must be a pretty dirty, bearded, ragged, hard-looking customer. The best he could do that night was to wash and shave, which helped mightily; but he seriously appreciated the fact that he must make a most advantageous deal in buying the supplies so that he would have money enough left for a new outfit. His boots had no soles and his trousers hung in tatters. He recalled a girl whose acquaintance he had made on a former sojourn in Salmon—what was her name?—and he could not present himself to her in this scarecrow garb.

Kalispel put on his coat, then had to remove it because he had slipped one arm through a rent instead of the sleeve. This was another rueful reminder of his poverty. He did not care about his appearance or even comfort while out on the range or in the wilds, but here in town among people he did not like his poverty. He blew out the lamp and left his room.

In the yellow flare of a hall lamp he saw two figures at the head of the stairway—a young woman standing with her back toward him, facing a man who had started down the steps and was looking back.

"Dad, please don't leave me alone. I—" she was entreating, in a voice that would have arrested Kalispel even if her small, dark, graceful head had not.

"You'll be all right, Sydney," replied the man, with a laugh. "You're out West now and must look after yourself. I want to talk to some miners. Go to bed."

He stamped on down the rickety stairway. The girl partly turned as Kalispel passed her and he caught a glimpse of a pale, clean-cut profile, striking enough in that poor light to make him want to turn and stare. But he resisted the desire and went quickly down, wanting to get another look at the father of that girl. He caught an odor of rum. There was a barroom connected with this lodging-house, but there was no doorway opening into it from the hall. Kalispel followed the man outside, where at the street corner under the yellow lights he met several men in rough garb, evidently waiting for him.

Kalispel approached them. "Howdy men," he said, genially. "I'm a stranger hereabouts. Where can I eat?"

"Reckon I've seen you before," replied one, a keen-eyed, hard-visaged Westerner who apparently missed nothing in Kalispel's make-up, especially not the gun hanging low.

"Yeah? All the same I'm a stranger an' hungry," retorted Lee, as he returned the searching scrutiny.

"Young fellow, there's a good restaurant a few doors below," replied the man Lee wanted a second glance at. He was beyond middle age, a handsome man with lined, weak

17

face and dark eyes full of havoc. His frame was not robust and his garb betokened the tenderfoot.

"Thanks. Would you have a bite with me?" returned Kalispel.

"I had mine early."

"Say, cowpuncher, mozy along, will you?" broke in another of the trio of Westerners. He had a lean sallow face, a long drooping mustache, and eyes that burned in the shadow of his sombrero.

That was sufficient to ignite the spark always smoldering in Lee's spirit.

"Why shore I'll mozy along—when I get ready," he replied, curtly.

"Ain't you thet Kalispel cowboy late of Montana?" queried the man who had first spoken, as with a slight gesture he silenced his lean-jawed companion.

"Yeah, I happen to be that cowboy—Kalispel Emerson."

"Wal, no offense meant," rejoined the other, hurriedly. "We jest want to talk business to Mr. Blair hyar. An' time's pressin'."

Kalispel did not trouble to reply. He fixed piercing eyes upon the tenderfoot, who appeared to sense something amiss, but could not gather what. "Excuse me, Mr. Blair, if I give you a hunch, usin' the advice I just heard you give your daughter. You're out West now an' must look after yourself."

With that pointed speech Kalispel wheeled to pass on down the street. "Dog-gone!" he soliloquized. "They'll fleece the socks off that tenderfoot. . . . An' the wolf-jawed hombre —where'd I ever see him? Gambler, I'll bet. . . . Well, it's none of my mix. I've trouble of my own. But that girl— now——"

Kalispel went into the restaurant to go about appeasing his ravenous hunger. He had not had a square meal for so long that he felt like a starved bear. His quick eye surveyed the assembled males, not one of which was a cowman. From long habit Kalispel always looked for that uncertain quantity. He fell to conversing with a miner and soon forgot the Blair incident. Then, in a few moments, he was attending to savory food set before him.

Then Kalispel, cheerful and responsive to exciting surroundings, strode out to see the town. How many nights had he ridden in off the range to make up for the monotony of a rider's life! But a voice cautioned him to remember the importance of his mission. No bucking the tiger—not a single drop of red liquor! This somewhat subdued his exuberance. Still, he would have a look, anyhow, and to that end he made the rounds of the saloons, the gambling-dens and dance-halls, winding up at the Spread Eagle, a composite resort at the edge of town on the bank of the river. This place was in full blast, and as Kalispel went into the big barnlike, gaudily-decorated dance-hall, full of smoke and the merry roar of music and dancers, he experienced a thought that had come to him many a time before—it would be well for him to have an anchor. He liked this sort of fling, which he argued would be all right, if it were not for the drink and fights and worse that seemed to attend a lonesome cowboy's infrequent visits to town.

Presently, at the end of a dance, he saw a girl detach herself from a burly dancer, to make her way in his direction. Kalispel had observed that, besides himself, there was not a young fellow in the hall. And this girl was hardly more than sixteen. She was little in stature, pretty in a birdlike way, with golden hair, and certainly was most inadequately clothed for such a cool night. She accosted Kalispel with a query as to where she had met him before.

"Gawd only knows, sweetheart. I'm shore a rollin' stone."

"You're not one of these mining galoots?" she asked, quickly. "I'll bet you're a grub-line cowpuncher out of a job."

"Plumb center, little girl. Gosh! but you're smart. An' you know the range, too."

"Put on your hat, unless you want to dance with me. I'm not used to bareheaded men," she returned, testily, while she fastened penetrating blue eyes on him.

"I'd like to dance with you, but I'm too much of a ragamuffin."

"That's no matter. Come on."

"Besides, I've no money to buy drinks."

"I don't want to drink. I can't stand much. I hate these club-footed, rum-soaked miners who slobber over me and paw me. . . . And I kind of like you, cowboy."

"Dog-gone it, I like you too," replied Kalispel, dubiously, feeling a wave of the old loneliness surge over him.

She was about to put a hand on his arm when a pale-faced, sombre-eyed man, approaching from behind Kalispel, with a slight gesture of authority, sent her hurriedly away.

"Young fellow, you'll excuse me," he said, coldly. "Nugget is much in demand."

"Nugget?" queried Kalispel, slowly.

"Yes, Nugget. Nobody knows her real name."

"Ah-huh. Suppose I take this act of yours as an insult. Your Spread Eagle is open to all."

"Certainly, but not over cordial to tramps."

"Your mistake, mister, an' damned risky," flashed Kalispel, changing to a menace the bitter range had fostered in him. "If I had intended to dance with your Nugget—an' she asked me to—you'd be dancin' to dodge hot bullets with your feet, right this minute."

Whereupon Kalispel lunged out of the glaring hall into the cold, dark night. It was getting late and the street was no longer crowded. He took to its center and made for his lodging-house. A familiar old sensation assailed him, a weakening, a sinking down, always in the past the precursor to a drinking debauch and a period of oblivion. But this had to be battled now. His status had changed. There was fortune to be made and happiness to achieve. In that clarifying passionate moment of vision he saw the future, and it was like a picture, beautiful and golden and rosy.

He reached the tavern. Men were passing in and out of the crowded noisy saloon. Kalispel went into the hall and up the rickety stairway. The lamp burned brightly on the landing of the second floor. As he turned toward his door he heard a low agitated voice, "Get out—of here!"

He stopped short. That Blair girl, whom her father had called Sydney! A man's voice, hurried and sibilant, answered her. "Sssch! Some one will hear. Listen to me——"

"No! Get out of my room!" she cried, her voice poignant with anger and fear.

Kalispel saw that her door was ajar. In two long strides he reached it and with forceful hand shoved it open violently. The act disclosed a tall man starting back from this sudden intrusion, and a white-faced girl, with dark eyes distended in fear, in the act of slipping off her bed. She was clad in a long nightgown and with one hand held the edge of a blanket to her breast. A lighted lamp stood on a little table close to her bed; a book lay face open on the floor.

"Pardon, Lady," said Kalispel, curtly. "Did I hear you order some one from your room?"

"Yes—you did," she replied, poignantly.

"All a mistake. I got in the wrong room," spoke up the man, with a short laugh that betrayed little concern for this intruder but considerable annoyance at the intrusion. He had to brush by Kalispel to get out the door.

"It was not a mistake," spoke up the girl, hotly. "He came

20

in. I asked if it were Dad. He saw me—in bed—reading. I ordered him out. Twice! But he—he came toward me."

"Aw, nonsense!" rasped the man, halted by her accusation to confront Kalispel. He had bold eyes that gleamed, a protruding, clean-shaven jowl, a forceful presence. "She's a tenderfoot, scared silly because I happened to open her door instead of mine."

"Ah-huh. Why didn't you step out quick when you saw the lady in bed?" demanded Kalispel.

"I was going to."

"Say, I heard her order you out. Twice!"

"Look here, are you questioning me, you——"

"Not any more," interrupted Kalispel. "But I'll take a whack at you."

A sharp left-handed blow sent the man staggering back off his balance. He might have gained his equilibrium, but Kalispel leaped after him and swung a terrific right to that prominent jaw. The sudden blow knocked him against the railing, which gave way with a crack. He went down the stairway, to fall with a resounding crash to the floor below. The jar that accompanied the crash brought the trample of heavy boots and excited voices of men entering below.

"Lady, shut your door," called Kalispel, and whipped out his gun. He hardly expected any trouble from the offending Romeo he had knocked down, but he had lived to distrust these incidents so often forced upon him.

"It's Borden," rang out a hoarse voice. "Dead—or damn near it."

"Back of his head all bloody," spoke up another man. "Must have been hit with an ax. Hold up, mebbe. Thet Casper outfit in town. He had a big roll on him. I seen him flash it today. Search him, boss."

"Hold the lamp, somebody. . . . Nope—no hold up. Here's his money an' watch."

"He's not dead, either. He's comin' to."

Kalispel stepped to the head of the stairway. "Hey, down there!" he called.

There followed a tense pause, then, "Hey yourself!"

"Who is that man?"

"What man?"

"Why, the one I just rapped gently on the chin."

"Ha! It must have been orful gentle, stranger."

"Wal, come out with it. Who an' what is he?"

"His name's Cliff Borden. An' he's well known hyar.

21

Part owner of the Spread Eagle. Buys minin' claims, and——"

"Forces his way into a young lady's bedroom," interrupted Kalispel, scornfully. "An' wouldn't get out when she ordered him out. . . . Now listen, you Salmon gentlemen. Drag Mister Borden out of this lodgin'-house an' when he comes to his senses tell him he'd better steer clear of me."

"An' who might you be, young fellar?" queried the gruff leader below.

"My name is Emerson an' I hail from Kalispel."

A whispering ensued, which soon gave place to the clearer voices of men engaged in lifting and carrying Borden out of the house.

After a moment Kalispel sheathed his gun and stood irresolute. Should he not assure the girl that the incident was past? The fact of her door being ajar emboldened him, and he knocked.

"Who is there?" came the quick response.

"It's me, Miss Blair."

The door opened wide. Kalispel had intended to inform the girl that all was well, but sight of her sent his thoughts whirling. She had thrown a dressing-gown over her shoulders, the effect of which simply enhanced a beauty he had only faintly grasped upon first sight.

"Oh! . . . Is—is he dead?" she faltered, with great, dark eyes upon him.

"Goodness no, miss!" exclaimed Kalispel, hastily. "I only hit him. Shore he fell hard an' must have busted his head below. They said it was all bloody. Don't you fear for him, miss. He's not hurt much."

"You misunderstand me. I don't fear for him. I wouldn't care—if—if you had killed him."

"Aw, now!" ejaculated Kalispel, staring. A flush came over the whiteness of her cheek. Her face was the loveliest thing Kalispel had ever gazed upon. He felt something terrible happening to his heart.

"I thank you for saving me—I—I don't know what," she said, tremulously.

"Maybe it wouldn't have been so bad as it looked," replied Kalispel, lamely. "He might have made a mistake about your door—an' then, after he was in—just lost his head, you know—which wouldn't be no wonder."

"You are generous to him, and—and——" she replied, suddenly to check her reply and to blush scarlet. "But I should

22

tell you that he followed me today. He spoke to me twice. He knew this was my room."

"I stand corrected, Miss Blair," returned Kalispel. "It will be just as well for Mr. Cliff Borden to keep out of sight tomorrow."

"I heard what you told those men to tell him."

"Yes? I'm sorry. That wasn't nice talk for a girl new to the West."

"I'm new, all right," she breathed, almost passionately. "I'm a most atrocious tenderfoot—and I—I ha-hate this West."

"I'm terrible sorry to hear that, miss," replied Kalispel, earnestly. "It's shore tough on newcomers. I know. I came from Missouri years ago. . . . But you'll love it some day. . . . Here I am keepin' you up! I only wanted to tell you everythin' was all right."

"But it's not," she said. "There's no lock on my door. That's why I was reading while waiting for Dad. His room is next to mine. Only, he stays out so late. And he comes in——"

She broke off confusedly, evidently in her serious train of thought about to betray something not favorable to her father.

"You'll be all right. Never mind when your Dad comes in. Shut your door tight an' brace it with a chair under the knob. My room is just at the head of the stairs. An' havin' been a cowboy, I sleep with one eye open. I'd hear if a mouse came sneakin' up this hall."

"Thank you," she replied, shyly. "I will see you tomorrow. . . . Good night, Mr. Kalispel."

He bade her good night and went to his room, to light his lamp and sit upon his bed, for long so absorbed that he had no idea where he was nor what he was doing.

Around midnight Kalispel heard voices below in the lower hall. He opened his door slightly. Blair had evidently been accompanied, if not escorted, back to the lodging-house by his Western acquaintances. They were hot on his trail. Kalispel heard him stumble over the broken steps and come up breathing heavily, to open and close a door. Kalispel undressed and went to bed.

He was up early, the first to await breakfast in the restaurant. From there he went to the largest store in town and presented his list of supplies, and told how he wanted them packed for a hard trip into the mountains. His next

23

errand was out to the pasture. This proved to be unfruitful, as the owner was in town, whereupon Kalispel went back.

He remarked to himself that he had seen the sun shine before, he had seen the pearly, fuzzy buds opening on the willows, he had been out on many and many a cold sparkling spring morning with the gold and rose on the hills; but no morning nor one of the things he noted had ever been so beautiful and heart-swelling as now.

"Must of been Sam's gold-strike," he mused as he swung along. But he knew that was a lie.

In front of the tavern he encountered Blair talking to the proprietor and another man.

"Here's your Kalispel fellar now," said the former.

"Kalispel?—I met this young man last night," returned Blair. "How do you do, sir? It appears I'm indebted to you for a service in my daughter's behalf."

"Mornin'. . . . Nothin' a-tall, Mr. Blair," replied Kalispel. "Some gazabo named Borden had been annoyin' Miss Blair all day. An' last night he busted into her room. I happened to be goin' up an' heard her order him out. But he didn't come, so I investigated."

"Haw! Haw!" laughed the proprietor. "Who's gonna pay for the damage to my stairs?"

"Damn if I will. You make Borden pay," retorted Kalispel.

"I'll gladly foot the bill," interposed Blair, hurriedly. "Young man, I'm greatly obliged to you. Excuse me if I persist. Sydney, my daughter, told me about it. Very different from your version. She's very much worried this morning. She fears there'll be a fight."

"Mr. Blair, your daughter didn't waste any fears on Borden last night. She'd been glad if I had shot him."

"Naturally. . . . But now it'd distress her—and me too—if Borden and you——"

"Not much chance, Mr. Blair," interrupted Kalispel, shortly. "I know his stripe."

The proprietor interposed. "Wal, young fellar, with all due respect to your nerve I'm givin' you a hunch somethin' will come of it. But sure I don't need to tell *you* to keep an eye peeled." After this trenchant speech he went indoors with his companion.

"Here's my daughter now," spoke up Blair.

Kalispel, with a strange sensation of dread and rapture combined, turned to see a slender, graceful young woman almost at his elbow. He did not recognize her. But the shy greeting she gave him, the blush that suffused her face, the way she slipped her hand under Blair's arm, appeared to establish the fact that she was his daughter.

He doffed his ragged sombrero in some embarrassment.

"Mornin', lady. I shore hope you slept well," he said.

"Not so very well," she replied.

In the bright sunshine, Kalispel discovered that the girl's hair was of a chestnut-gold color, and the eyes which he had imagined matched her dark tresses were violet in hue. In her street clothes she seemed taller, too, but somehow Kalispel began to associate her with the lovely creature of last night.

"What's your name?" asked Blair.

"Emerson. Lee Emerson. I got the nickname Kalispel out on the Montana range."

"Pray overlook my curiosity, Emerson. . . . There seems to be an idea in this town that you're—what did they call it?—a bad hombre. Last night, one of those men you met with me—Pritchard—he gave you a hard——"

"Pritchard!" interrupted Kalispel, sharply. "I knew I'd seen him somewhere. Mr. Blair, that man is a gambler—a shady customer. Look out for him an' all of them. Don't drink with them, or gamble, or consider any deals whatsoever."

"Thanks. I'll admit I'd grown a little leary. There might be a reason for Pritchard calling you a bad hombre."

"Aw, I am a bad hombre," admitted Kalispel, coldly. "But that's no reason why I can't do a good turn for newcomers to the West."

"May I ask just what *is* a bad hombre?" inquired Sydney Blair, her disturbing violet eyes searching his.

"It's no compliment, Miss Blair, I'm sorry to say," replied Kalispel, returning her intent glance.

"Don't embarrass him, Sydney," said Blair. "See here, Emerson. I've got considerable cash on my person. Is it safe for me to carry it around?"

"I should smile not. If you're going to be here after dark, put your money in the bank pronto."

"Thanks. That's straight talk. I'll ask you another. I came West to go into a mining deal with a Boise man, a promotor named Leavitt. I met Pritchard on the stage coming from Bannock. I told him. He discouraged me. And he and his partners are endeavoring to interest me in mining enterprizes here. What do you think of it?"

"Highway robbery, in the majority of cases. Of course some minin' claims pan out well. But if I were you I wouldn't risk it."

25

"Emerson, I'll go deposit my money in the bank at once. Then I'll want to talk to you again."

"All right, Mr. Blair. I'll be around town today an' I reckon most of tomorrow," called Kalispel after him as he hurried away.

"I'd like to talk to you, too," said the girl, shyly, yet with sweet directness. "We are strangers, and I'm beginning to realize we're such tenderfeet. . . . Won't you come somewhere with me, so we can talk? Not in here. How about the restaurant? It's lunch-time and I haven't had any breakfast."

"You'd take me to lunch—even after I've admitted I'm a bad hombre?" he asked, smiling at her.

"Yes, I would. You don't seem so—so very bad to me," she replied, returning the smile.

"But I shore look disreputable," he protested, with a gesture inviting her to note his ragged apparel.

"I haven't seen any dressed-up Westerners yet," she rejoined, demurely, and with a flash of eyes took him in as far down as the cartridge-studded belt and swinging gun. "Perhaps you mean—that," she went on. "It is rather fearful. . . . Please come. I don't care what your reputation is. I *know* there's no reason why I—I should be ashamed to— to ——"

"How do you know, Miss Blair?" he interposed, gravely.

"I— You . . . Well, it's the way you look at me. . . ."

"Miss Blair, I've been a pretty wild cowboy, but there's no reason I can't look you straight in the eyes."

"Well then, what else matters?"

"But mine's a Westerner's point of view," he rejoined, soberly, driven to stand clear in his conscience before this girl. "For a range-rider in these days, rustlin' a few cattle, gamblin'-hells an' dance-hall girls—red liquor an' gun-play— all in the day's work!"

"It's honest of you to tell me," she said, losing her color. "I'm sorry I forced you to. . . . But if I am to live in this— this beautiful, terrible West, I must learn. I must meet people —see things. I feel so—so lonely, and you're the only person I've met that I've wanted to talk to. . . . Won't you come?"

And that was how Kalispel Emerson found himself seated at a table in the corner of the little restaurant, opposite this lovely violet-eyed girl. He accepted the miracle and tried to battle against his sensations, to be worthy for the moment of the trust she placed in a stranger and to help her. Ordering the lunch from the waitress took a little time and added to his composure, after which he faced the girl across the table.

"I am Sydney Blair," she began, impulsively. "You may not believe that I'm only nineteen. We are from Ohio. Owing to an unsatisfactory partnership and poor health, my father decided to sell out his business and go West. I was the only child. My mother is dead. I had a—a—something happen to—that made me want to leave Ohio forever."

As she paused, almost faltering, Kalispel saw a slight bit of color come and go in her cheeks.

"Miss Blair, that's to the great gain of the West," he replied, gallantly, as she hesitated. "People come out here from everywhere—to begin anew, to make the West what it will be some day. . . . I reckon you feel lonesome an' homesick an' scared. It's hard on young women—this West, especially if they are pretty like you. But you'll learn to stand what seems so rough an' crude now—you'll fit in, an' some day love it. . . . Reckon I speak for all Westerners when I say I just can't be sorry you came."

"It's not so much to me just now—my comfort, my adapting myself to new people and conditions. It is concern for my father. He has responded strangely to Western influences that we knew nothing of. He drinks, he gambles, he makes friends with any and everyone he meets. He leaves me alone at night, as you know. And I am beginning to worry myself sick over what to do."

"Ah-huh. An' that's why you wanted to talk to some one," replied Kalispel, kindly. "Well, that happens to 'most every man who comes out here. In your case, Miss Blair, you've got just two things to do to keep him from goin' plumb to hell."

"Oh!— What are they?" she exclaimed, eagerly.

"You must get hold of his money an' hang on to it."

"Yes. I thought of that myself. I can do it. . . . What's the other?"

"Let him get to hard work at whatever his heart is set on."

"It is this gold-mining. Dad is mad about that. Please tell me all about it."

Kalispel did not need to draw upon imagination or hearsay to acquaint the young woman with the facts. He painted a graphic picture of the hardships, the failures of thousands of gold-seekers to the fortune of one, the rough camp life, the wildness of the gold-diggings. And despite his deliberate sticking to realism, upon the conclusion of his discourse he found himself gazing into such radiant, shining eyes that he was astonished.

27

"Oh, I would like that!" she cried.

He spread wide his hands, as if to indicate the hopelessness of tenderfeet and his inability to discourage this one. Then suddenly a query flashed into his mind—why not induce Blair and his daughter to go back with him into the mountains and share with him and his brothers the marvelous opportunity there? It struck Kalispel almost mute. He managed to finish his lunch, but his former simplicity and frankness failed him. Fortunately, the girl was so thrilled with the prospect of gold-seeking that she scarcely noticed Kalispel's lapse into pondering reticence.

Soon they were out on the street again, Kalispel biting his tongue to keep back a rush of eloquence, and Sydney babbling away as if the hour had made them friends.

Halfway to the tavern they encountered Blair. "Sydney, where have you been?" he queried. His face and demeanor betrayed agitation.

"I took Mr. Emerson to lunch," she replied, gayly. "We had a . . . Dad, what is the matter?"

"Emerson, you are being hunted all over town," declared Blair, hastily.

"Ah-huh," replied Kalispel. His wary eye had noted a circle of men in front of the tavern. On the moment it split to let out Borden and a wide-sombreroed individual with a star prominent upon his vest. Kalispel recognized him and cursed under his breath.

"Blair, take your daughter inside—pronto," he called, tensely, and striding up the sidewalk, he faced the crowd.

Chapter Three

Borden's bold front altered manifestly in his swerving aside. The crowd, too, split behind the two men, the larger half going out into the street and the smaller half lining against the walls of the buildings. These significant moves had their effect upon the sheriff. His big bulk appeared less formidably actuated. He slowed down, then halted.

"Howdy, Kalispel," he called, in a loud voice.

"Not so good, Lowrie," replied Lee, bitingly, and he stopped within fifteen steps of the sheriff. "Kinda sore these days."

"You're under arrest."

"Say, man! Are you gettin' dotty in your old age?" rejoined Kalispel, derisively. "You didn't arrest me in Montana. How can you do it in Idaho?"

"I was sworn in this mornin'."

"Bah! You can't bluff me. You couldn't be sworn in short of Boise."

"Wal, I've been deputized by citizens of Salmon. An' I'm arrestin' you an' takin' you back to Montana."

"What for? Throwin' this dirty skunk, Borden, out of a respectable young woman's room last night? Where he'd forced himself! . . . If I know Salmon citizens, they won't back Borden an' you for that."

"No. It's a case of long standin'."

"*What?*" flashed Kalispel, suddenly blazing. "Sing it out so this crowd can hear you. I've got friends in this town."

"Wal, it's—rustlin' cattle," returned Lowrie, hoarsely. All at once he realized that he was skating on thin ice.

Kalispel leaped as if he had been stung. His face flamed red and then turned white.

"I shore did. I admit it. I'm proud of it. But what *kind* of rustlin' was that, Hank Lowrie? I helped steal cattle from the outfit who first stole cattle from mine. Why, that kind of rustlin' is as old as the range! Nothin' but an exchange of beef!"

"Wal, you followed up thet exchange by spillin' blood, didn't you?" queried Lowrie, sarcastically, his little gimlet eyes wavering like a compass needle.

"Forced on me, damn you! An' you know it. Your lousy K Bar foreman hounded me all day. He was drunk an' crazy. I had to meet him. At that it was an even break. An' there's some decent Montana cowmen who patted me on the back for doin' it. . . . I left Montana to save my outfit from fightin' on my account."

"Thet's your story, but——"

"It's true," interrupted Kalispel, in ringing passion. "An' you're a liar!"

Borden propelled himself into the argument by advancing a couple of nervous strides and exploding furiously. "Lowrie, are you going to arrest this cowboy beggar?"

"Shore I am," replied the sheriff, gruffly.

"Like hell you are!" rang out Kalispel, contemptuously.

"Handcuff the bully!" shouted Borden, his discolored face ugly with ungovernable fury.

"Shet up," rasped Lowrie, giving way to more than exasperation. Uncertainty sat visibly upon him.

"Put irons on me? Haw! Haw! That's funny. . . . Why, you damn fools! Where is this bluff going to get you?"

"Emerson, I'm arrestin' you. If you submit peaceful I'll take you along without irons. We're goin' on the noon stage. An' this time tomorrow you'll be under the roof of a Montana jail."

Kalispel believed he had gauged his man correctly. But slowly he froze to the consciousness that he might be wrong and that Lowrie, egged on by Borden and his stand before the gaping crowd, might try to go through with it. Kalispel sank a little in his tracks and stiffened, all except his quivering right hand, now low at his side.

"Lowrie, long before tomorrow you'll be under the sod—if you press this deal any farther."

"What! Air you threatenin' me?" blustered the officer.

"No. I'm just tellin' you."

Lowrie edged a foot forward.

"*Look out!*" cried Kalispel, piercingly. Then, as the other became like an upright stone, Kalispel went on, coldly. "Old-timer, if you'd moved your hand then, instead of your foot, it'd been all day with you."

"What!" bellowed the sheriff. "You'd draw on—me?"

"I'll kill you!"

Lowrie's visage turned a livid white. His attitude appeared suggestive of inward collapse. It was plain that he had not expected resistance, let alone a deadly menace that held the spectators rooted in their tracks. A moment of intense suspense passed. Then Kalispel relaxed out of his crouch.

"I had you right, Lowrie. You're just what they call you in Montana—a blow-hard sheriff, yellow to your gizzard. Now get out of Salmon. If you don't, an' I run into you again, you throw a gun or I'll shoot your leg off."

"I'm not matchin' gun-play with a killer," replied Lowrie, hoarsely.

"No? Then what the hell kind of a sheriff are you in these days?—Rustle now."

Lowrie wheeled as on a pivot and rapidly strode down the street. Borden backed away as if desirous of losing himself in the crowd.

"Hey, you! Hold on!" called Kalispel.

Borden turned a distorted face expressive of an impotent wrath.

"Did you get a message from me last night?" demanded Kalispel.

"No," replied Borden, harshly.

30

"Well, I sent one. An' here it is. . . . You steer damn good an' clear of me."

"Emerson, you add insult to injury," fumed Borden, his pale eyes glaring. "Last night you assaulted me for something I was innocent of. A mistake. . . . I opened the wrong door. . . . An accident misunderstood by a tenderfoot girl scared out of her——"

"Accident, hell!" shouted Kalispel, just as keen to have the crowd hear as was Borden "You hounded that girl all day yesterday. She told me so. Then late at night you busted into her room. An' you wouldn't leave till I heard her an' went in to drive you out. I should have shot you. Forcin' yourself into the bedroom of a fine little lady at midnight! My Gawd! what are honest pioneer folks goin' to think of us Westerners if we stand for the likes of that? . . . I never learned rotten cuss-words enough on the range to fit you. So I won't try. But you steer clear of me. If I get the littlest chance in the world, I'll shoot you."

Borden hurriedly shouldered his way through the crowd and disappeared. Kalispel stood there at the edge of the sidewalk, running his eyes over the faces turned his way. He espied Blair and his daughter in the entrance of a hallway just opposite his position. The girl's pale face and wide dark eyes proved that she had seen and heard the encounter with Lowrie and Borden. It had been a bad enough situation without that. Kalispel experienced a sickening reaction. What miserable luck dogged him! What kind of an unfavorable opinion would the girl have of him now? On the moment, when this thought waved hot over him, he glanced back at the hallway. Blair was emerging with his daughter. She was still staring, as if fascinated, at Kalispel, and catching his eye she nodded with a wan little smile. They passed on into the lodging-house. That smile held hope for Kalispel. He stood there on the spot until the crowd dispersed. Then he strode off with the idea forming in mind to hurry his purchases, pack, and leave town before nightfall.

He found that the additional three burros had been acquired for him, but pack-saddles were in the process of repair and would not be finished until the morrow. The fact that the man from whom Kalispel got the burros offered to let him have a horse and saddle on credit put a different light on the journey back to the gold claim. A sure-footed, staunch horse could travel where packed burros could go. He gratefully accepted the offer. And an hour

31

later he was tightening the saddle-girths on a bay horse that he liked.

Gradually the wrath which weighed upon Kalispel wore away. He had moments of dejection when he remembered Sydney Blair, but each time he reasoned away his wild romancings and satisfied himself with having rendered a service to the loveliest and sweetest girl he had ever met.

"Gosh!" he sighed. "If I'd seen her a couple of more times it'd been all day with me. . . . Maybe so, anyhow. . . . Well, I owe Borden somethin'. I oughtn't kill him, just for that."

Kalispel watched the cloud-ships sailing in shadows along the mountain-sides; he sat a long time on a log while the sunset curtains fell into the valley; he walked on the river bank, listening to the low mellow roar of deep current over rocks. All was certainly not well with him, for these things stirred a new and pervading melancholy.

Finally he returned to town, not forgetting to be his vigilant, wary self. His supplies were all packed and ready to be delivered to his order. Upon leaving the store, Kalispel strolled down the long street as far as the Spread Eagle, and up again on the other side. This was a gesture such as might be expected of him, and which he had made before under like conditions; but this time it did not afford him any satisfaction. To Sydney Blair it would have been the act of a braggart. Kalispel was divided between a longing to see her again and a dread that he might.

He met a number of acquaintances, only one or two of whom evinced any avoidance of him. On the contrary, most of them greeted him cordially. Kalispel felt that he had not done Salmon a bad turn. Lowrie had certainly left town and Borden was conspicuous by his absence.

Kalispel quietly slipped into the lodging-house and up the stairway. A bright light came from Miss Blair's open door. He heard her talking to her father. The mere sound of her voice had an unaccountable effect upon him. He went into his room, closing the door softly, and stood a moment in the darkness, conscious of a pang. Then he lighted his lamp.

As he turned he espied something white on the floor just inside the threshold. He stared. It was an envelope. Picking it up, Kalispel found it open and unaddressed. A faint perfume assailed his nostrils, and recognizing it, he experienced a swift, strong vibration all through him. With clumsy shaking hands he extracted the folded sheet of paper from the envelope and spread it out in the glare of the lamp. The page appeared to be covered with fine, even, graceful handwriting.

Dear Mr. Kalispel:

Father and I saw and heard everything. If it had not been you, it would have been a show for us. But I was terrified. I thought you were going to fight them, and I was divided between sudden hate for that pompous, beady-eyed sheriff and fear for you. Not until I was safely here in my room and could think did I realize that *you* weren't in much danger. I also found that I had caught a glimpse of the other gentleman's discolored face, which somehow afforded me a peculiar satisfaction.

However, the purpose of this note is to assure you that I did not believe one word the sheriff said, and— please do not leave town without seeing us again. I feel directly responsible for Borden's having put the sheriff after you. Likewise I am elated that he failed to arrest you. I want to entreat you, despite this newborn savage something in me, to avoid meeting either of those men, for my sake.

Won't you have supper with us tonight? You can tell father about gold-mining.

Sincerely,
Sydney Blair.

Kalispel sagged against the bed and sat down limply. He read the note again. There was no doubting the written words that ran on so firmly and beautifully under his bewildered eyes.

"She didn't believe that liar," he whispered, raptly. "She trusts me. . . . She wants to see me again. . . . She likes me. . . . Aw, I'm plumb loco! She's just a little lady, too fine and kind to let me go off feelin' sick with shame an' disgrace. . . . An' by Heaven! that's too good for me!"

Kalispel took a few moments to wash his face and brush his hair, and then, blissfully oblivious of his ragged garb, he went out bareheaded to knock at Miss Blair's door.

"There he is now," announced her father. "Come in, Emerson."

Kalispel presented himself in the doorway, and bowed. "Good evenin'," he said. "I'll be happy to have supper with you."

Miss Blair had changed the brown street dress to one

of white and she looked so lovely to Kalispel that the blood rushed back to his heart with a shock.

"Oh, here you are!" she cried gayly, though a vivid blush stained her cheek. "Good evening. I—we feared you had run away—after that sheriff."

"No. I reckon I'm not much on runnin'. Fact is I shore forgot Lowrie," drawled Kalispel, growing cool now and sure of himself, conscious that the havoc had been wrought in him and glorying in it. "I've been out lookin' over my burros an' tryin' a new saddlehorse."

"Go on down, Sydney. I'll catch you," suggested Blair.

"Of course horses are an old story to you," said the girl as she and Kalispel started down the stairs.

"I reckon. But I've never outgrown livin' that story. Do you ride, Miss Blair?"

"Yes. But I wouldn't take any prizes for horsemanship," she rejoined, with a laugh. "I'd love horses if I had a chance. Perhaps here in the West I may find it."

"How'd you like to ride a horse for days an' days out into those wild hills? Lonely camp fires at night! Meetin' never a soul, not even an Indian, on the way! Seein' deer an' elk an' bear so tame they stand to watch you ride by! Two hundred miles almost out into these beautiful mountains—an' then a valley like one in a dream—where you can scoop up gold by the handful!"

She turned in the yellow flare of the tavern light to look at him.

"Heavens! Don't torment me!" she exclaimed, breathlessly. "But you're not teasing. You're serious. . . . Oh, I would be mad with joy!"

Blair caught up with them before Kalispel could find a reply for Sydney's astonishing response.

"Emerson, I gather that the less said to you about today's little fracas the better," remarked Blair. "So all I'll say is that it tickled me. And it might not displease you to learn that at least a dozen men spoke to me about it—to your credit. Lowrie is partial to Morman cattlemen, I hear. And Borden is not liked any too well in Salmon."

"Ah-huh. . . . Well, I reckon it'd be kind of hard to displease me this minute," replied Kalispel, with a laugh.

They entered the crowded restaurant, where a miner gave up his table to them. Kalispel saw every man in that place before he followed the Blairs to their seats. Sydney was about to take the seat facing the room, when Kalispel intercepted her with a smile.

34

"Excuse me, Lady," he drawled, coolly. "Reckon you had better let me sit here. Maybe it's not strict etiquette, but it's important. You see—there are some poor devils who can't sit with their backs to a door."

"Oh—really?" she returned, blankly, and then suddenly she understood. Her color paled, and when she took the chair he held for her it was with downcast eyes.

"Blair, I reckon I want to pay for this supper," said Kalispel. "It's my turn."

"I'll match you for it," replied Blair.

"Gosh! you're lucky. I'd hate to match you for a bag of gold nuggets."

"I hope you get the chance," declared Blair, gayly. "Sydney has been raving about your talk."

"Yeah?—She didn't strike me as particular enthusiastic."

"Kalispel Emerson, that's not true," interposed the girl, with a doubtful look at him.

"Wal, I mean from my side of the fence," he rejoined, lamely. "Here's our waitress. Let's order. An' for me it's to be a meal I'll remember. . . . But not for what I eat."

Presently, with the orders given, they were free to talk.

"Emerson, what have you been putting into my girl's head?" queried Blair.

Kalispel leaned his elbow on the table and looked across at Sydney. She met his glance, and a little by-play he had intended to be teasing developed into the thoughtful look of man and girl in whom some magic current had leaped from hidden springs. It decided Kalispel to make a reality of the wild dream he had cherished.

"Blair," he began, turning to him, "it'll cost you about fifty dollars for two horses an' saddles. An' about a hundred for supplies, beddin', tent for Miss Sydney, an' other stuff, not includin' trail clothes, guns, an' such. Say, an outlay of two hundred dollars at the most."

"Yes? . . . You certainly are a sudden fellow. What are you drivin' at?"

"Would you risk so much on the chance of a gold claim where you can dig your two-hundred-dollar investment in one day?"

"Emerson, are you serious?"

"I reckon. Never more in my life. This *is* serious, for me. . . . I said—*in one day!*"

Blair turned to his daughter. "Sydney, is our newfound Western friend panning out like the others?"

"No, Dad. He's honest," she replied, in hurried directness.

35

Her bright, shining eyes did not need that warm, fascinated regard to complete Kalispel's undoing.

"No offense, Emerson," said Blair. "I was joking, of course. All the same, I'd take you or your word on Sydney's say-so any day."

"Thanks, Blair. . . . But—Miss Sydney—do you give him your say-so?" rejoined Kalispel, earnestly, and again he met the eloquent eyes.

"Yes."

"You trust—me?"

"I do trust you."

"But I'm a stranger. I've admitted I'm a bad hombre. You've had evidence of—of my wild range life."

"Are you trying to undermine the—the——"

"No. I only want to be sure. I reckon it's a pretty wonderful thing for me."

"I am out West now," she countered. But her eyes were intense.

"Meanin' you must level yourself to us Westerners. That's true. . . . But if you really mean what you said—if you can believe me worth makin' a friend of—wal, I'll put something wonderful in the way of you an' your father."

"I do trust you—and I will go with you," she returned, paling again.

"That makes this hour the biggest of my life," declared Kalispel, stern yet radiant. "Now listen," and he bent over the table to whisper. "Not many days ago my two brothers an' I struck gold over here in a valley of the Saw Tooth Mountains. It is rich diggins. There'll be a million in gold dust panned out of that valley, an' no tellin' how much from the quartz lode. . . . We left Sam there. My brother Jake has gone to Boise to sell a half interest in our quartz mine. We're askin' one hundred thousand. I am here to pack in supplies. We planned to keep the strike secret as long as possible. That won't be very long. Such strikes leak out. There'll be the wildest gold stampede Idaho ever saw. But we'll have time to clean up a fortune before the rush."

"My word!" ejaculated Blair, incredulously. "Great! You sound like a book! No wonder you upset poor Sydney!"

"Blair, will you pack in there with me?" asked Kalispel.

"Will I?— Say, do you mean accept a chance like this—on an outlay of a few hundred dollars?"

"I reckon that's what I mean."

"You don't want to sell me a claim—or get backing?"

"No. An' I don't aim to knock you in the head an' steal

36

your money, which is precisely what Pritchard an' his pards would do if they couldn't get it any other way."

"Then why offer strangers such a wonderful opportunity?" asked Blair, gravely.

"There's more gold than we can ever dig—an' the idea appeals to me."

"Have you fallen in love with my daughter?"

"Oh—Dad!" gasped Sydney. A burning blush obliterated the whiteness of her face. "How perfectly terrible of you!" She tried to hide the hot cheeks with her hands. "Kalispel—please don't—mind his rudeness."

Kalispel suffered for her poignant embarrassment, but the feeling was nothing compared to the torment of his own emotions. He had laid a trap for himself. He wanted to base this whole interview and offer upon his honesty, his sincerity.

"Blair, you call my hand—pretty hard," he replied, with strong agitation. "I—I reckon I have . . . but I mean I never knew it till this minute. . . . That needn't make any difference to you an' Miss Sydney."

"Hell! as you Westerners say," exclaimed Blair, frankly. "You needn't apologize for it. Lord knows I'm used to men falling in love with Sydney. She had three proposals on the way out here. Sudden? Say, one of them was on a stagecoach. It came from a man as big as a hill, with a voice like a bull. He was a rancher. But he was bluff and honest. . . . You had to like him. . . . I've made up my mind that Sydney will be a disturbing element out here in the West."

"Any girl is that, I'm proud to say," replied Kalispel. "But Miss Sydney will create havoc wherever she goes."

"Is that a cowboy compliment?" demanded the girl, lifting her face to look at him with inscrutable eyes.

"I reckon I meant it so."

"Listen, young folks," interposed Blair, good-humoredly. "First Kalispel takes my breath away. And then Sydney confronts me again with the awful responsibility of having her on my hands."

"Dad, that isn't nice!" she protested.

"Well, where are we? Sydney, we've just had a magnificent offer to make our fortunes. With no strings on it! . . . But does this perfectly natural and perhaps unfortunate state Emerson finds himself in make any difference to you?"

"I am amazed—and sorry if it is true—which of course it really can't be," she replied, haltingly, her gaze falling. "But in any case, Dad, if you are really so keen to dig gold—it need not make any difference."

37

"Fine! Sydney, you are a thoroughbred. . . . We'll go!—Kalispel, shake on the deal."

"Wait. I've a little more to tell," returned Kalispel, deep stirred. "Here's my story. I was born on a farm in Missouri. My mother died when I was little. My father married again. I wasn't happy after that. When I was fourteen I ran away from home. Joined a wagon-train. At Laramie, Wyomin', I got in a fight an' left the wagon-train. I'd been used to horses all my life an' naturally I became a cowboy. I rode all over Wyomin', in some of the hardest outfits on the ranges. Then I drifted to Montana, an' the same applied there. My quickness with guns, my propensity to get in trouble, especially over some girl, earned me a name I wish I could shake. . . . That range-ridin' of mine lasted ten years. I'm nearin' twenty-seven now. My brothers Sam an' Jake had been prospectin' gold in Montana. They got wind of my shootin'-scrape at Kalispel, an' they hunted me up, an' persuaded me to quit the ranges. So I went with them, an' after long discouraging months we made this strike over here in the mountains. . . . I can't see anything but a fortune for all of us. Wal, when I get mine, I'll buy a ranch. I have the place picked out up the Salmon, a beautiful valley where the river makes a bend, an' there are groves an' lines of trees, long low slopes for cattle grazin', an' in short, just the most amazin' wonderful ranch in the West. I'll settle in there an' live down this Kalispel name. . . . Now that's about all to tell. I just wanted you to know."

"Emerson, I appreciate your frankness and confidence," said Blair, warmly. "You didn't say so, but I gather that you're not so black as you were painted. . . . And here's my hand."

Sydney offered hers without hesitation. Kalispel could only press the soft little hand in his. In that moment he could not trust his utterance.

"I thank you, too," she said, softly. "I'm sure I understand your wish to tell us. This West must indeed be a savage, bloody country. But even if you had been wilder than you intimated—that would not mean anything to me. It is what you are *now!*"

Kalispel's heart swelled with the contact of her hand and the significance of her words. The future seemed to beckon with enchanted promise. After all the lean, hard, wasteful years he had his chance for all a man could work and fight for.

"We don't appear to be hungry," concluded Kalispel. "Let's

go back to the hotel an' plan. We absolutely must keep secret your goin' with me. That'd excite suspicion. Pritchard an' his outfit would follow us. You must let me buy everythin' except maybe clothes for Miss Sydney."

"You certainly are not going to buy *them*," she replied, laughingly. "But you may give me hints about boots, overalls, gloves, sombrero. . . . Oh! what fun! . . . Dad, I'm reminding you that this adventure came through me."

Kalispel turned often in his saddle to look back down the winding river road. Certain events the last day in Salmon had convinced him that Pritchard and his cronies had some-how found out he was taking the Blairs with him. But this was late in the second day of the journey and there had been no sign of men on their trail.

Blair lagged behind, changing from one side of the saddle to the other. He was rather heavy and unused to horseback. Now and then he got off to walk a little. Sydney rode ahead, driving the burros. Already she was a surprising success. Young, strong, supple, and vividly elated with this adventure, she made play and romance of what was really hard work. Then her appearance alone had transformed the world for Lee. In a light sombrero, with her dark hair hanging in a braid, and wearing red scarf, buckskin blouse, fringed gauntlets, overalls, and boots like any Western girl, to Kalispel she was an object of adoration.

If anything, she drove the heavily-laden burros a little too fast. But Kalispel, having reproved her once over some trifle, did not care to risk it again. She could do anything she chose, just so long as she did not drive the burros into the river or endanger her life or limb.

Before sunset that day they arrived at the widening of the valley and the ranch Kalispel had decided would be his some day. He particularly wanted to get Sydney's opinion of the place, and to that end he tried to keep from talking about it. Nevertheless, even before she had dismounted, something she said, or the way she looked, prompted him to transgress.

"Wal, Lady, look the ranch over, 'cause—who knows— you might be mistress of it some day," he drawled, in cool audacity, though he carefully avoided her eyes.

He heard her catch her breath, and then, a little too long afterward to seem convincing, she uttered a silvery peal of laughter. It jarred on Kalispel, until he reflected that he deserved just such a rebuke.

During the camp tasks she was as helpful as on the preceding night, but she made no response to his several remarks and he observed that she held her chin pretty high. He wondered what she would do when, sooner or later, something happened to frighten her. That time would surely come. The girl had scarcely any conception of what lay in store for her.

The sun went down in golden splendor that evening. Kalispel could not have ordered a sunset more calculated to enhance the natural beauty of that impressive bend in the river and the slow-swelling slopes of silver to the gold-fired peaks. A troop of deer stalked out of the woods to stand on a gravel bar, and a flock of ducks winged swift flight along the shimmering water. Kalispel was quick to call Sydney's attention to the wild element that made the picture perfect. If she deigned to look, she certainly did not make any comment. After supper she stole away to disappear along the river bank. Kalispel had the satisfaction, presently, of feeling that she would indeed have to be blind to miss the extraordinary afterglow of sunset.

The expanding, slow-moving clouds spread a canopy of burning rose over the scene. And the valley filled with clear lilac light that seemed more enchantment than reality. Diamonds of rose shone on the willows, and the winding river slid along, murmuring and singing, mirroring the blaze from the sky and the fading purple of the slopes.

Dusk fell on the valley floor, while high on the black-fringed, white-capped peaks the gold still lingered. The lowing of the cattle, the raucous he-haw of a burro, the baa-baa of sheep broke the solitude and kept the wilderness from laying its mantle over the valley.

Kalispel put up Sydney's little tent and unrolled her blankets inside, then went over to renew acquaintance with the settler. He was to learn that he might take a shorter route to the Middle Fork, and save miles farther on a trail cut into the hills on the west side of the Salmon, and thirty miles over the hills graded down into a valley called The Cove. From this point the trail followed down Camus Creek to the Middle Fork. The settler assured Kalispel that he would have no difficulty working his way up the Middle Fork as far as he cared to go. The valley boxed here and there into canyons, but these could be traversed by fording the river.

When Kalispel returned to camp, the fire had burned low, and as the Blairs were not in evidence he concluded they had gone to bed. He unrolled his own blankets back near the road so that in case any riders came along they would surely awaken him.

He was up at dawn and had the horses and pack-animals in, and breakfast ready by the time the sun burst red up the cleft in the valley. Blair rolled out, lame and sore, but cheerfully grumbling, and he gasped at the ice-cold water.

"Say, what a morning!" ejaculated Blair as he ferociously used a towel on face and hands. "This isn't water! It's ice. . . . Enough to make a man out of me! . . . Have you called Sydney?"

"Reckon I'd better risk it," replied Kalispel, anxiously, and making a bold front before the little tent he called out, lustily: "Miss Blair! . . . Miss Blair!—come an' get it!" No answer. After a moment he tried again, louder. "Miss Sydney!" Receiving no reply, he shouted, "Hey, you Sydney!" And as that elicited no response, he yelled, bravely, "Hey, *Syd!*"

A moment's rather pregnant silence was finally broken by a clear, cold, wide-awake voice. "Mr. Emerson, are you calling me?"

"I reckon—I was," replied Kalispel, confusedly.

"What do you want?"

"Wal, the fact is it's long past time to get up. Breakfast is waitin'—nice buckwheat cakes an' maple syrup. Here's some hot water I'll set by your tent. An' the horses are waitin'!"

"Oh, is that all?" she inquired, slightingly.

"Wal, not exactly all," he drawled. "I'm shore powerful keen to see you again in that spankin' cowgirl outfit."

As he had calculated, this speech surely suppressed her. He dispatched his breakfast before Blair was half finished, and was saddling the horses when Sydney appeared. She deigned him a rather formal good morning, but to her father she was gay and voluble. Kalispel went on serenely with his work, somehow divining this glorious morning that all was well. Sydney did not come near him. She studiously averted her face when occasion made his approach necessary, but when he was quite distant, then her dark glance sought him and hung upon his movements. In less than an hour he was packed and ready to go.

Blair had to mount his horse from a stone. But Sydney swung herself up, lithe and agile. Then Kalispel took advantage of the moment to approach her.

"Did you tighten your cinch?" he asked, casually.

"Oh, I forgot. I'll get off an' do it."

"Didn't I tell you always to feel your cinch before climbin' on?"

"Yes, I believe you did, Mr. Emerson," she replied, curtly, and the dark eyes lowered coolly upon him.

"Wal, why didn't you, then? Shore I don't care if your saddle slips an' you get a spill. But you hate so to be taken for a tenderfoot. An' some day we'll be meetin' people."

"Pray don't concern yourself."

"Will you move your leg, please, an' let me tighten this cinch? . . . Wal, it shore was loose. Do you know a horse is smart? He'll swell himself up when you saddle him. . . . There, I reckon that will hold."

Kalispel transferred his hand to the pommel of her saddle and gave it a shake, after the habit of horsemen, then he let it rest there and looked up at her.

"Are you havin' a nice time?"

"Lovely, thank you," she replied, with averted face.

"Do you want our ride to last for days?"

"I'm not tired of the *ride*—as yet," she returned, distantly. "Sydney."

"Were you not in a hurry to start?" she queried, icily.

"I made you angry with that fool speech. Please forgive me."

"You are quite mistaken, Mr. Emerson."

"Tell me, Sydney," he implored. "Don't you like this place? Couldn't it be made a wonderful ranch—an' a beautiful home?"

Then she turned to look down into his eyes.

"It has not struck me particularly," she replied. "There have been pretty places all along the river."

"Aw!" he exclaimed, in bitter disappointment, and he wheeled to his horse.

Soon Kalispel faced the winding strip of road, the shining river, the notch of the valley; and the vigilant habit of looking back reasserted itself. Two hours of leisurely travel passed. According to landmarks he had been told to look for, he was approaching the point where he soon must strike off the road on the trail to The Cove. He had spied the green-willowed mouth of a gully in the hills and felt relieved that soon he would be leaving the river, when, upon looking back a last time, he espied three horsemen with pack-animals not far behind.

Kalispel was in the lead. He reined his horse and let the string of burros pass by. Blair caught up with him, and lastly the reluctant Sydney.

"Slow today, eh? Not steppin' high an' handsome like yesterday," gibed Kalispel.

"You took the lead, so I fell behind," replied the girl.

"Wal, you can go ahead now, 'cause if my eyes don't fool me I'm in for trouble," retorted Kalispel.

"Trouble?— What do you mean?" she rejoined, quickly.

"Emerson! There are three horsemen coming. Are they following us?" ejaculated Blair, anxiously.

The three riders came on at a trot. Their seat in the saddle, their garb and general appearance, proclaimed to Kalispel's experienced eye that they were Westerners. In a few moments more he recognized the leader and had no doubt as to the identity of the other two.

"Just as I figured," muttered Kalispel, angrily.

"Who are they, Emerson?" asked Blair, hurriedly.

"Pritchard an' his pards."

"Oh!" cried Sydney.

"Blair, go on with your girl till I catch up."

"I don't want to do that, Emerson," rejoined Blair, nervously. "I ought to stick with you. . . . Do you think they mean violence? . . . Sydney, you ride on."

"I shall not," she declared.

"Blair, drag her horse to one side—pronto!" ordered Kalispel, sharply.

He slid out of his saddle and blocked the road. The approaching trio slowed to a trot, then a walk, and finally halted in front of Kalispel. Pritchard's lean, gray visage needed no speech to confirm Kalispel's suspicion.

Chapter Four

"Howdy, Kalispel," called the gambler, coolly, making a point of deliberately lighting a cigarette. "Have you turned road-agent, along with your other accomplishments?"

"Now I got you placed, Pritchard," snapped Kalispel. "I set in a game with you once at Butte. An' my pardner reckoned you slick with the cards."

"Case of mistaken identity," returned the other, puffing a cloud of smoke. Evidently he thought he had the situation in hand. His companions sat nervously in their saddles. "I ain't denyin' any compliments about my game. Those days if a man wasn't slick with the cairds he'd be a lamb among wolves. . . . Are you holdin' us up?"

"I reckon you're trailin' me."

"Wrong again. Haskell an' Selby here are goin' to Challis with me."

"You're a liar, Pritchard."

"Wal, I'm not arguin' the case with you, Kalispel. If you'll let us pass we'll ride on, mindin' our own business."

Kalispel concluded that it would be a wise move on his part to let the trio get ahead. Pritchard manifestly would avoid a clash, but there was little doubt that he wanted to keep track of the Blairs.

"Pritchard, you an' your pards mozey along. An' don't make the mistake to come slippin' along on my back trail again," snapped Kalispel, and strode aside to let the restive pack-animals and saddle-horses go by.

"Blair," called Pritchard as he rode on, "you'll regret exchangin' our deal for whatever this cowboy has sprung on you."

"All right, Pritchard," replied Blair. "It couldn't be much worse than yours and it's my business."

"Wal, *we* wasn't after your girl, anyway. You'll wake up some mornin' to find her gone."

Kalispel was not of a caliber to let that gibe pass. He concluded that the whistle of a bullet by the gambler's ear would be more effective for the future than any verbal threat. Whereupon he whipped out his gun and took a snap shot at the top of Pritchard's high-crowned sombrero. He knocked it off, too. The horses plunged. The man on the off side shouted: "Rustle, you damn fool! Thet fellar is rank poison."

Pritchard did not even look back, let alone halt to get his sombrero. He spurred after his galloping comrades, who already had the pack-horses on the run. Kalispel flipped his gun and, sheathing it, he walked forward to pick up the gambler's hat. The bullet had cut a furrow across the crown. Returning, he hung the sombrero on the pommel of Blair's saddle.

"Just to show you I wasn't intendin' him any hurt," he said. "But I ought to have shot his leg off. Reckon I was mad enough to. . . . Blair, they were followin' us as shore as you're born. But it hasn't struck them yet that we're turnin' off into the mountains pronto. They'll find out, though, an' if they track us again there'll be real trouble. I'm darn sorry. For two bits I'd call the deal off with you. If I had the money I'd pay you what——"

"See here, Kalispel," interrupted Blair, earnestly, "this incident didn't please me, but I'm getting hunches, as you call them. If Sydney and I *have* to get used to these nice

44

gentle ways you Westerners have—well, I think we're lucky to be with you. That's all."

"It's pretty straight talk. But look at Sydney's face."

That sweet face had indeed not recovered from the fright of the meeting and Kalispel's sudden termination of it.

"A little pale around the gills," laughed Blair. "Why, boy, three days ago she would have fainted! Sydney's doing fine."

"I shore say so, too. But with me it's a question of what she thinks." Kalispel stepped close to Sydney's horse and looked up at her. "Girl, for a tenderfoot you've got nerve. I admire you heaps. . . . But if you've got the littlest doubt of me I won't go on with this deal. I'm askin' you to be plumb honest."

"Doubt of—you?" she asked, tremulously.

"Yes. You heard what that hombre said. I reckon my deal with you an' your father does look kind of fishy. It's not too late to turn back. If you go on into the wilds with me you couldn't find your way back."

"I don't want to turn back. I told you I trusted you."

"Wal, I'm not shore ya do. You hardly spoke to me this mornin'."

His simplicity might have been responsible for the break in her gravity. At any rate, she flushed and smiled.

"After all, I have to obey Dad," she said. "And he seems to swear by you."

"All flatterin' enough. But your dad hasn't a ghost of a show to see these gold-diggin's unless you swear by me, too."

"That's asking a great deal, Mr. Kalispel."

"What do you think of me?" demanded Kalispel, stubbornly.

"Well, if you compel me—I think you are a devil and a flirt."

"Aw—Miss Sydney!" burst out Kalispel, in dismay.

"And very impudent—and inclined to be conceited—and an atrocious cook—and a domineering fellow—and a bloodthirsty Westerner—and——"

"Wal, the deal is off," interrupted Kalispel, throwing up his hands.

"But I willingly trust my honor and my life in your hands," she concluded, changing from jest to earnest.

Kalispel felt the hot blood smart in his weather-beaten neck and face. Unconsciously he had demanded the very answer she had granted, but now that it was delivered he seemed to have overstepped himself again.

"Sydney, I just had to know," he returned, huskily. "I'm

the doubtin' one. An' I shore don't deserve your kindness, though I swear I do your trust. . . . So now if you say we'll ride on—wal, we'll ride."

She betrayed sympathy for him and evidently appreciated the complex situation. He was proud, sensitive, fiery, and would not tolerate any word against himself, yet had confessed grave faults and facts.

"Let us ride on, and be friends," she said, simply.

Kalispel found the burros resting under the cottonwoods. Little danger of them straying or traveling along without being driven! Far ahead at the bend of the road slight clouds of dust marked the progress of Pritchard and his men. They were already well out of sight. This fact, however, meant little to Kalispel, for he felt sure that they would not abandon the track of the Blairs. He would encounter them again sooner or later, and not improbably the issue would be serious. But he had no fears that they would ever track him as far as the gold-diggings.

Presently he came to the mouth of a gully out of which flowed a brook. An old trail seldom traveled followed the watercourse. It led up gradually, winding through groves of cottonwoods and copses of willow, to emerge into a wide valley. This was open country, the haunt of elk and deer. The trail led up the rolling slopes to a forest of pines. The Blairs kept Kalispel in sight, but when they caught up with him on top of the divide, where he decided to camp, they were pretty weary and quiet.

It was cold up there. Patches of snow showed under the pines. Kalispel's first task was to build a fire for his companions, after which he plunged into his duties with a will. Blair, lame as he was, lent a hand, but Sydney sat before the fire, a rather weary and dejected girl. To unsaddle and hobble the horses and unpack the burros took only a few minutes, as likewise the pitching of Sydney's tent, but when it came to preparation of the supper, Kalispel was slow and deliberate. Sydney's remark as to his status as a cook rankled in Kalispel. It was impossible for her not to observe his care, especially as she was obviously hungry. Blair frankly came out with the fact that he would "starve pronto." When presently Kalispel served them he had no misgivings about this supper. At its conclusion Sydney lifted her dark eyes and murmured: "I'm sorry I said you were a poor cook. I suppose—when you get your ranch back there on the river— you will not want any woman to do your cooking."

Blair laughed heartily at that cryptic bit of flattery, but

Kalispel was nonplused and bewildered. He had never been very successful in understanding girls, and this one was wholly beyond him. What had she meant by that? Not want any woman! Was she telling him that he could never get her or that she would like to be the woman? Kalispel pondered it a moment.

"Wal, since you tax me, I'll say that I'll never want a Lemhi squaw or a bronco-bustin' cowgirl to cook for me."

The night bade fair to be a cold one. Kalispel heated a stone and wrapped it in a canvas for Sydney to put at her feet. He and Blair did not make a very good night of it. Off and on he was up replenishing the fire, and welcomed the gray dawn. Sydney was up before sunrise and declared she had slept snug and warm.

They were all that day riding down through the pines to The Cove. It was a big round basin of several thousand acres, surrounded by bold bluffs and high mountains. They camped on Camus Creek, and next morning following the rushing stream down into a rugged canyon, which augmented its characteristics until it grew to be a magnificent chasm with great colored cliffs, eddying pools and foaming rapids, intersecting brooks that trembled white over the banks to swell the Camus, long gullies splitting the stupendous walls up to the black patches of lodge-pole pines, huge caverns hollowed out by wind and water, grassy and fern-clad benches where white goats watched the intruders go by down the trail.

For some reason beyond Kalispel's ken, Sydney rode directly behind him most of the way down this canyon, and she plied him with innumerable questions. And at many a place, where the stream roared over a fall or the pines and flowers and shade invited rest, or a beautiful glade opened up she would say: "Let's camp here. It's too lovely to pass by."

And Kalispel would say: "Ride your hoss, lady. This shore is no picnic."

"But if I was particularly crazy about a place, wouldn't you stop?"

"Wal, I reckon so, if you could persuade me you could be crazy about anyone—I mean thing."

"Oh!" she replied, enigmatically.

Blair had a bad trip. He was so saddle-sore that he had to spend more and more time walking. The trail led up and down, endlessly, and it was rough, and in spots, dangerous.

Before sunset the bronze-walled canyon with its pine-fringed rims opened out into a wider and grander canyon from which came a low sullen roar.

"Hear that?" called Kalispel, turning to Sydney.

"Do you think I'm deaf? Oh, it makes my skin prickle."

"That's the roar of the Middle Fork," declared Kalispel. "An' dog-gone me! I'm shore afraid the meltin' snow has raised the river."

"Will we have to swim our horses across?"

"Gosh! I wish we could. But the danger is we'll have three or four feet of swift water slidin' over slippery rocks. An' if a hoss rolls with you—good-by!"

"Heavens! . . . I should think you'd want to keep me with you a little while, anyway."

"Sydney, I don't savvy you," he retorted. "But I'm tellin' you I'd shore love to keep you with me always."

"Yes? And you're so wondrously brave with men. . . . Oh, the river! beautiful!— How wide and green and swift! . . . Dare we ever try to ford that?"

"We shore have to. But not here," replied Kalispel, his keen eyes ranging the canyon.

Camus Creek spread wide and shallow over yellow ledges to flow into the river. At this junction the Middle Fork was twice as wide as the Salmon, and presented a thrilling and formidable spectacle, roaring around a dark-walled bend to slide green and hurrying onward, down under a colossal bronze-faced mountain wall into a purple gateway beyond. On the Camus Creek side sage-covered benches sloped down to banks where tall lofty pine trees bordered the river. The whole scene had a bigness and roughness that emphasized this opening into the wild Saw Tooth Range.

They forded the Camus to climb a sage-bench, from which a view of the vast, smooth, grassy slopes on the left, swelling and mounting to gold-mantled peaks, capped the climax of that splendid wilderness scene.

"I'm going to camp right here," declared Sydney, and she dismounted.

"Alone?" queried her guide, smiling.

"But it's sunset. We've come so far. Dad is ready to drop. And I—oh, I've deceived you. I'm ready to die."

"Shore a couple more miles up river won't kill you."

"Kalispel, have you no heart?"

"Reckon I did have one awhile back. Come, pile on again, Lady."

"Don't you love beautiful places? Oh, I'm disappointed in you. Won't you camp here—to please me?"

"Wal, if you put it that strong I reckon I will," he drawled.

48

"Fact is I'd camped here, anyhow. I just wanted you to coax me."

"Indeed!— I wonder if my trust is misplaced."

"*Quién sabe,*" he ended, sagely.

"Go away," she waved. "I'll take care of my horse."

To Kalispel's amaze and secret glee she not only unsaddled her mount, but hobbled him, too. She must have watched Kalispel at this task, for she executed it neatly. She scolded her father and drove him out to fetch in firewood. And then she essayed to help Kalispel at his manifold camp tasks.

"Dog-gone it! Get out of my way," he ejaculated, mildly. "How do you expect me to get supper pronto?"

"But I want to help," she protested.

"Wal, you're terrible disturbin'."

"How? I'm certainly not clumsy."

"Gosh! You're gracefulness itself. I reckon it's your good looks."

"Nonsense! You should be used to my looks by now. . . . Please, Kalispel, let me learn. It fascinates me—the way you mix dough for biscuits."

And she plumped herself down on her knees beside him, and rolling up her sleeves to expose strong round arms, she put her hands with his into the pan.

"Take yours out," she said, presently.

"Reckon I can't. They're fast."

She giggled. "Was there ever such a man?— You are *holding* mine."

"So I am. Dog-gone! . . . Sydney, if you don't want me to love you, this is no way to act."

"We must eat, little boy. And I must learn to be a camp cook. . . . And for that matter a—ranch cook."

"Yeah?— If I had any nerve——"

"Kalispel, never fear. You are the nerviest person I ever met in my whole life."

"With men an' guns, you mean?"

"I mean with helpless, innocent, trusting, tenderfoot girls," she retorted. "The proof is in the pudding. No, the dough! You are still holding my hands."

Kalispel surrendered and removed his floury hands from the pan.

"You ab-so-lute-lee don't want me to love you?" he asked, sternly.

"I ab-so-lute-lee don't," she mimicked.

"Wal, you bake the biscuits—an' be a murderer in another way," he said, and got up.

49

Supper was late that night. Neither Kalispel nor Blair appeared to note that the biscuits were burnt and soggy. Kalispel heroically made way with several.

The wide canyon with its dark sky-high walls was an impressive place. The Blairs sat up for an hour around the camp fire.

"You're gettin' a touch of the real wild West here," remarked Kalispel. "But the lonesomeness, an' that strange feeling for which there's no name, don't grip your soul here like they will over in my valley. The voice of the stream is different. Wolves mourn on the slopes. An' the old mountain thunders."

"Thunders! How can a mountain thunder? Is it a volcano?" rejoined Sydney, greatly interested.

"I can't say how it thunders, but it does. Makes you shiver when you wake up in the middle of the night. It's the mountain on the north side of the valley. Twice as high as that an' amazin' to see. The whole front of it is a mile-high slope of many colors, bare as weathered earth can be. A terrible slant of loose dirt an' gravel an' clay. Seems like it is alive an' growls deep inside."

"Uh! Sounds kind of spooky," declared Sydney.

"Reckon you've hit it, spooky!"

Next morning Kalispel rounded up the stock in the gray of dawn and had his party on the way early. The trail leading up the river was not so well defined as the one they had been following. In some places of rocky foundations it disappeared altogether. But the travel was fairly good and almost level, so that the little caravan made perhaps three miles an hour.

Kalispel soon called the attention of the Blairs to a tremendous slope of weathered rock on the other side of the river. It was a slide of talus so high that the ledge from which the mass of loose shale and rock had eroded could not be located from below. Deer and elk and bear trails bisected it low down. It terminated, not many rods below, in a rough white rapid that swept quickly into a deep eddy. If a horse was carried that far he could not scale the steep bluff of rock and would unquestionably be lost in the heavy rapids below.

They plunged on. The icy cold water splashed up in Kalispel's face. Sydney had not yet realized actual danger. Then suddenly her horse slipped. The water surged up to her saddle. She shrieked and appeared about to throw herself off.

"Stay on!" yelled Kalispel. The animal righted himself. "Pull him downstream a little."

"I thought I—was a gone gosling then," she called, and turned a startled face toward him.

"You're doin' fine. . . . Not much more now. We'll make it."

He kicked and spurred his own mount, that was scarcely doing better than Sydney's. And they entered the bad stretch, slanted a little downstream. Kalispel urged his horse on ahead and closer to hers.

"Give me your hand," he shouted, reaching precariously for her. And he caught hers just in the nick of time, for her horse went down and rolled. Kalispel dragged the girl free from the saddle. His own animal labored, slipped, plunged and snorted furiously. Sydney's weight in the racing current was too great. Besides, the current pulled her head under. Kalispel dragged her up, caught her blouse, and would have succeeded in drawing her across his pommel, but his horse fell. Kalispel swung his leg and slid off. He went almost under. Then with his boots touching the bottom he drew Sydney's head out of the water, and leaning back against the current he used it to hold him up and push him along while he edged toward the shore. When he was about to be carried off his feet a boulder helped again to catch him. By accurate calculation and prodigious effort he reached the shallow water just above the rapid.

He lifted the girl in his arms, and staggering over the slippery stones he gained the bank and laid her down on a mat of pine needles. She was conscious and not in any way harmed.

Kalispel stood erect to gaze upstream to see how Blair had fared. To his relief the big horse was wading out in the shallow water. Both the other horses, unencumbered with riders, were doing likewise. The burros were already out on the bank.

"Lucky! Wal, I guess!" exclaimed Kalispel as he knelt beside the girl.

"Sydney, it was a close call. . . . How are you?"

"Frozen—stiff," she whispered.

"No wonder. Gee! Wasn't that water cold? I'll have a fire in a jiffy. . . . Shore you've no hurts?"

Her wet face was pallid and her great violet eyes beginning to lose their dark shade of terror.

"You saved—my life," she said, in wondering gratitude.

"Sydney, shore we both darn near went over the rapids. . . . An' that would have been all day."

She smiled wanly and clung to him. "I'm sorry I said

51

that—last night. . . . You know—about what I didn't want—you to do. . . . It isn't true."

Next morning Kalispel found the trail he and Jake had made with their burros coming down off the mountain. He rejoiced. Somehow a vague fear had attended him. Now all was well. He had but to travel slowly and husband the strength of the Blairs, and in four days, or less, he would be back with Sam in the valley of gold. He had no fear that his generous-hearted brother might resent the coming of Blair and Sydney. Sam was right, however, in wanting a month or more of staking claims and digging gold before the stampede came. Eventually a stampede was inevitable.

Kalispel did not trifle with his happiness by importuning Sydney about her shy confession. That had been enough to lift him to the seventh heaven. She seemed to be a girl of an infinite variety of moods, the last of which, since the river episode, was one of shyness and reserve. She no longer teased him or made ambiguous remarks or met his worshipful eyes. Moreover, the strain of the strenuous horseback ride had begun to tell upon her. That night, high up on the windy, grassy hilltop, at the end of the day's climb, she said: "Lift me down, Kalispel."

The next day provided easier travel, owing to a winding trail around the slopes of the round bald mountains. He found, too, that he was getting on faster than he had expected. The horses made half again as much progress as he and Jake had made on foot.

Toward the middle of the afternoon of the third day Kalispel ascertained that they were almost over the divide, from the ridge of which they could look right down upon Sam's valley.

He had dreamed a good deal this last day, so that the hours had been as minutes. A thousand times he had glanced back to make sure Sydney's slender graceful form was a reality, that the pensive face with its dark, challenging eyes was there to gladden his sight. And many of those times had been rewarded by a smile, a gleam or flash, or wave of gauntleted hand, something sweet to enhance his dream. Love, fortune, happiness were within his grasp. And he would gaze about him, over the vast spread of jagged peaks and forested domes, or down into the rough gulches, or out upon the colored bare slopes so characteristic of the region, or up at an isolated ledge where the sheep and goats kept motionless vigil—all with a sense that the thing which had saved

52

him was this continual reversion to nature, to the lonely silence of the hills, to the heights and the depths of the rocks which called for- endurance, for the infinite breathing whole that had given him faith.

As he approached the last few rods of the ascent to the summit of the divide he slowed down to let Sydney catch up. The burros passed on over out of sight. On the left rose the bulk of a bronze peak, and on his right towered the mighty half of the stupendous slope of defaced mountain-side.

"Oh, how wild and ghastly . . . but beautiful!" panted Sydney as she joined him. "Kal, I shall hug you—maybe—for fetching me here—giving me this—this tremendous experience."

"Kal?" he echoed, in a transport.

"Yes, Kal," she retorted, archly.

"Let me tell you somethin'," he pleaded.

"Well, you've been pretty good lately—for *you*," she temporized, but her eyes were eloquent and warm.

"Sydney, in a moment more we'll be lookin' down into my valley. An' it'll be the happiest moment of my life."

"Little boy, why so pale and solemn? It certainly will not be the unhappiest of mine." She stretched a gloved hand to him. They went on.

Kalispel saw the fringed tip of the south slope rise about the divide.

"I smell smoke," said Sydney.

"So do I," replied Kalispel, in surprize. "That's strange."

The horses stamped up on top. Kalispel swept his eager gaze downward to the gray valley of rocks, the silver winding stream, the grand bare slope looming sinisterly beyond. But what was it that flashed and moved? White tents! Columns of blue smoke rising! Men wading in the stream!

"My Gawd!" burst out Kalispel, his heart contracting.

"Oh! Your valley is full of people!" cried Sydney, in dismay.

Chapter Five

Kalispel stared down into the valley with a terrible sickening realization that the spectacle below represented a stampede of miners. Long before Jake could have gotten to Boise and back the gold-diggings had been discovered.

53

"Smoke! Tents! Men puttering in the brook! What does it all mean?" exclaimed Blair, in amazed consternation.

"Look! There's a pack-train coming down the valley," cried Sydney.

"Of all the cursed luck!" exclaimed Kalispel, in bitter passion. His sweeping gaze took in a new and well-defined trail coming in from the south. Heavily laden mules wagged their canvas packs, bristling with shovels and picks, along this trail. Prospectors swung behind them, with the stride of men who had found the pot at the foot of the rainbow. Kalispel at last turned to his friends.

"Folks, I'm so sorry I want to die," he said, huskily. "Our diggin's have been discovered . . . an' the stampede has begun."

"Oh, Kalispel—don't look—so—so dreadful!" entreated Sydney. "We know it couldn't be your fault."

"Hell, boy! If what you say is true—and, by golly! it looks like it—why, there's enough gold for all," added Blair, manfully swallowing his disappointment.

"Let's rustle down," replied Kalispel. But he was inconsolable. He divined a blow, the crushing extent of which he could not grasp. Sam would tell him.

He urged his horse down after the burros. The Blairs followed. As Kalispel descended his gaze sought to encompass all the activity in that valley. Tents glanced white and gray in the afternoon sunlight. They appeared to run in two long lines down the middle of the bench, leaving a lane between. That lane was a street. Already a town had been laid out. A keener survey gathered even more dismaying facts. Camps had been located close together all the way down the stream as far as he could see. That meant claims. All available gold-bearing ground could not have been taken up yet, but no doubt the rich claims had been staked.

The descent of that pass seemed interminable to Kalispel. He never looked back once at Sydney. He pushed the string of burros at a pace that threatened slipping of their packs. At last he drove them out on the level bench, not far from the stream, where they began to crop the green grass. Kalispel dismounted. Whatever he had to encounter here he wanted to face on foot. Thought of Sam's rich quartz claim somehow did not mitigate his queer misgivings. As he threw his saddle, a familiar low deep rumble brought him up with a start. The old bald-faced mountain had growled ominously.

"Hear that, Blair?" he asked, as his followers arrived.

"Hear what?"

"Oh, I did. Thunder!" cried Sydney. She was wide-eyed and agitated, and gray of face from fatigue. She reached out her hands for Kalispel to lift her down, and as he leaped to her side she almost fell into his arms.

"You poor kid!" he said, thickly. "Set here an' rest. . . . Blair, you watch the burros while I go see what's what."

Kalispel strode over the rocky bench down to the stream to the nearest camp. Bed-rolls, packs, utensils and stone fireplaces, picks, and shovels, piles of wood, all kinds of camp paraphernalia, appeared to line the stream. Of the two nearest miners one was bending over a rock in the stream, and the other, a tall, bearded, wet and dirty young man, evidently having espied Kalispel, advanced a little to meet him.

"Howdy, stranger. See you found a new way in," he replied, genially.

"That's the way I went out two weeks or so ago," replied Kalispel, curtly.

"Was you in hyar—two weeks ago?" queried the other, incredulously.

"Yes. Me an' my two brothers."

"Wal, it's a pity you didn't stay on. Mebbe one of you fellars was responsible for the news of a gold strike that hit Challis about a week ago."

"I wasn't. I went out with my brother to pack in supplies. Maybe he got drunk an' gave the snap away."

"Rand Leavitt got wind of it first, an' a stampede rustled after him. Leavitt beat us all to it. Bonanza! He struck a quartz vein packed with gold. The rest of us are placer minin'. An' believe me, stranger, no kick comin'."

"Shore you know my brother, Sam Emerson?"

"Nope. Not by name, anyhow."

"Sam found that rich quartz vein, an' Jake an' I packed out a piece worth five hundred dollars."

"What?— Stranger, are you drunk or crazy?"

"Neither. But I'm most damn curious," snapped Kalispel.

"Bill, come out hyar," yelled the young miner. His call fetched the big, bearded, red-shirted man on the run. "Say, Bill, listen to this. Hyar's a fellar who says his brother made a gold strike hyar weeks ago, an' thet he an' another brother packed out a chunk of quartz worth five hundred."

"It's true. Do you know my brother, Sam Emerson?" flashed Kalispel. "We left him here, located on the quartz vein."

"Sam Emerson? Don't know him. An' he's shore not located on the quartz vein now, for Leavitt staked thet. He

55

got in hyar first with Selback an' outfit. You're shore haidin' fer trouble, young man, if you make thet claim to them."

Kalispel abruptly wheeled and almost ran across the bench toward the location of Sam's quartz vein. As he neared it he slowed up to catch his breath and to take the lay of the land. In the first place he had difficulty finding the outcropping ledge under the looming bare slope. It appeared to be hidden by tents and a large framework of peeled logs, which manifestly was a cabin in course of construction. Kalispel heard the blows of an ax. He passed the end of the lane between the tents. It ran west the remaining distance of the bench. He heard the crash of falling timber and the hoarse voices of men. These came from behind him, down by the stream. The tent town appeared deserted, except at this end, where he espied men actively engaged in labor around the cabin.

In another moment Kalispel stalked upon the scene of Sam's strike. He did not need to look twice at the long outcropping ledge. A tall man with a rifle across his knees sat significantly in the foreground.

"Are you Rand Leavitt?" called Kalispel, in a voice that rang, as he passed the open tent to confront this guard.

The man rose quickly. He stood coatless and hatless, young, bullet-headed, swarthy-faced, and his deep-set eyes appeared to start.

"No, stranger. My name's Selback. The boss is down town," replied the man. "An' who might you be, bustin' up hyar like a bull out of a corral?"

Kalispel was slow to answer, but swift and sure in his estimate of this guard, Selback. There was something expected, furtive, cold, and calculating in the man's eyes, yet no gleam of intuitive sense of Kalispel's status.

"I'm Kalispel Emerson—brother of Sam . . . Where is Sam?"

"Are you askin' me? I don't know your brother—or you, either."

"Shore you haven't seen Sam Emerson?" rang Kalispel, piercingly. The builders had ceased their tasks to come down on the ground.

"There are a lot of miners hyar whose name I never heard."

"Name or not, you shore seen Sam when you hit this valley . . . because he was here on this claim. He found this quartz. I was with him when he struck it. So was Jake, my other brother."

"Man alive! You've gone gold mad," declared the guard, with a gruff laugh. But there was no sincerity in word or mirth. He did not ring true.

"By Gawd!" cried Kalispel, "this has a queer look!"

"An' so have you, stranger!" retorted Selback, probably misled by Kalispel's poignant exclamation. "Just you rustle along or Leavitt will run you out of Thunder River."

"We Emersons don't run."

"Wal, walk, then, an' be quick about it," ordered the guard, making a move to swing the rifle around.

"Hold on!" cut out Kalispel.

But Selback did not heed the warning. The rifle barrel continued to swerve beneath the man's paling visage. In a flash Kalispel drew and fired. The guard's head sank, and, stumbling, he fell forward over his clattering rifle.

Rapid footfalls cracked on the rocks. Kalispel wheeled to confront a man who yelled as he cleared the tent. He ran almost into Kalispel's smoking gun.

"Line up with your gang. Pronto!" ordered Kalispel, with a wave of the gun. He knew his man. This was Leavitt, who lost no time lining up beside the three laborers, but he did not put up his hands.

"You see I'm unarmed," he said, coolly. "What's the deal?" and he swept a glittering gray glance from Kalispel to the man on the ground and back again.

"You're Rand Leavitt," confirmed Kalispel as he instinctively recognized a shrewd, nervy, resourceful leader. Leavitt was under forty, a man of lofty stature, whose pale, cold, boldly-chiseled face denoted intelligence and force.

"Yes, I'm Leavitt. What's this hold-up mean?"

"Wal, your man Selback didn't get a hunch, as you see," returned Kalispel, sarcastically.

"If you're a bandit, hold up the miners. We've got a quartz vein. No gold yet. I've sent out for a stamp mill."

"I'm no bandit, an' damn well you know it."

"How the hell do I know who and what you are?" demanded the other, in pale anger. "What'd you kill Selback for—if it's not a hold-up?"

"The damn fool tried to throw his rifle on me, after I warned him."

"Who are you?"

Kalispel did not answer. He backed against the wall of the tent. Miners, led by the couple whom he had accosted upon his arrival, were hurrying to the scene, drawn, no doubt, by the gunshot. Kalispel fought down his fury and despair.

57

Whatever the justice of his claim, it would never be recognized. He was too late. He had to decide whether or not to kill this man Leavitt.

"Boss, he said his name was Kalispel Emerson," spoke one of the laborers, hurriedly. "Thet he was brother to a Sam Emerson, whom he swore had located this quartz vein."

"Sam Emerson!" shouted Leavitt, loud-voiced and protesting. "Where in the hell was he, then? I found this claim, opened up to be sure, gold shining in the sun, pick and shovel, camp duffle and stuff lying around. But no miner!"

"You lie!" hissed Kalispel.

"No I don't lie," stormed Leavitt. "There wasn't any miner here. I swear that. I could have proved it by Selback."

"You made away with my brother an' jumped his claim."

"I jumped it, yes. I had a perfect right to. But it had not been worked for days. . . . When you accuse me of making away with your brother you're the liar—or you are out of your head."

He was steady of hand, pale-faced, but fire-eyed, and his voice and demeanor carried conviction, if not to Kalispel, to the others present, a constantly growing crowd.

"Leavitt, I reckon I'll bore you."

"You'll murder an innocent man, then," replied Leavitt. "I'm not threatening you, as was Selback. You've no excuse to kill me, except your suspicion, which is rank injustice. . . . And these miners will lynch you."

Kalispel had put him to a crucial test. But Leavitt had not weakened. If he was guilty, as Kalispel believed, he was too shrewd, too quick-witted and iron-nerved, to betray himself to Kalispel or lose his prestige with the crowd. Besides, there was a remote possibility that Sam had wandered out of the valley or had met some inexplicable tragic end. Kalispel felt that he was not omnipotent. In his torturing disappointment and frenzy he might have erred in judging Selback. He dared not force the issue here and lose forever any chance of reclaiming the mine. Jake would return with proofs that he had packed out the gold-veined quartz.

"Leavitt, I'll let you off because men like you hang themselves," declared Kalispel, bitterly. "But I'm accusin' you before this crowd. You're crooked, you made away with my brother an' jumped his claim. I call on all here to witness my stand against you an' my oath that I'll live to prove it."

Kalispel backed away from the tent and from the gaping miners. He was keen enough to see even in that moment that sentiment of these men was divided. Turning presently, he sheathed his gun and had headed for the spot where he had left his burros, when he remembered Sydney. In that exceeding bitter moment of hopeless despair it seemed he could not face her with blood on his hands, with the fear that these miners, and surely Leavitt, would convince her that he was a murderer. As truly as that had his hasty deed made him an outcast! Plunging away in the other direction, he leaped the creek and hid far across the valley, in a clump of firs, and there lay like a deer mortally wounded and seeking to die alone.

Long after darkness fell he went back to the place where he had left the Blairs and the burros. He found only his own packs. The Blairs, with their supplies and equipment, had left. Kalispel welcomed that fact. He searched in his pack for a flask of whisky and finding it he sought to kill the cold, sick misery in his marrow and to blot out the insupportable loss of brother, fortune, love.

When Kalispel recovered a consciousness with which he could remember, it was another day, and he believed the second or third after his arrival. The sun had blistered his face as he lay unprotected in the open. Ill, shaken, in a horrible mental state, he drank the last swallow of liquor.

Then he looked about him. The packs were intact, his saddle lying on the ground, his bed unrolled. The horse and burros were gone from the grassy bench. This location was as good as any, he thought, and after a survey of the bench he concluded he could not do better. He was far back, close to the base of the divide, and over a half-mile from Leavitt's camp, which stood about even with where the great bare slope began its terrifying rise to dominate the valley. The new trail coming down the stream forked into the one he had made up the divide just below where he elected to camp. Forthwith he spread his tarpaulin across a narrow space between two high boulders, and moved in his supplies. Behind him and up the gradual slope were quantities of dead and fallen lodge-pole pines. He could not eat, though his thirst was intense, and in a mood to drive himself to exhaustion, he packed down one tree after another until he had a huge pile of them. Then, spent and wet and hot, he flung himself down and importuned heart and consciousness with hopeless query—what was it that had happened and what could he do? Footsteps roused him to sit up, braced against a boulder. Blair confronted him.

"How are you, Kalispel?" he asked, not unkindly.

"Mornin', Blair—or is it afternoon? . . . I'd be better off dead," replied Kalispel.

"Don't say that, lad. It's not like you at all. You must pull yourself together and shake the terrible passion you must have had—and the debauch afterward."

"Blair, am I still drunk, or are you speakin' kindly to me?" queried Kalispel.

"I am, son, and I mean it," went on the elder man, taking a seat near Kalispel.

"Wal, if I can be grateful for anythin', I'm thanking you."

"Listen, cowboy. I've seen a good deal of life, and life anywhere, east or west, is the same when it comes to misfortune, loss, grief. If ever a young fellow had a tough thing to face, you certainly had. But you gave in to it in wild West fashion and it has ruined you. Leavitt stands high with these miners. They elected him judge of the camp—an office, as I understand it, to determine gold claims and all the accepted rules of mining-camps. Your denouncing him apparently hurt you more than killing Selback. For as I got it, Selback was a hard, grasping man, not at all liked. Then to make the situation worse for you, our friends Pritchard, Selby and Haskell rode in yesterday morning. They made friends at once with Leavitt. I heard them, especially Pritchard, denounce you as Kalispel Emerson, notorious gunman from Montana, a bad hombre in every way."

"Interestin'—an' about to come true, I reckon," replied Kalispel, with the ice in his soul cutting his voice. "An' I'm calculatin' that you come out to give me a hunch to leave?"

"No," declared Blair, emphatically. "I might have felt that way a couple of days ago. But not now. Something has changed me. I'd stay. . . . You see, I'm convinced of your honesty, Kalispel. I believe you and your brothers have been robbed of this claim. Probably I'm the only man in camp who does. I've always been a contrary cuss, prone to take the under dog's side. By heaven! I'd stay and find out."

"I'll stay, all right," returned Kalispel, grimly. "Blair, set me right. How long have we been here?"

"This is the third day."

"Where did you an' Sydney go? What did you do?"

"Well, after you left us we heard the shooting and followed the crowd into camp. There we met Leavitt. He was very agreeable and helpful. Asked us to supper. Pretty much taken with Sydney, of course. He gave us a tent, sent out for our packs, made us comfortable. Yesterday I bought my gold claim from him. It's one of the best, they say. Twenty dollars a foot. One hundred feet. All the claims are divided into sections of that size. . . . I've been panning gold. Dug two ounces of dust today before I gave out. It's the hardest work I ever undertook. But great fun. Sydney is crazy about it. Leavitt showed her how."

"Wal, that doesn't improve his chances of long life," muttered Kalispel, somberly. "It's hell enough to lose her—without——"

"Kalispel," interrupted Blair, hurriedly, "we were out here yesterday. Sydney wanted to see you. She seemed driven. I caught her looking out this way often. She was pretty hard hit, son. . . . Well, we came, and found you dead drunk, lying there—not a pleasant sight. Sydney was horrified. And then disgusted. I wanted her to stay—help me do something for you. She wouldn't. . . . I'm going to tell you what she said, because I believe it will do you good. 'Dad, I—I cared for that cowboy, Kalispel!—— But this isn't he. Or if it is I am disillusioned. . . . To protest love for me—then, scarcely out of my sight—give way to his terrible passion to kill—and drink. . . . To lie here like a sodden beast. . . . He did not love me.' "

"Aw, Gawd!" groaned Kalispel, hanging his head. This was the last, the most exceeding bitter drop of his cup of gall.

"Kalispel, that's tougher than loss of your mine. I don't share Sydney's disillusion. She is young and this is her second hurt. By far the deepest, I am sure. If I know the Blairs, she won't soon get over this one. . . . Now, boy, a last word, then I'm through this painful talk. Adversity either beats us down or brings out the latent in us, the unquenchable spirit of manhood. This is not a question of your physical courage. It seems you are notorious for that. But a question of whether or not you are going to succumb to drink—and such abasement as that in which we found you."

"Blair, don't say any more, please," replied Kalispel, hoarsely. "Only tell me, why did you talk this way?"

"I like you and I think you have had a rotten deal. Besides, I know the horror of the bottle, myself."

"Were you ever a drinker?"

"Yes, I was. And I have never been safe."

Kalispel recalled what Sydney had betrayed to him about her father's conviviality.

"Ah-huh. So that's why. . . . Wal, red liquor never had me down till this time. . . . Blair, you've got another reason for all this plain, kind talk"

"Yes. I've taken a sudden dislike to Leavitt."

"How come?"

"I don't know, except what revealed it to me. And that was a look I saw him give Sydney when she was unaware of it. If I were your kind, Kalispel, I'd pick a fight with him and shoot him. This illustrates my peculiar streak. But as I look back over my life I find that seldom or never has my distrust of a man been unjust. Or my faith wrong. It's a gift."

"Wal, I had the same hunch about Leavitt. Yet I couldn't lay a single proof of its being fair."

"Leavitt has a powerful personality," declared Blair. "He might have that two-sided nature so common to many men. If he is crooked he'll never fool me. But he could Sydney. She thinks he is handsome, well educated, fascinating, the biggest Westerner she has met yet."

"I reckon that's easy for me to see, but most damn sickenin' to swallow."

"Leavitt is taken with her. He may get her on the rebound. Funny how strange and weak women are that way. Perhaps it is self-preservation. It worries me. I tried to give Sydney a hint of my suspicions. She shut me up pronto."

"Wal, Blair, don't talk against the man. That'll only make Sydney contrary. Women are shore strange an' weak. But sometimes strange an' wondrous strong, too. I'd class Sydney among the last. An' *if* she really cared for me I can't conceive of her goin' to Leavitt, whether or not I'm a bloody gunman an' beast. Rebound or no rebound!"

"She did care for you. She said so, right out. And that implies more than she confessed."

"My Gawd, man! Stop torturin' me."

"I'm sorry," rejoined Blair, hastily, as he arose. "But she is my daughter. And she *was* your sweetheart. . . . Hell! don't glare at me like that. I know her better than you. . . . You can't get out of this fact. We had a common cause. This West is hell. I can't go back. I must meet what comes. And I'm scared. . . . I took a shine to you, Kalispel, and I felt I could lean on you."

"You can—so help me Gawd!" cried Kalispel, fiercely. The father of the girl he loved had called to the best in him —to what had seemed utterly destroyed. But—for her sake he might perform a miracle.

"Atta boy! That's the talk," ejaculated Blair, warmly.

"But how—Blair? How?" gasped Kalispel, haggardly. "I'll be an outlaw now. Every miner's opinion, if not his hand, will be against me. Leavitt will see to that. He stole our mine. An' he'll be crafty as hell."

"Yes. But this camp will grow like a mushroom overnight," declared Blair, earnestly. "In a month there'll be thousands of people here. They are streaming in. Twelve pack outfits yesterday. Old-timers here say Thunder Mountain will bring the biggest gold rush Idaho ever saw. . . . A tent town, a saw-log, clap-board town full of miners, gamblers, adventurers, women, merchants, pack-drivers, freighters. All bent on gold. An awful mess, they say. It's fascinating to think of. I'd like the idea but for my daughter. . . . Well, you lay low. Dig gold yourself. Cut the drink and don't use your gun except in case of self-defense. Wait for your brother Jake to come back. He may shed some light on this stampede. And all the time you will be working for proof of Leavitt's guilt. But *that* will not be your main objective."

"What will be, Blair?" queried Kalispel, thrilling despite his agony.

"Sydney! To win back her confidence and respect. To show her that you are a man. That you can take a blow like this, yet still come up to make your fortune. That no defeat can keep you from winning her and the ranch your heart was set on."

"You're diggin' my guts out of a vise," returned Kalispel. "Blair, it's not hard to see why Sydney is such a wonderful girl. You're her father. . . . I'll play the cards as you have dealt them to me. An' win or lose, I shall owe to you an' Sydney the great lesson of my life. . . . You go back now. I've work to do an' some mighty desperate thinkin'."

Kalispel's acts, in great contrast to his inertia for three days, attested to the spell which beset him. At least the interest taken in him by the miners along that end of the stream proclaimed he was an individual of marked interest in Thunder Mountain Camp. He bathed and scrubbed himself in the ice-cold creek; he packed water up to his camp; he shaved his bristling face; he burned his ragged clothes and donned the new outfit he had purchased; he put his camp in ship-shape, and then cooked supper, all with feverish haste and in plain sight of his neighbors.

He thought that they would be vastly more astounded if they could have read his mind. It seemed to him to be a whirling chaos of consciousness, a continual stream of ideas, plans, hopes, fears, of deduction and calculation, of intuitive reasoning and rejected imaginings. And a fight against the deadly menace he felt for Leavitt. He divined presently that any effort of will directed against that mood was wasted. Leavitt was responsible for Sam's disappearance, probably his death. He would get back Sam's quartz mine from that suave and resourceful robber and kill him afterward, or he would kill him, anyhow. Proof was the imperative necessity.

Finally he grasped the wisdom of Blair's reasoning. What he had to do was to live down an undeserved reputation for reckless shooting and evil motive, for all the hard idiom the frontier had cast upon him. How to set about that seemingly impossible task was the imperious question. Kalispel cudgeled his brain. Long after dark he paced to and fro under the black sinister mountain and the stars, and long after he lay in his bed he pondered the problem. In the end he remembered his earlier years of cowboy life on the Wyoming ranges, where he had been popular with everybody with whom he came in contact. Drinking, gambling, his appeal to dance-hall girls, and the inevitable gun-play—these had been his bane. The man who made the same mistake twice could never cope with the terrific problems that confronted Kalispel. At midnight he heard the faint thunder of the mountain, and it seemed to record the passing of time, the brevity of life, the fact that nature audited her secret books—that now was the day to seize.

Morning came. Kalispel awakened to it, mindful that a resolve made in the white heat of misfired passion could be kept through the gloom and tedium of recurrent moods. He was equal to his task. He laid stone walls; he chopped wood; he washed and dried his blankets; he built a fireplace; and to his watchful neighbors he made plain that he had adopted his camp as a permanent abode.

He had supplies for a month, but not a dollar to his name. His resentment powerfully combated the idea of working a poor claim, when by rights he should have owned the best. Yet he yielded to the exigency of his plan. Once decided, he had the thought that there must be hundreds of fine claims left. But where? Anywhere in that valley of treasure, he argued. Seldom did the mile stretch of winding trail up the valley fail to show pack-trains. The prospectors, the miners, the adventurers were coming. He had as fair a chance as they.

A few minutes later he was deepening the gravelly pit of his fireplace when a gleam of yellow caught his eye. "What the hell!" he muttered, falling on his knees. The bright gleam had resulted when his spade cut into a dusty gold nugget. Incredulously he stared. The blood fled back to his heart and appeared to dam up there; a muffled drumming pounded in his ears. Then with eager, grasping hands he clawed into a pocket of nuggets, a few large and many small, coarse-grained and dull, but gold, gold, gold.

Chapter Six

The town of Thunder Mountain grew as if by magic.

Only a little while back the valley had been a wilderness of solitude and silence, undisturbed save for the scream of the eagle on the heights, the bugle of elk on the slopes, and the strange rumble, like distant thunder, deep under the earth.

The old beaver, answering to the instincts of nature, had taken her cub and had left the valley. The Indians, creatures of the wild, in touch with the elements, had listened to the mysterious voice of the Great Spirit, and they too had fled.

But the white man came. The magnet was gold. And no voice, no warning, no spirit, no God could drive him away.

From Challis and Salmon, Boise and Bellair, from Washington and Montana, from the south across the black lava deserts, from the Wyoming ranges, from everywhere that men heard that siren call, enchanting and irresistible, they came deepening the trails; prospectors, engineers, promoters, miners, followed by the adventurers, the gamblers, the women with hawk eyes, the dive-keepers and rum-peddlers, until Thunder River hummed with a raw, bold, happy, excited greedy throng.

Tents sprouted like white weeds and shacks and cabins followed suit. Two enterprising carpenters packed in a portable saw-mill and made more money than the gold diggers. Like grass before the scythe the willows, the cottonwoods, the pines and firs, the lodge-pole pines and the spruces went down. In peeled logs and sawed clapboards they went up again, almost as swiftly as they had come down, and from dawn to dark the incessant pound of hammers resounded through the valley. The solitude that had beguiled the Indians vanished in the roar of a thriving gold-camp, and the beauty perished in the stark, ghastly, hideous defacement of nature by white men.

In less than six weeks after its discovery, Leavitt Mine was in operation, grinding out the precious yellow metal. A tenton stamp mill in sections had been hauled by wagons to within a hundred miles of Thunder River. From there the greatest freighter in Idaho, one Juan Uriquides, had packed the mill over perilous trails and down into the valley on the backs of mules. He received ten cents a pound for this packing, and thereby set a price for all supplies and merchandise to be freighted in.

The once crystal stream of mountain water ran low and muddy; the big-horn sheep that had watched from the lofty ledges deserted their haunts to escape the noise and smoke; the elk and deer went across the divide.

Every available claim for two miles along the creek had been staked. Up the slopes and in the gullies miners dug in the loose earth blasted in the rock. By day and by night the long wide street of Thunder City roared. On each side of this long wide street stores and restaurants, saloons and gambling-dens, lodging-houses and dance-halls, made bid for the custom of the populace, and each and every one of them was full. Thunder City, in its early bloom, was rich. The atmosphere was one of swift, gay, ruthless, happy-go-lucky life, under which burned the fever of gold. There were no drones in that beehive. A restless tension strung each and all as if they unconsciously knew Thunder City would not last and they must make hay while the sun shone.

The time came when Thunder City achieved the dignity of a miners' meeting, during which, as was the custom of progressive mining-camps, a judge, sheriff, and recorder were elected. The former's duty was to preside at each meeting of the gold-diggers; the second was supposed to maintain law and order; and the third had the task of keeping records of claims. All claims went by numbers. Leavitt's mine was No. 1, and all the others, up and down the valley, were numbered accordingly.

Rand Leavitt was the judge; Hank Lowrie, the sheriff; and Cliff Borden, the recorder.

One sunset hour in early summer Kalispel Emerson sat in the door of the little cabin he had erected between the boulders that had served as his shelter.

He had a double motive for occupying this favorite seat during his leisure hours—first he could watch the trails in the hope of seeing his brother Jake some day; and secondly, from this vantage-point he could look down the gradually descending bench to the cabin of the Blairs, located on the bank of the stream, and on the site of Blair's gold claim. Tents and shacks were scattered all along the stream and over the bench, but the cabin of the Blairs stood out conspicuously by reason of its yellow peeled logs and pretentiousness. It had a wide porch on the eastern side, where Sydney spent a good deal of her time working and resting.

Kalispel watched her at this distance, perhaps an eighth of a mile, and knew that she knew he watched her. The young miners going by her cabin always stopped to chat a moment, and Rand Leavitt often visited her there, especially on Sunday afternoons, but Kalispel never went near enough to catch the expression of her eyes. They appeared to be black gulfs in a pale face the sun did not tan.

Two months had gone by for Kalispel on the wings of his strenuous gold-digging and his passionate devotion to the Herculean task he had set himself. The former had been successful beyond even the dreams he had entertained before his loss. Every place he struck his pick yielded gold in some quantity, and he had so many little buckskin bags of dust and nuggets hidden away that he was afraid to count them. But in his serious reflection he knew beyond doubt that his dream of a ranch could be realized, and that if his star continued to shine all through summer and fall he would be rich. It did not affect him much, except when he indulged in a melancholy dream of what might have been.

His passionate devotion to the ideal set up by Blair had not been entirely futile, but he had found that to live down a bad name kept alive by enemies in high places was something well-nigh impossible. The sole hope that now inspired Kalispel hung upon the fact that Sydney Blair watched him from afar.

Always at the back of his mind was the consciousness that he still was Kalispel Emerson and would one day stalk out to face Rand Leavitt. That seemed inevitable. Jealousy had been added to what he considered a stern passion for justice. Leavitt's attention to Sydney Blair was unmistakable and if she had not responded she had at least accepted it. Gossip of the gold camp had it that Leavitt would marry the girl.

Each and every honest miner in the diggings was too busy with his own labors to know what the other fellow was doing. The saloons and gambling-dens were objective proof of whether a miner was rich today and poor tomorrow. As they earned prodigiously, they wasted prodigally. But this fact did not apply to Kalispel. He did not drink or gamble or spend; and therefore was considered poor, one of the many unsuccessful diggers. Moreover, his story was known, and his absurd claim and loss were an outstanding joke with those miners who did not know him.

Thunder City, however, was overrun with adventurers, and miners who labored for gold only as a blind, while by stealth they stole and robbed. Kalispel had come under the cold, watchful eyes of those parasites, and many had been the time his gun hand had itched. But if they were suspicious of him, they had no ground to substantiate it, for he was just as shrewd and infinitely more watchful.

On a late afternoon Kalispel pondered a plan to further his interests; and this was to begin to hunt game with the idea of supplying meat to the miners. Deer had been run out of the valley. Good hunters were few, and most miners would not take the time to hunt. Yet they were greatly dependent upon meat, for food prices in the stores were abnormally high. Kalispel thought his plan would serve several purposes —to give the impression that he needed money, to enable him to become acquainted with many miners and win their confidence, and to hide his secret motive to work out the truth of Leavitt's guilt. As the weeks passed Kalispel grew more sure of this. Leavitt might be another Henry Plummer of Alden Gulch fame. Murder of miners had so far not occurred, but the finding and stealing of stored gold dust, and robbery by masked men at night had grown increasingly until it was something to contend with.

As he revolved these thoughts the valley became steeped in a luminous golden sheen, the last reflection from the sunset flush upon the heights. And at that moment Sydney Blair appeared upon the porch, to lean against the rail and gaze out. This had become such a habit of hers that Kalispel waited for it. She wore something which shone faintly blue. He got up to pace to and fro, and at last to stand where she could not help but see him. Always he was alone. And she must know that his heart was yearning for her—that degradation was impossible for him now. But did she know, and if she did, what were her thoughts?

Kalispel had talked often with Blair, and somehow their positions had become reversed. The advice and solicitation now came from Kalispel. After all, Blair had not made as good a deal in his gold claim as he had fondly believed. His gravel bar had suddenly panned out. And digging among the rocks of his claim for nuggets or quartz had not been successful. He had begun to drink and gamble, moderately, as was common among the better class of miners, yet even that little had lately made a subtle difference in him. Wherefore Kalispel, summing up, decided that it was about time for him to step out of his quiet, watchful isolation.

He walked down to the stream, to the big camp where Hadley and Jones, two progressive miners, maintained a mess for eight of their comrades. Kalispel dropped in on them at supper-time. He was not exactly friendly with these men, but knew that through the weeks they had unlearned some of the lessons gossip and ill-will had taught them.

"Jones, I've an idee," said Kalispel. "How are you off for meat?"

"Meat?— Jehoshephat! Costs us more than ham an' bacon."

"How'll it be when the snow flies?"

"If it grows any harder to get we'll blow this grub-shack, an' thet's no lie."

"I'm thinkin' of huntin' meat to sell. What'll you pay a pound for fresh venison an' elk?"

"Thet's a good idee, Emerson. Are you serious?"

"Shore. I've got to live. I'm a poor miner, but a good hunter. Will you pay ten cents a pound till fall, an' more when the snow flies?"

"You bet I will. An' jump at a hundred pounds a week, an' double thet when winter comes."

"Done. It'll be no trick for me. I've a horse an' burros."

"Kalispel," spoke up Hadley, the young partner of Jones, "you'd be doin' us a service. Lack of meat is the drawback in this mess. An' thet holds all over town."

"Wal, I'll see if I can drum up some more customers. An' if I can, I won't trade for any of your claims."

"Small chance of you gettin' a whack of mine," called out a miner, cheerfully. "Look at this."

Kalispel stepped over to have placed in his hands a bright smooth nugget weighing in excess of three ounces.

"Gosh! That's the biggest I ever saw," exclaimed Kalispel, as he returned it.

"This ain't a marker to the one sold to Leavitt by a miner. Three hundred dollars he got for it. An' you can gamble thet if Leavitt paid so much it was worth a good deal more."

"Yes, an' our hard-fisted judge grabbed the Woodbury claim today," interposed another miner.

"I hadn't heard," replied Kalispel, quietly. "You fellows know I'm particular interested in how Judge Leavitt acquires land, gold, claims, an' quartz veins."

"Haw! Haw!— Wal, this was easy. Leavitt has the

decidin' of all claims, you know. An' he took over most of Woodbury's because thet hombre stepped high, wide, an' handsome when he stepped off his claim. Course the miners in on the meetin' were thick with Leavitt an' voted Woodbury out. There's some gossip floatin' about. Leavitt, Borden, Lowrie, an' a few more are playin' a high-handed game these days."

Kalispel went on down the trail, pondering what he had heard. He stopped at camps of miners he knew and got not only orders for fresh meat, but also sincere thanks for the offer.

There were several trails leading into town and the one on which he found himself happened to pass the Blair cabin. This time Kalispel did not avoid it.

The hour was almost dusk, but the magnificent afterglow of sunset reflected down into the valley, bathing it in rosy light. The day had been hot, and now the drowsy heat had begun to yield to the cool air from the heights.

Blair sat on his porch steps, smoking. Kalispel heard voices, and as he recognized Sydney's, he felt his breath catch in his throat.

"Howdy, Blair," drawled Kalispel, as he leisurely halted. "Any dust these days?"

"Hello yourself," replied Blair. "Where you been keepin' yourself?"

"Me? Aw, I been meditatin' on a misspent life," said Kalispel, coolly.

Sydney stepped from the back of the porch to the rail. She wore white. Kalispel bowed and greeted her.

"Good evening," she rejoined, in perfect composure.

Kalispel's quick glance noted the sweet, troubled face, and the dark eyes that swept over him. Then he looked back at Blair, striving to hide the tumult sight of her had roused in him.

"Kalispel, the only dust around this claim is what blows in from the trails," said Blair, disgustedly.

"All panned out?"

"Ha!— My neighbor, Dick Swan, an old miner, says the bar in front of my claim was planted."

"Dad, you should not say things you can't prove," interposed Sydney, quickly. "Especially to an enemy of Rand Leavitt."

"Oh, well, what's the use?" returned Blair, wearily. "I'll have to buy another claim. . . . How you making out,

70

Kalispel? Never saw you look so fine. Still digging up in the rocks?"

"Not much. I hate it 'most as bad as I did diggin' fence-post holes back in Wyomin'. Blair, what I dropped over to see you about is this. I'm goin' to hunt game an' sell fresh meat to the miners. Would you like some?"

"Fresh meat? Lord, yes! We've been living on canned stuff. But ask Sydney here. She does the buying."

"How about it, Miss Blair?" inquired Kalispel, easily. "Would you like a nice fat haunch of venison now an' then?"

"So you intend making honest use of your one talent?" she said, in a level voice that irritated and mystified Kalispel. Why could she not be civil?

"Butcherin', you mean," rejoined Kalispel, in a voice as controlled as hers. "Shore. I'm gettin' out of practice handlin' guns. An' sooner or later now I'm shore to buck into Borden or Lowrie—or Leavitt."

She vibrated slightly to that, but her reply was an inscrutable gaze from eyes now shadowy and deep. Then she wheeled away from the rail.

Blair laughed, not without a tinge of bitterness. "Sydney's testy these days, Kalispel. No wonder. But you fetch the venison."

"Thanks, Blair." Then Kalispel bent close to whisper. "If you get up against it in any way—come to see me."

Blair regarded him with haggard eyes. "Son, I'm ashamed to do it, after that spiel I gave you weeks ago."

"Hell! Never mind that. It served its turn. . . . Are things goin' bad?"

Blair whispered, after a glance back on the porch. "I've lost a good deal of money gambling."

"Aw!" and Kalispel made a passionate gesture. "Pritchard?"

"Mostly to him. But others, also. I was way ahead at first. If I'd only had sense enough to quit then! Now I've got to play to get even."

"You never will, Blair. Take a hunch from me. Never with this gang. They'll fleece the skin off you."

"Fleece! Do you mean to imply the game is crooked?"

"Good Heavens, man! Don't you know that?"

"No, I don't. But by Heaven! I'll watch them next time." Blair appeared to be stubborn, somber, thick, and hard to reach. Kalispel had seen that change in hundreds of genial and wholesome men. It came from drink. Kalispel sustained a sudden sharp misgiving about Blair. So many Easterners were too soft to tackle the adversity of the West. Yet he was not a man who could be criticized. Kalispel thought rapidly.

"All right. I'll watch them with you," he replied, curtly, and turned to go.

"Hold on, Emerson," called Blair, rising and taking Kalispel's arm. "You won't go in these gambling-halls on my account, will you?"

"I shore will. Sydney's goin' back on me is no reason for me to go back on you."

"But, son, listen," returned Blair, in distress. "Sure as you do that you'll be using your gun again."

"Like as not. Will that jar you?"

"Not by a damn sight!" retorted Blair. "I was thinking of . . . Never mind now. Anyway, I appreciate your friendship. And, by thunder! I think you have been unjustly maligned. They've all got you wrong, and that goes for my own daughter."

He squeezed Kalispel's arm and abruptly returned to the porch, turning at the steps to call back: "I'll let you know when I'm going to buck the tiger again."

"Fine. I might set in the game myself," called Kalispel, which remark was inspired by Sydney's white form once more against the rail.

"Dad, is *he* persuading you to gamble?" came in Sydney's high-pitched voice.

"Hell no!" rasped Blair. "He's been trying to stop me. That boy is the only friend we've made. You don't savvy the West. You don't appreciate that cowboy. You've allowed your absurd squeamishness and that blighter Leavitt——"

Kalispel passed on out of hearing. He would like to have heard Sydney's reply to that last reproach of her father. Kalispel found his blood racing unwontedly and a choking sensation in his throat. He had been responsible for getting the Blairs into this unhappy situation. What would be the end?

He went downtown. Thunder City was having its supper hour; nevertheless, that in no wise detracted from the appearance of activity. The yellow lights of the main street flared brightly; it was crowded with moving figures; music and laughter vied with the hum of conversation. The saloons were full of drinkers, loungers, miners selling and buying claims, gamblers on the lookout for prey, adventurers of every type.

Kalispel started in to make a round of all the stores, halls, resorts, houses, on the street. He took supper in the third

72

place, a restaurant of pretensions, newly started. There were several women present, not of the dance-hall stripe, and one of them, young, handsome, richly clad, manifested interest in Kalispel, and bowed to him with the freedom prevalent in the mining-camp. He doffed his sombrero and approached her table.

"I reckon you ladies are shore lost here in Thunder City," he said, with his winning smile.

"We would not have missed it for the world," returned the handsome young woman. The other two smiled their corroberation and frankly flattered him with their glances. The man accompanying them was obviously not a mining-man. He said they were travelers going home from California and had not been able to resist the lure of a gold stampede.

"Did you enjoy the ride in?" queried Kalispel, of the youngest woman.

"It was terrible, but wonderful," she replied, enthusiastically. "We rode, walked, fell off, and rode again."

"An' now you're here—what?"

"I'd like to stay," she said, frankly.

"Wal, you'd shore be an asset to Thunder City," drawled Kalispel, admiringly. "No trouble drawin' yourself a husband! Now if you're lookin' for one I'd——"

They interrupted him with merry laughter, in which their escort joined.

"The delightful simplicity and suddenness of you Westerners!" exclaimed the pretty one. "You don't look like the rest of these miners, though."

"I'm no miner," rejoined Kalispel, in his coolest, laziest voice, enjoying the incident hugely and playing up to it. "My name is Kalispel Emerson. Used to be a cowboy. Sorry to add, lady—just now a desperado."

"Indeed? How thrilling! . . . So I have a proposal from a desperado? Are you one of those Mr. Leavitt said were to be run out of Thunder City—or hanged?"

"I reckon not, lady," replied Kalispel, stiffening, and passed on, to their evident disappointment. He could not escape Leavitt's name. Everywhere he went Leavitt somehow intruded upon any word.

Kalispel passed out upon his round of the street, with a consciousness that it did not require much to kindle the old spirit of fire. About the only thing that could save Leavitt and Borden and Lowrie from facing him soon was for the mountain to slide down and bury the gold camp. In the

Dead Eye Saloon he ran straight into Lowrie, but saw that individual first.

"Howdy, Sheriff," he said, with careless nonchalance that had a bite in it. "Are you still trailin' Montana cowboys?"

"Howdy, Kalispel," returned the other, gruffly. "No, I reckon not, so long as they keep the peace."

"Wal, I'm not drinkin' or gamblin', these days."

"What are you doin'? Look fit an' pert to me. An' prosperous, too."

"Shore, I'm all three. Just hangin' around for my brother to come. Then we'll hunt for Sam, my other brother, who made this gold strike."

"So I heard, Kalispel," rejoined the sheriff, ponderingly. "You don't look loco. But thet talk shore is."

"Lowrie, you know damn well I wouldn't make that claim if it wasn't true," snapped Kalispel, coldly, and backed out into the throng on the street.

He watched gambling games in several halls. Then he went into Bull Mecklin's, reputed to be the toughest den in the gold-diggings; and was there invited by gamesters to join them. Kalispel smilingly responded that he hated to win money from anyone. And as he did not play or approach the bar he attracted the attention of the proprietor, a massive-headed, thick-necked man whose name fitted him. He gruffly asked Kalispel what he wanted there.

"I'm lookin' for a man," replied Kalispel, significantly, and was severely let alone after that. Some one recognized him, however, and he heard the whisper: "Kalispel, Montana gun-slinger!"

Thunder City was a bonanza gold-strike, the scene of Idaho's great stampede, and it was full of raw, bold characters, many of whom were dishonest; but it had nothing of the menace Kalispel had known in cattle towns of Wyoming and Montana. Here he was an object of curiosity, a notorious person to be let alone, a doubtful and sinister figure. Back there he would have been encountered in every saloon and gambling-hall by some hard-lipped youngster or lean-faced man who did not like the look of him or the way he packed his gun. Thunder City was new; it would grow wild if the gold lasted.

Finally Kalispel strolled into the most pretentious resort of the street, one that had just been erected and not yet named. It occupied the largest structure in the mining-town, a barnlike frame outside and a markedly contrasting gaudy interior. Music, gay voices, shrill mirth, clink of gold and crash of glass, a shuffle of rough boots—these united in a roar. Kalispel was surprised to run into the pretty little girl he had met in the Spread Eagle at Salmon.

"Howdy, Nugget," he greeted her pleasantly. "What you doin' away from Salmon. Did you shake the Spread Eagle?"

"Say, was I drunk when I met you—somewhere?" she asked, flippantly.

"You shore wasn't. Why? That's not flatterin'."

"Because I wouldn't forget a handsome gazabo like you. What's your name?"

"Kalispel Emerson," replied he, and related the incident of their meeting.

"Oh, I remember now. But you don't look the same. Except your eyes. . . . Struck it rich, I'll bet. All spruced up, bright-eyed and pink-cheeked!— Say, boy, you'd better let me alone."

"Don't you like me, Nugget?"

"If I didn't, would I give you a hunch?"

"Let's dance. I reckon I'm rusty, but I shore used to be slick."

They joined the whirling throng on the wide dance-floor, and they had not progressed far when she said: "You may be rusty, Kalispel, but you're pretty good. My God! what a relief to be free of these clodhoppers, heavy with liquor, bearded and dirty!"

"Nugget, it struck me over in Salmon that you were too nice a kid for this dance-hall life."

She looked up at him, but made no reply.

"Who fetched you over here?" he went on, presently.

"I came with Borden's outfit."

"Borden? Oh, yes! He ran the Spread Eagle over there. Is there anyone in this deal with him?"

"Say, are you pumping me?"

"Sounds like that, I reckon. But listen, an' then tell me or not, as you like." As they danced around he briefly related the part his brothers and he had played in the discovery of gold there in the valley, about his leaving with Jake and returning alone to find Sam gone, and the claim lost, his shooting of Selback and accusing of Leavitt.

"So you're that fellow!" she whispered, excitedly. "You're that bad hombre, then? You look it, Kalispel. . . . Well, go ahead and make love to me. It will make Rand Leavitt wild."

"Ah-huh.— Is he sweet on you?"

"I wouldn't call it sweet. He has reasons of his own for

not being open about it. And I don't mind telling you that he's Borden's partner here, on the sly, too."

"Wal, thanks, Nugget. One more question. But don't be hurt even if you won't answer. . . . Is this man Borden responsible for your being here?"

"No. I can't lay that to him exactly. I have to earn my living. But he's a slave-driver. Ask the other girls."

"Nugget, suppose you let me be your friend."

"You mean make love to me?" The bitterness in her voice touched a deeper cord in Kalispel's kindly nature.

"I don't want to be that kind of friend, Nugget. I can be a better one. I admit, though, I'd shore have made love to you if my heart hadn't been broken. You're as pretty as the dickens. An' nice. I like you."

"Well, you're a queer duck. But I like you, too. And you're on. I won't promise, though, not to fall in love with you."

"I'll risk that, Nugget."

"You'll risk more. It's bound to look like you were drinking and making up with me. And if you get—well, too thick with me, Borden will rare. And so will Leavitt."

"I reckon. Wal, I've made the offer."

"You're a deep one. What's your game?"

"Didn't I confide in you—trust you?"

"So you did," she returned, wonderingly. "I've got a hunch. . . . Kalispel, I'm yours for jest or earnest. . . . Say, it's nice to dance with you. You're clean and decent"

"I'll stick with you all evenin'. We'll pour the drinks on the floor. . . . Reckon it's awful nice to dance with you, too, Nugget."

Chapter Seven

Jake Emerson's case against the Leavitt Mining Company was scheduled to be heard on the night of the very day he got back to the valley, a gaunt, haggard ghost of the man who had left there two months before in the prime of life and ambition. It was significant to Kalispel that Judge Leavitt, furious at the claim, rushed the hearing of the case.

The law of the mining-camps was that in case of a dispute over a gold claim as to ownership, the case was to be heard before the judge in the presence of the other miners, all of whom were to listen to the testimony and then vote. Which-ever claimant received the most votes got the gold claim.

Borden's dance-hall, being the most commodious place in the camp for a courtroom, was selected for the trial. This was to be its initiation in such proceedings.

Even without much time for advertising, the case attracted a throng. Kalispel had personally notified hundreds of miners to be present. He realized that Jake and he had no chance of winning the claim. But Kalispel's purpose was to establish a contest of Leavitt's right to the property.

A thousand and more miners assembled in the street before Borden's dance-hall. Less than a hundred of these were admitted, however, and that augmented the growing curiosity in the case.

"Fellars," sang out one man, "thar's room for three or four hundred of us in thet hall, packed like sardines."

"Wal, every consarned one of us has a right to vote," said another.

"Wake up, tenderfeet," called a cool ringing voice from the shadows. "This case is fixed."

That voice belonged to Kalispel, who had remained outside to see how many miners came and what their comment might be. Then he pounded to be admitted. He required only a general survey of those present to be assured that very few friendly to him were there. Blair had promised to come, but could not be located. Lowrie, the sheriff, the two deputies, all armed, stood conspicuously before the orchestra platform of the hall, where at a table sat the judge and his recorder.

Leavitt, pale and stern, stood up and rapped on the table.

"Gentlemen," he began in a loud voice that carried out of the open windows into the thronged street, "the case at hand is that of one Jake Emerson, claimant, and the Leavitt Mining Company, defendant. The property contested is the quartz lode, claim Number One. . . . We will hear Emerson's argument."

When the judge sat down Jake came forward. His appear-ance carried conviction of two facts—first that he had endured almost mortal illness and the privation and toil of a desert wanderer; and secondly that his white face and eyes of fire, his heavy irresistible strides forward, pronounced him a formidable person absolutely sure of the right of his cause. He halted in front of the platform, and after a long steady stare at Leavitt, he turned to face the hall.

"Men, you are all miners like myself," he began, in sonorous voice. "An' if you are honest, an' live by the rule

77

'do unto others as you would have them do unto you,' I could ask no more than to be judged by you.

"I arrived in Idaho 'most a year ago, comin' from Montana with my elder brother Sam, an' my younger brother Lee, who is standin' there. Sam an' me had been prospectin' for years an' knew the minin' game from A to Z. Our young brother, however, was a cowboy. He took to the wild life of the range, an' as he survived one hard outfit after another he earned the name Kalispel Emerson, gunman, bad hombre, rustler. He may deserve the first, because the fact thet he is alive today proves it. But the other names are undeserved. The fact thet Sam an' I believed in the boy's honesty is responsible for our bringin' him with us to Idaho.

"We prospected the Lemhi Range before we wandered over here into the Saw Tooths. It was on the second of April, as I figgered out afterwards, thet we dropped down over the south slope into this valley. . . . Now, men, I can prove thet we came, though not the date. As I've only just returned here today, so tuckered out thet I fell in my tracks, it stands to reason thet I couldn't have seen any of the things I'll enumerate. . . . Some of you miners will remember signs of an old beaver-dam on the far side of the creek, where the little brook curves in. . . . There used to be some rings of ground, earth banked up in circles. These were made by the Sheep-Eater Indians who camped here many years ago. . . . There used to be a pine tree across the creek on the high ridge, an' it forked at the trunk so low down you could step up in it. . . ."

"Thet big pine furnished lumber for my cabin," interrupted a miner. "I cut it down myself."

"Silence!" ordered Judge Leavitt, pounding the table. "And, Emerson, you confine yourself to your claim. We haven't time for all this rigamarole."

"The first night we camped here we heard the old mountain thunder," continued Jake. "An' the next day we struck gold. I took a hundred an' more pans of dust an' nuggets out of the creek. An' before sunset Sam came staggerin' into camp with a chunk of quartz showin' heavy veins of gold. He had uncovered a ledge thet carried a quartz lead.

"We made our plan. Sam was to stay here to guard our claim. Lee an' I were to go out. I was to take the quartz to prove our claim an' sell a half interest for one hundred thousand dollars. Lee was to pack supplies back into the valley. . . . We left, workin' up over the pass at the east end of the valley, an' we crossed the Middle Fork, an' got to

Challis. There, as we decided it took so many days to get out, an' Sam would soon be needin' supplies, Lee left Challis for Salmon, where he was to outfit an' go back over the trail we had made. I was to go to Boise an' make our deal.

"Men, I never got to Boise. I never got away from Challis. . . . We must have been watched an' suspected. Mebbe some sharp-eyed claim-jumpers saw me unpack my burros. It was all I could do to lift thet chunk of quartz. I hid it under my bed. . . . Wal, I had a few drinks thet night. But I wasn't drunk or near drunk. I was in possession of all my faculties. An' when I was slugged from behind I fell an' seen the man who hit me before he knocked me out. He was youngish, had a big round head with short hair, an' deep eyes like gimlets———"

"Gentlemen," Kalispel's voice rang out, "that description fits perfectly the man Selback I shot here the day I arrived. He was a guard at the quartz mine an' tried to throw his rifle on me."

Leavitt pounded the table furiously. "Another interruption will end this case," he shouted.

"Wal, men," resumed Jake, "when I come to I was lyin' in a shack an' damn near dead. An' old fellar named Wilson had took pity on me an' took me in. I'd been crazy for weeks. You don't have to look close to see where I was hit." Here Jake bent his head to show bare, livid scars over his temple. "An' it was weeks more before I was strong enough to start back here. Accordin' to Wilson, the day followin' my accident Leavitt an' Selback packed in a hurry an' left for parts unknown. Some more men, known to be thick with Leavitt, left the next day, then mules loaded down with supplies an' minin'-tools. Thet started the stampede. . . . Then, the rest you know. An' as Gawd is my witness I have told the truth!"

Emerson ended amid a breathless silence and Leavitt arose. His strong face was white with suppressed emotion which might have been anger. But to Kalispel it was that and more. Leavitt had no fear of losing the quartz mine. But he did have fear that he would lose his life. The menace of Jake Emerson could be felt by all. Moreover, Leavitt had for a second time, met Kalispel's steely-cold gaze.

"Gentlemen, I represent the Leavitt Mining Co.," he began, clearing his throat. "And I am the only one living of the two men who found the open quartz claim. . . . So far as Emerson's testimony reflects upon me, I merely deny. He did arrive in Challis. He did get drunk. He did talk and he did get into a brawl in a saloon. But I heard about that after the stampede was well on here. Selback had the hunch to come in here. I never knew where he got it. That, however, is of no importance, because when we got here we found the quartz mine open. The ground had been stripped, the lode exposed, and the gold vein was shining in the sun. But there was no miner. He had been there days before, but he was gone. Gone, gentlemen! We hunted and hunted, yet found no other trace of him than the few tools and camp equipment he had left behind. I had a perfect right to take the claim, which I did. That's my testimony and that is all. You will please vote as you see fit."

In silence the miners dropped their votes into the hat Lowrie passed. When the contents were emptied on the table Leavitt said: "I cannot take part in the counting. Emerson, you are invited to sit with the recorder and count these votes."

Borden presently called out impressively: "Leavitt Mining Company sixty-six. Emerson twenty-two."

Kalispel riveted his gaze upon Leavitt. That individual, despite an iron nerve, showed the stress of the climax, and that fury had been added to his other feelings.

"Give me those twenty-two names," he hissed livid of face, and snatching the papers from Borden he scanned them with a mien that boded no good for these voters. Some miner yelled out the window: "Leavitt sixty-six. Emerson twenty-two."

Loud huzzahs did not drown yells of derision. The verdict was not unanimous. Leavitt could not have failed to hear that vote of discord.

Then Jake Emerson confronted the three officers on the platform.

"You win, as we knowed you'd win," he boomed in his sonorous voice. "But you haven't heard the last of this deal."

Kalispel leaped to the side of his brother.

"Leavitt, that last will come when Sam returns—or we find his body!"

Jake Emerson located an obscure claim and went to work, a gloomy, taciturn, defeated man, brooding revenge. Kalispel took to hunting, and packing elk and deer meat down off the high slopes and swales. About half his time was required to fulfill the obligations he had made. The rest he utilized working his claim, which still yielded gold. He had become obsessed with the idea that somewhere inside the claim he had walled off there might be another and the largest pocket of nuggets. These nuggets he had found appeared to have been melted and therefore must have encountered volcanic action.

In midsummer the peak of the stampede was reached and Thunder City saw its heyday. Gambling-dens, saloons, and dance-halls, reaped a rich harvest. Several shooting escapades, and a fatal encounter between Lowrie and a drunken miner, with an increase of banditry, augured ill for the future of the gold-diggings.

Kalispel celebrated the first of August by taking a full tin can of gold nuggets out of a hole no deeper than his waist. He did not tell Jake, much as he wanted to help that morose brother. The last thing Kalispel desired was for miners and robbers to learn he had struck gold. Besides, of late, Jake had taken to searching for Sam's body, which he claimed to have seen in a dream.

Two or three times a week Kalispel would go to the town in the evenings and develop his interesting and risky friendship with Nugget or watch Blair's gambling vicissitudes.

At length Kalispel's opportunity arrived when he found Blair sitting in a game of poker with Pritchard, Selby, and two miners he did not know. For a change Blair was winning, which fact was obvious to all from his radiance and frequent call for drinks. Pritchard was a loser, but that fact could not have been deduced from his cold pale face and impenetrable eyes. Kalispel saw how the fickle luck went against him; and as the stakes were heavy, the gambler would certainly have to resort to trickery to recoup. Coin, currency, and small ounce-sacks of gold dust furnished the medium for betting, and the game was one of table stakes.

Kalispel watched from a vantage point behind Pritchard and out of his sight. It appeared evident that Pritchard's ally was aware of Kalispel's presence, yet nothing came of that fact.

Finally the tide turned against Blair and he lost the pile of gold in front of him, most of which flowed to Selby. One of the miners was under the influence of drink and scarcely knew one card from another. The second, a sharp-eyed young giant, had begun to get suspicious. Then a jack-pot was started which progressed inordinately before it was opened. Pritchard was the dealer and this was his chance. As cards were dealt Kalispel casually stepped forward. Only an eye like his could have detected duplicity on the part of the gambler. At the right instant Kalispel shoved his gun hard into the gambler's side.

"Pritchard, if you move a finger I'll bore you," he called, in a voice to silence the room.

"What the . . . Who—?" gasped Pritchard, his face becoming ashen in hue.

"You know who. . . . Blair, turn his hand upside down—the left one."

Blair, staring aghast, did as he was bidden, disclosing neatly palmed in the long white hand the aces of spades and diamonds. Selby cursed under his breath. The young miner leaped to his feet with an imprecation.

"Steady, all," warned Kalispel, "else you'll spoil the fun or scramble this cheat's gizzard. . . . Now turn over the cards he dealt himself."

In these five cards were the two other aces.

"Only four aces!" drawled Kalispel. "Pritch, you pulled one at the wrong time."

"———— ———— ————!" cursed the young giant, in a rage, and he threw his cards in the face of the gambler. "We'll run you out of town for this."

Selby, on the opposite side of the table, broke his stiff posture to jerk suddenly. He drew, but before he could get the gun above the table Kalispel shot him in the arm. He screamed with frenzy and pain, while the gun thumped to the floor. The gambling-den rang with loud shouts and scraping of chairs and stamping of boots. Selby appeared to be fainting and fell over the table.

"Push him off," ordered Kalispel, who did not trust that move of Selby's.

The stalwart miner gave him a shove, sending him to the floor, where it was manifest that Selby was not shamming. The young giant's next move was to lunge across the table and knock Pritchard ten feet out of his chair. Moreover he leaped after the prostrate gambler and, seizing him with powerful hands, he dragged him across the floor, making a furrow in the saw-dust. And he threw Pritchard bodily out of the hall.

"Rustle, Pritchard, or you'll get shot," shouted the miner. "Some of us are gettin' damn sick of gamblers, robbers, claim-jumpers, an' such in these diggin's."

He strode back to the table and shoved a hand out to Kalispel, who could not accept it, as he still had his gun extended.

"Emerson, you don't know me, but I know you," declared the miner, in no uncertain voice. "My name's Jeffries. Thanks for interferin'. I'm strong for you. An' there are a good many more in the same boat."

"Much obliged, Kal," added Blair, pale and shaken. "I should have taken your advice."

"Damnation!" ejaculated Jeffries. "Can't we play a little poker in this camp without bein' skinned?"

Kalispel waved Blair out and backed away from the crowd. Haskell might still have to be reckoned with. Gaining the outside, Kalispel joined Blair and hurried away up the street. Kalispel cursed him roundly.

"Man, you'll be ruined if you're not shot," he ended, passionately. "An' that'll leave Sydney at the mercy of Leavitt. Then I'll have to kill him an' get run out of town myself."

They found Sydney on the porch in the moonlight with the very man Kalispel had mentioned. Anyone with half an eye could have seen that Leavitt had been making love to the girl. Kalispel certainly had murder in his heart.

"Leavitt, you better hurry downtown," said Blair. "Kalispel shot another man. It happened in your crooked gambling-joint."

"Oh, Dad!" cried Sydney, as Leavitt, leaving her abruptly, strode off the far end of the porch and went around the cabin.

Blair sat down upon the steps and wiped his wet face. Kalispel stood in the moonlight, gazing up at the girl.

"You—you devil!" she cried, in a low choking voice.

"Hey, do you mean me or your dad?" drawled Kalispel.

"I mean you. And Dad is as bad—only he's a coward instead."

"Wal, if you mean me—shore it takes devils like me to save bull-headed old geezers like your father."

"Dad, what have you—done now?"

"Nothing. I was playing cards. Got way ahead. Then lost. That gambler Pritchard cheated. Kal showed him up. And then Pritchard's partner Selby pulled his gun. Kal shot him, that's all."

"Killed—him?" whispered Sydney, in horror.

"For Heaven's sake, no! Just shot the gun out of his hand. It'd been a damn good thing if he had killed the blighter. . . . Kal, come to think of it—who ought to clean up on that last deal?"

Kalispel threw up his hands as if to indicate to Sydney that her parent was hopeless.

"Daughter, it looked mighty like Leavitt was making love to you," went on Blair.

"Yes? Well, if he was, you may be sure that I sanctioned it," she retorted.

"I won't have it," stormed Blair. "Leavitt is not what he seems."

"Unfortunately, that applies to the majority of men," replied Sydney, bitterly. "I have found it true of two, at least."

"Sydney Blair, I never was two-faced," exclaimed Kalispel, with passion. "If I were that kind, I could tell you something about Leavitt which would make you despise him."

"Rand Leavitt is a handsome, generous, splendid man," she flashed, "and I am considering his offer of marriage."

"Wal, darlin'," drawled Kalispel, cool and hard, "consider all you like. But you won't marry him."

"Don't dare call me—that. I am not your darling. And why have you the—the effrontery to say I won't marry him?"

"Do you see this lovely little plaything, shinin' in the moonlight?" taunted Kalispel, as he flipped his gun up and caught it.

"Oh-h!—You are a monster—or you are mad."

"Shore. Good night, darlin'."

The next day was Saturday, a drowsy summer day, with a hint of blue haze in the air and the smell of fall. Kalispel happened to meet Nugget on the street. In everyday costume, free of the scant and alluring attire of the dance-hall, she made a pretty graceful figure. Kalispel did not need to be asked twice to accompany her to Reed's store. As luck would have it, Leavitt and Sydney appeared coming down the street.

"Look! There's my secret admirer with the Blair girl," said Nugget, laughing. "Funny thing—life! . . . Kalispel, do you know her?"

"I've met her," replied he.

"She's lovely. What a damned shame if she's stuck on that hypocrite!"

"Nugget, when we pass them I dare you to speak to him."

"Never took a dare in my life. . . . It might be a hunch to her."

Perhaps twenty paces distant, Sydney looked up to espy Kalispel and his companion. Suddenly a blazing scarlet blush suffused her face. It waved away as swiftly, leaving her pale, with great tragic eyes staring straight ahead. Because of her strange reaction, which staggered Kalispel, he could not look at Leavitt.

"Howdy, Rand," called Nugget, with the most innocent, smiling naïveté.

Then the couples passed each other and Nugget turned to

her companion. "Gosh! but he'll murder me! . . . Did you see her blush. . . . Why, Kalispel, you're as white as a sheet!"

"Am I? Wal, I feel yellow."

"Ashamed to be seen with me?"

"Not on your life! I was glad, an' don't forget it. . . . Nugget, that's the girl who broke my heart."

"You don't say! The Blair girl!" she whispered, excitedly. "Oh, Kalispel, she *is* lovely. You poor fellow! Now I understand you and I like you better than ever. You're true to that proud girl, though she passes you scornfully on the street. And Leavitt, the skunk, parades along with her, doing the elegant—and after dark, late at night, slips in the back door to try to make love to me. . . . I'll be darned if I don't tell her!"

"Nugget, that'd be doin' her a good turn," replied Kalispel, hopefully.

"Boy, if I know girls, she didn't burn like a house afire for nothing when she recognized you. Kalispel, I'll bet she's in love with you."

"Aw, Nugget, don't handle words so horrible careless."

"I'll bet it," she went on, vehemently. "Did she *ever* love you?"

"I reckon so. A little."

"Then it's a lot now. Nothing like jealousy to show a woman's heart! She saw us—she thought you were sweet on the little blond dance-hall girl. She gave herself away."

"No—no! It's only worse. She'll like him all the more."

"Listen, pard," whispered the girl, wickedly. "If she does I can tell her something that will kill it pronto. And if not, I can tell *you* something that will make you kill him pronto."

"Nugget!" cried Kalispel.

"That's all now. Here's the store. Don't give up, cowboy. . . . Tell Dick I'll meet him tonight, right after supper."

Chapter Eight

Kalispel was scraping and stretching an elk hide when his young friend, Dick Sloan, put in an appearance.

"Howdy, Dick. You're not pannin' gold while the sun shines," was Kalispel's greeting.

"I don't care," replied the youth, flinging himself down.

It was then that Kalispel glanced up from his work. Dick was a fair-haired and frank-faced young fellow of twenty-two, lately come to Thunder City, and had at once taken a liking to Kalispel. The mining-camp was not the best place in the world for Dick, and this morning he looked it.

"Had a scrap with Nugget?" asked Kalispel, intuitively.

"Not exactly. But she—dished me," rejoined Dick, miserably.

"Dished you?—Wal, the fickle little devil! She swore she liked you."

"I thought so, too."

"Did she meet you last night?"

"Yes. An' we walked across the bridge. She was different, somehow. Sort of cold an' gloomy. Wouldn't let me touch her. I smelled liquor on her. I hate thet, an' I scolded her fierce. She took it so quiet I was sorry. Then she said: 'Dick, my boss says you interfere with my business. You take my time. An' you don't drink or gamble. There's nothin' in it for the house. So I'll have to give up seeing you any more.'"

"Wal, I'm damned! Doesn't sound like Nugget. . . . An' what'd you say to that, Dick?"

"I told her I'd drink an' gamble. My claim is comin' out fine, Kalispel. You can never tell about gold-diggin's. My neighbor, an old miner, says I'll strike it rich. So I can afford to take Nugget's time."

"Ah-huh. An' what'd she say to that?"

"She wouldn't hear of it. First she talked sense to me, an' seein' that was no good, she pitched into me proper. Then I told her there wasn't any use—that I loved her an' wanted to marry her an' take her away from the rotten dance-hall."

"The devil you did? Gosh! Dick, you are gone. An' all my fault! What'd I do it for? . . . An' how'd Nugget take that?"

"Kind of shocked her," replied Sloan. "We were walkin' back an' had just got to the bridge. She stopped to lean on the rail. Burst out cryin'. . . . I was plumb near cryin' myself— she looked so forlorn an' pretty in the moonlight. But she got over it quick an' walked on. 'Thanks, Dick, for askin' me. I'm sorry I can't.'— I asked her why she couldn't an' she told me she didn't care for me. An' I said she had cared at first. She'd admitted it, an' kissed me, too. I kept naggin' her all the way back. Finally she laughed sort of mockin' an' said: 'You poor kid! Mebbe I'm in love with Cliff Borden!' —Then she left me."

"I'm a son of a gun!" ejaculated Kalispel.

"Borden runs the hall where she dances, doesn't he?" went on Sloan.

"Yes. An' Rand Leavitt is his silent pardner."

"Do you think she told the truth? I can't believe it."

"No. I should smile not," declared Kalispel, vehemently, slamming his knife down. "Nugget is as good an' fine an' clean as the gold she's named for. Aw, I don't care if she is a dance-hall girl. That's her job, her misfortune. . . . She dished you, Dick, because you were serious an' she wanted to save you from trouble with Borden."

"Kalispel, I shore was serious."

"Better forget her, boy, an' go back to your pannin' gold."

"But I can't forget her," Dick protested, miserably. "I love her!— Pard, didn't you ever feel thet way about a girl, an' couldn't forget her?"

"Yes, I did, Dick. I do!"

"Then you must understand, Kalispel. I've got to figure a way. If I go to hittin' the bottle an' buckin' the tiger she'll see there's no help for me—an' be nice."

"Dick, you'd be fool enough to do that," snapped Kalispel, furiously. It was as if he were caught in the trap, too.

"My mind is made up, unless you can do somethin'," answered Sloan, simply. "Nugget thinks a powerful lot of you. I hoped mebbe you'd coax her to change her mind about givin' me up. I don't ask much. But I've just got to see her."

"All right, I'll make her see you," decided Kalispel, goaded by his conflicting emotions. "Go back to work. An' I'll fetch Nugget to the bridge tonight if I have to pack her. Right after supper."

Sloan lunged up with glowing face, about to burst into grateful acclaim.

"Cheese it!" yelled Kalispel. "Get out quick, or I'll change my mind."

Sloan fled, and Kalispel returned to his work. But often his hand dropped listlessly and his busy mind cogitated the strangeness, the mystery, the terror, and the glory of love. Kalispel knew what yearning for a girl's lips meant. He knew, and hated himself while he confessed it, that he would be madly glad for Sydney Blair's kisses even though he had to share them with other men. But his portion seemed more bitter than that. For Sydney surely despised him now. She could not but believe that he was in love with the dance-hall girl.

Perhaps such trend of thought had more to do with Kalispel's impotent rage than poor Sloan's predicament. At any

87

rate, he worked himself into one of his cool, reckless, dangerous states, and towards sunset he left his cabin and paced swiftly down the trail.

As he passed Blair's cabin Sydney came out on the porch, with a pan or dish in her hands. She wore a blue gingham apron, her sleeves were rolled to her elbows, and she looked bewitching. Kalispel was in a mood for anything. He would confront her, make her furious or sick or something, cost what it might. Sloan's miserable love, so devastating and all-powerful, had called to his own.

Kalispel went up on the porch, to Sydney's amaze. He had never done that before. Her violet eyes, suddenly dilating, appeared to search his face for signs of intoxication.

"Where's your dad?" asked Kalispel.

"I don't know. He left in a huff."

"How are things goin'?"

"They could not be worse. . . . But as Dad is out—please——"

"Please rustle, eh? Ump-umm. I'm hopin' you'll ask me to supper."

She laughed contemptuously. "You flatter yourself, Mr. Emerson."

"Do you expect to be alone?"

"Yes. Dad will not come back. And I don't care. . . . Oh, I hate the way things are turning out."

"Tell me, Sydney."

"No. You may be Dad's friend. He thinks so. But you are certainly not mine."

"Is Leavitt comin' over tonight?"

"I'd like to lie to you. But he is not."

"An' you'll be alone till late?"

"Yes."

"I don't like it a damn bit," declared Kalispel, forcibly.

"*You* don't! As if it were any of your business," she returned, and again her mocking little laugh scorned him.

"Wal, take your choice," said Kalispel, with the chill in his voice. "Either you let me come back here or I'll drag your father out of that gamblin'-joint an' beat him so he'll be laid up for a spell."

"You cannot mean that—that last," she protested.

"I shore do."

"You would hurt Dad?"

"Hurt him? Isn't he hurtin' you more an' more? Isn't he slippin' more every day? Isn't he leavin' you alone for this slick-tongued Leavitt to——"

"Yes," she interposed hurriedly. "But that is no reason for violence. Your kindness is misplaced, Mr. Emerson. *You* are not my champion."

"Not with your consent, I shore can see. But I am, anyhow."

"You are, in—in spite of my scorn for you?"

"In spite of that. . . . I've had a rotten deal, Sydney. From life, from luck, from this liar, Leavitt—from *you*. But deep as it all has sunk into me, I'm still a man. An' I'm goin' to raise hell around these diggin's pretty pronto."

"In my behalf, Sir Galahad?"

"Aw, Sydney, that doesn't become you!" he ejaculated, reproachfully. "Scorn me all you want, but don't bemean yourself."

"I declare—you are the most amazing person. I simply cannot understand you."

"Wal, that's because I'm simple an' honest. An' you're deep an' deceitful. You're a woman. You don't play fair. . . . But as always we get into a fight. I'll be goin'. Make your choice. Do I come back here or——"

"Very well, you may come. I prefer even your presence to having my poor, misguided dad beaten."

"Oh no. You can't say cuttin' things. Not at all! . . . All right, I'll come, unless I can persuade your dad to," replied Kalispel, and he leaped off the steps and strode away, smarting under her gibe, sick with his impotence. Yet as he recalled that last unfathomable gaze, his nerves seemed to quiver. When she hated him so flagrantly why did she look at him like that? It seemed as if some part of her personality was in conflict with another. But whatever complexity of emotion ruled her, the effect on Kalispel only added to his somber state. He felt the old swamping wave roll over him—the need to drown his woe in drink. As he could not resort to that, he ceased to rail against passion and bitterness. He was just Kalispel Emerson, kicked by fate, and he could not stay the inevitableness of things.

He went into the Chinaman's little shop and passed some time over a biscuit and a cup of coffee. Then at half after six o'clock he wended his somber way toward Borden's dance-hall. It was the hour when fewest of Thunder City's thousands were abroad, yet there were enough of the motley crew to cause Kalispel to take to the center of the street. The yellow lights cast their flare out into the night; music thrummed and beat somewhere; the saloon emitted a ceaseless hum; the smell of smoke and sawdust and rum filled the drowsy summer air.

Kalispel sensed events. He could no more stave off the ominous violence of the time and the place than he could the fire in his spirit. Restraint and resistance seemed spent.

"Wal, things happen this way," he muttered. "Just now I wouldn't budge a step to avoid Leavitt or Borden."

The music-hall building occupied considerable space, and as it was only one story high, the dining-room, kitchen, and other rooms were on the ground floor. Kalispel presented himself at the door of the dining-room. Half a dozen young women were at supper, but Nugget was not with them.

"Evenin', girls. Where's that golden-headed Nugget?"

"She just left the table," replied one of them. "Down the hall, last room on the right. But she don't receive gentlemen in her budwar." The last sentence had something of a sneer in it.

Kalispel thanked the girls, but made no other reply. He found the narrow dark hall, and at length reached the end and knocked.

"Who's there?" came the answer.

"It's me, Nugget."

"So I hear. But who's me?"

"Kalispel."

The little door swung open to let him step into a small room, well lighted and furnished. Nugget welcomed him with glad eyes.

"Howdy, cowboy," she said, gayly, as she closed the door. Then as she observed him more closely: "Kalispel, what's wrong? Oh, you look——"

He reached for her with powerful hand and pulled her close, to peer down into the startled face.

"For two bits I'd wring your white neck."

"Why, Kalispel!—you're drunk!" she gasped.

"Nugget, you've seen too many drunken men to make a mistake about me. No, I'm sober, an' as mad as I'm sober."

"Mad!—At—me?" she faltered, her hands catching at his arms.

"Wal, I reckon it's you. I've a mind to beat you good, drag you out of this hell-hole, an' shoot it up proper."

"Oh, my friend, you wouldn't hurt me!" she cried. "What have I done?"

"You've played fast an' loose with my pard."

"Dick—I did not. I played square with him. Poor boy! He wanted to *marry* me."

"He's crazy about you."

"Dick will get over that."

"I reckon not. If I thought so, I wouldn't be here after you. *I* don't get over my case."

"After—me?"

"Yes, after you," he replied, giving her an ungentle shake. "Nugget, you're going to break Dick's heart."

"Kal, don't—don't hurt me," she begged, like a child. "I can't stand to be beat. That's why I ran away from home.— Choke me—shoot me—if ` you think I deserve it. But don't——"

"Do you care for this boy?"

"No! No!—Not any more than I do for you," she protested.

"That's not what I mean. I'm your big brother."

"Oh, I know that!"

"Wal, he loves you, too wonderful to . . . Nugget, don't lie to me. You love this boy?"

"I—I like him terribly," she sobbed. "But I don't want to—to get him into trouble with these men."

"He's ruined now. An' we've got to save him. Put some clothes on. I'm takin' you to meet him."

"Where is he?"

"He'll wait at the bridge."

"Fetch him here—to my room. I'd keel over if—I went with you."

As Kalispel released the girl she sank on the bed, weak and white, with her blue eyes fixed in tragic solemnity upon him.

Kalispel ran out into the alley, and had almost reached the street when he remembered that such hasty procedure was perilous for a man with enemies. Resuming his habitual vigilance, he went on across the street and down to the bridge. Dick loomed out of the darkness.

"Pard, I was afraid she wouldn't come," he said dejectedly.

"Come on, idiot. It's all right. An' if you open your face, I'll punch it," growled Kalispel.

In a very few minutes he and Dick entered Nugget's room and closed the door. She had not moved since Kalispel's departure. But there had come a subtle change in her.

"Nugget," began Sloan, huskily.

"Don't call me that. My name is Ruth," she replied as she slipped off the bed to confront him.

"All right . . . Ruth," said the young man, hopefully.

They forgot Kalispel. They stood with glances locked, tense in that uncertain moment, searching each other's souls.

It was the girl who swayed. Sloan caught her to his breast.

"Oh, Dick! I do love—you for wanting to—to marry me," she whispered, brokenly.

"Darlin', there's only one way to save me."

"Don't—don't make me!"

"Kiss me!" he demanded, emboldened by her entreaty.

She flung her arms round his neck and pressed her lips to his. Kalispel saw the tears streaming from under her closed eyelids. And then she was looking up at him, as beautiful as any woman could be, transfigured.

"Mad boy! . . . Oh, why do you love me?" she whispered.

"I just do."

"Can't you get over it?"

"Never."

"Borden will be wild," she whispered, wavering.

"Does he own you?"

"He thinks he does. Kalispel will have to kill him. And that——"

"Enough. Say you will leave—this place."

"Oh, if I only dared!"

"Say you *will!* Or I'll carry you out of here this minute."

"Yes. I—I will come."

"Say you will marry me!"

"If—nothing—else will do."

"Nug—Ruth, darlin', you leave here right now. Pack your things. I'll help. You can have my tent. It's quite comfortable —board floor an' all. You can keep house for me while I dig gold for you. I'll sleep at my neighbor's. An' then the very first parson who comes will marry us. . . . I'll make my fortune here. Then we'll go far away. My parents are dead. I have no one to look out for. . . . You'll be my wife!"

Kalispel stepped out and softly closed the door.

"By heaven! there's one good mark for Kalispel!" he whispered.

On the street he searched for Blair. Eventually Kalispel located him in the most disreputable gambling-hell in the gold camp. He was already under the influence of drink and the elation of winning. Blair was a poor gambler for many reasons, but his chief fault was to lose his head when fortune smiled. Kalispel surveyed the room and then approached the table to lean over and whisper in Blair's ear.

"Come home soon as you start losin'. Hell to pay!"

"Huh? . . . Oh yes—all right—all right," returned Blair, slowly comprehending.

Kalispel went out. "Wouldn't do for me to stay down town

tonight," he soliloquized as he made his way through the noisy throng. He was like a man that could see in the dark, and on all sides at once. The atmosphere of the gold town seemed charged with fatality for him. It was, for all these gold-grubbers and parasites. Mirth, song, and guitar, the discordant squeak of fiddles, the gay, soft murmuring inside and the coarse roar outside—these belied the truth that only a step away from this life loomed defeat, ruin, death.

Kalispel felt this, and deeply his relation to it. He had drawn the Blairs into the vortex of this maelstrom, and he doubted that he could avert a tragic end. As for Sydney, he was in a state of desperation. She had seemed at first so self-contained, so strong and fine and balanced. But who could understand a woman? Sydney might do anything.

As Kalispel left town the moon came out above the bold black dome of Thunder Mountain. Its hue was orange and it had a weird, threatening aspect. The whole dark mass of the slope lay in shadow, looming as always, menacing as always, waiting. And on the moment a low hollow rumble pealed from subterranean depths.

"Thunder an' grumble, old man," muttered Kalispel, grimly. "You're not foolin' me. You'll never bury me an' my gold."

When he ascended the steps of the Blair porch Sydney was not in sight. Lighting a cigarette, he paced to and fro, heavily, so she would hear his footfalls. The door was open and a faint light shone in the far room. But she did not come out. He was about to call when he heard quick steps on the ground. He turned to see Sydney appear in the moonlight, coming from the trail. His pulses leaped again. Slowly she ascended to the porch, leaned against the post, panting. He, approached her.

"Somebody chase you?" he queried, sharply. "Don't you know enough yet to stay away from that gold camp after dark?"

She did not answer. Kalispel stepped closer, to peer into her face. The moon shone at her back, so that all he could descry in the shadow were two dark eyes that electrified him.

"Where you been?" he demanded.

"I followed you," she replied, as swiftly, and the low, rich voice shook.

"Where?"

"Downtown. Never lost sight of you for a moment."

"Wal, I'll be dog-goned! . . . Flatterin', Sydney—but I don't savvy."

93

"You may call it flattering if you like."

"Where'd you follow me?"

"To Borden's dance-hall."

"An' then what?"

"I followed you in."

"My Gawd! . . . Sydney, what possessed you?—That joint! To *go in* it!"

"I was possessed, yes, of several things—the only one of which need concern you is that I had a determination to know."

"Ah-huh. I'm some flabbergasted. . . . Wal?"

"I went through to the dining-room," she continued, hurriedly. "Those girls!—I asked where Kalispel Emerson had gone. They looked queer. But one of them laughed and said: 'He's gone back to Nugget's room. Down the hall—last on the right!' "

"Then—what?" gasped Kalispel.

"I ran out. On the way up the street I thought I'd make a good job of it. I went into all the—the gambling-places and asked for my father. But he had not been seen in any one of them tonight. Oh, I am so—so frightened."

"Wal, you needn't be—about him, anyway. I found him in Flannigan's. He was all right. He'd won a lot. I told him to quit soon as he began to lose. Told him there was hell to pay—which wasn't no lie. He'll be home pronto."

She murmured something in relief. Then silence fell. Kalispel threw away his cigarette, in a slow, uncertain gesture which betrayed the conflict of his thoughts. The yellow moon, the black slope, the pale squares of tents, the faint roar of the stream, and the fainter hum of life in the town—all seemed unreal to Kalispel, like the objects remembered from a dream.

But as he attended once more to the girl he found she was real—so real and intense that his consciousness fixed sternly on one obvious fact—her conviction of his utter shamelessness.

That did not greatly shock Kalispel, because he knew his innocence and could prove it, but what staggered him was her motive in wanting to determine this supposed guilt of his.

"Miss Blair, your trailin' me 'pears a powerful strange proceedin'," he drawled, stifling his agitation and playing for time. She would commit herself.

"Yes, it was—for me—more than *you* could dream. But this West is strange—this raw camp—these gold-mad men—all are strange. And I have been upset by them."

94

"Wal, what'd you do it for?"

"I'd never tell you, but for the fact that I must clear myself of something brazen. . . . When I met you on the street with that—that—with the girl called Nugget I was so distressed and shamed that I realized I had not utterly lost faith in you—that in my heart I still cared. . . . Even your prompting her to speak familiarly to Rand Leavitt—even after he said she was your sweetheart—even then I still fought for you. Oh, it was hard to kill. I had to be sure, so tonight I followed you."

Into Kalispel's slow and mounting ecstasy there burnt, at the mention of Leavitt, a passion that held all softer emotions in check.

"So Leavitt told you Nugget was my sweetheart?"

"Yes, he did."

"An' that confirmed your suspicions?"

"It told me what a fool I was. Still I had to find out for myself."

"An' you believed I put Nugget up to speakin' intimate to Leavitt?"

"That was how he explained it—and I believed."

"Wal, for once you were right," replied Kalispel, coldly. "I did put her up to it."

"How contemptible of you!" she exclaimed, hotly. "He is a gentleman. He is insulted."

"Ah-huh. An' you are perfectly shore Leavitt is too much a gentleman—too far above us poor miners—to have any interest in a girl like Nugget?"

"Yes, I am. More than that—he is too fine and clean to come to *me,* if he had been with *her*—as you have done."

"An' whatever decent feelin' you ever had for me is dead an' gone?"

"Yes, thank God. You are a strange mixture of chivalry and baseness. You don't know what honor means. You have no morals. You saved me from a ruffian. You make love to me and pull me out of the river when I was drowning. Then you kill an innocent man and become a drunken sot. Lastly you become transformed, apparently. At least your appearance underwent some great change. No more ragged garb or unkempt locks! You win my father. You win the miners to your side. You take up the hardest job of all, to pack meat down to these madmen who would starve before they'd give up gold. . . . And then *all* the time, no doubt, you were going to—to the room of this Nugget. And worst of all you come to me with her kisses on your lips. . . ."

In her denunciation Kalispel grasped the undercurrent—the betrayal of her jealousy.

"Sydney, how do you know that Nugget is not as good as the very gold she's named for?"

Sydney gasped. "Do you imagine *I* am mad, too?" she cried, incredulously.

"Couldn't a man—couldn't I go into Nugget's bedroom without having you think something wrong?"

"No!" she replied, violently.

"Suppose I told you she needed a brother an' I'd tried to be one? That she'd run off from home when only a kid, an' drifted into this dance-hall business to earn a livin'? That some one had to save her from ruin—from dyin' of drink an' violence—from men like these brutal miners—an' Borden—an' *Leavitt?*"

She laughed in mocking astonishment.

"I'd think you a monumental liar."

"Wal, the funny thing is—I could prove it."

"Kalispel, you lack a great deal, and one thing is brains. Can't you see how—how cheap it is to intimate that Leavitt— Oh, I wouldn't repeat it!"

"Shore I can see what I lack," he rejoined, in the might of gathering wrath. "One thing is common sense. Another was to keep on lovin' a girl who failed in the big things—faith, love. But whatever I had for you, Sydney Blair, is as dead as whatever you had for me. An' cold as ashes!"

Her passion spent, she backed away from him to the porch rail. He loomed over her, peering down into the white face.

"All the same, I can prove my innocence," he went on. "I can prove it two ways."

"How can you?" she whispered, as if she could not hold back the words.

"Wal, I reckon this way suits—me—best," he replied, hoarsely, and seized her in powerful, relentless arms.

Sydney struggled violently, but in a moment she was in such a vice-like clasp that she was unable to move. He bent to kiss her, but she twisted her face this way and that, so that his lips swept her cheeks, her closed eyes, her hair.

"How—dare you?" she cried, in fierce anger and dawning fright. "Let me go! . . . You shall suffer—for this. . . ."

Kalispel reached her lips with his, ending her outcries, her struggles. Suddenly she sank limp on his breast. And he kissed her with all the despairing passion of his innocence, with the agony of renunciation, with mad hunger for what he knew was lost to him.

When he released his hold she sank upon the bench, drooping and spent.

"There!" he said, huskily, "I reckon—that's my proof. I couldn't be—villain enough to do that—if I was the—what you called me. . . . An' I'll never forgive you, Sydney Blair."

Kalispel wrestled himself erect, and at that juncture Blair came staggering and panting up the steps.

"Wal, old-timer, I see you're drunk again," remarked Kalispel, stepping forward doubtfully.

"That you—Emerson? . . . No, I'm not drunk. . . . Where's Syd——?"

"Here, Dad," cried the girl, rising with her hands on the rail. "Oh, you look so white!"

"Blair, where'd the blood come from?" queried Kalispel, sharply, as he put his finger to a dark splotch running down Blair's face.

"I won all—their gold," panted Blair, heavily. "Stacks of it! . . . And I was hurrying home with it all—got beyond the camp—heard steps behind—men—three men—they hit me—ran off with the gold."

"Ah-huh. Wal, this crack won't kill you, but maybe it'll be a lesson. Sydney, better wash an' tie it up."

"Dad, I knew it would happen," faltered Sydney.

"Wal, I reckon some gun-play is just what I need," said Kalispel, and strode off the porch.

"Come back!" called the girl, poignantly.

Kalispel did not even turn his head, though her voice was like a dragging weight.

"Oh, don't go! . . . *Kalispel!*"

He walked on, his formidable self again, out into the weird moonlight.

Chapter Nine

September came with its frosty mornings and purple-hazed afternoons. Kalispel spent less time hunting game on the heights, though meat brought almost as high a price as gold. It had been inevitable that Jake would retrograde. After he lost hope of finding Sam's body or some clue of his having left the valley, Jake seemed on the verge of ruining all their chances. Kalispel, finally in desperation, confided in him, and that worked a great change in the despondent miner. He became amenable, and willingly set his hand to the task of accumulating firewood for the winter, no small need when the snow began to fly.

Events had multiplied. Kalispel did not watch for Sydney on her porch any more, and when by accident he happened to see her, he suffered a wrenching pang. Blair had been laid up with his injury, which had induced fever; and Kalispel thought that was a good thing. He sent Jake with meat and firewood to the cabin, and also had his brother do what tasks and errands Sydney would permit.

Miners with mediocre claims were working like beavers to clean up as much as possible and get out before winter locked the valley.

This had been added incentive to the small clique of bandits who were operating in the diggings. Kalispel had been unable to discover Blair's assailants, and had come to the conclusion that they were under the dominance of a clever and resourceful leader. While Kalispel was not hunting, he haunted the town by day and night, a somber, watchful man who had become marked by the populace.

One morning Kalispel had a call from a miner who brought a request for an interview from Masters, the new sheriff. Kalispel regarded that as something to expect and told the messenger he would see the sheriff.

A little later Masters approached leisurely. Kalispel had never encountered the man at close range. He was tall and lean, in his shirt sleeves, without any star on his vest, and walked with a limp. He wore a huge black sombrero, that at a distance hid the upper part of his sallow face, and he packed one gun prominently where it ought to be. Kalispel's sharp eyes made sure he had another inside his vest.

"Howdy, youngster," he drawled, with the accent of a Texan. "Shore am obliged to you for seein' me."

"Howdy, yourself," replied Kalispel as he met the other's deep gray eyes. One glance at them and this man's lined, quiet face told Kalispel that he did not have to do with another Lowrie. "You sort of surprised me. A sheriff usually don't ask to call."

"Wal, I reckon he ought to, if he happens to want to see a youngster like you."

"Ah-huh. That sounds friendly, Masters."

"I'd like to be friendly with everybody heahabouts. I didn't want the job, Kalispel. But since thet rock busted my laig I can't do hard work. I got a man workin' my claim on

98

shares. An' I let the miners elect me. There was some opposition from the big mugs, but thet didn't keep me from bein' elected."

"Good thing for Thunder City, I'd say," rejoined Kalispel, thoughtfully. He liked the man. "Who were the big mugs?"

"Wal, who'd you say? You've been heah longer than me."

"Masters, I'm a pretty blunt-spoken fellow. Borden an' Leavitt, with their backin', run this camp. An' if they didn't want you elected I don't see how'n hell you ever got in."

"Lowrie was their man, as you know, an' after you drove him out of town they moved to set up Haskell. Do you know him?"

Kalispel grunted an unfavorable affirmative.

"Wal, my friends canvassed the diggin's an' got the jump on the opposition. So I was nominated at the meetin', an' elected, as you must have heahed if you were there."

"No, sorry to say I missed that. I'd kind of enjoyed it."

"Youngster, why'd you drive Lowrie out of camp?" queried the Texan, deliberately.

"What do you want to know for, Sheriff?"

"Wal, I don't want thet against you."

Thus importuned, Kalispel told him in full the details of his entire association with Lowrie.

"An' you'd killed him if he'd hung on heah?"

"I shore would. That job of his, tryin' to arrest my friend, Dick Sloan, for no reason on earth except that Sloan dragged the girl Nugget out of Borden's dive—that soured me for good an' all on Lowrie."

"What'd you have to do with Sloan's takin' up the girl?"

"I had a lot to do with it. They love each other. She's a good kid. An' Sloan means to marry her."

"Wal, thet puts a different light on the matter. I'm glad you told me. . . . Youngster, I don't mind tellin' you I like you. I'm from Texas, an' thet oughta explain. You're in bad heah with most of the miners an' thought wal of by the rest. I'm one of the rest. You an' me ought to pull together."

"My Gawd!— Me pullin' with a sheriff. About as funny as death!"

"There are sheriffs an' sheriffs. I don't need to tell you thet Lowrie was a four-flush. He couldn't have lasted a day in Texas. Wal, outside of my likin' you, there are some good reasons why I'd hate to clash with you."

"Masters, I can name one myself," replied Kalispel, heartily. "I just don't want to clash with you. . . . Suppose you name some of your reasons."

"Wal, youngster, I'll tell you one, an' if you stand for it we'll shake on it. Then I'll tell you the others."

"Shoot, Texas, dog-gone it, I kind of like you!" exclaimed Kalispel, frankly.

"I've seen twice the frontier life you have, an' most of it spent with a harder shootin' outfit than you ever met up with. When I was your age I rode for McNelly an' his Texas Rangers. Later I trained with gun-fighters like King Fisher, Wess Hardin', an' others of thet Texas ilk. . . . Wal, the point of all this gabbin' aboot myself, which I ain't much given to, is thet if you an' me clashed heah, I'd pretty shore beat you to a gun."

"How do you know?" queried Kalispel, voicing the old, dark, insatiable curiosity of his kind.

"Wal, it stands to reason. An' besides, I seen you draw on Selby."

"Masters, you can bet I'm not askin' to put it to a test. An' here's my hand on that."

"An' heah's mine, youngster," drawled the Texan, with satisfaction.

"All right. I'm lucky for once. Now give me another reason for not wantin' to lay me out cold."

"I don't like Leavitt."

Kalispel made one of his swift passionate gestures. "Ha! . . . Go on. You're the most interestin' sheriff I ever met."

"Wal, another is I don't like Borden."

"Ah-huh. I reckon one more will about do me."

"I don't like the rumor thet's spreadin' heah."

"What rumor?" flashed Kalispel.

"Thet you're one of these bandits who are holdin' up the miners."

Kalispel leaped up with a curse. "—— ——, Masters! This is the last straw. An' what'n hell did you tell me for—if you want me to be a law-abidin' citizen?"

"Set down again, youngster. You shore air hot-haided," replied the Texan, in his slow, quiet way. "Listen. I made up my mind since I been heah with you thet you have been lied aboot. I had a hunch before I came, but wasn't sure. . . . Give me the straight of this camp gossip aboot the Emerson claim to Leavitt's property. On your honor, youngster. This is shore a critical time in yore life. You're young. You're no fool. You don't drink an' gamble—which shore surprised me. Now come clean an' straight."

Whereupon Kalispel, stirred to his depths, related in detail and holding to absolute facts, the discovery of the valley, of the placer gold, of the quartz vein, and the events following, up to Jake's return and the trial.

The Texan nodded ponderingly, pulling at his long drooping mustache.

"Youngster, I believe you," he returned, at length. "Leavitt has jumped your claim. But it's just as possible thet yore brother Sam was gone as it is thet he was heah. You've got to admit thet. An' like as not you'll never know. But you can never tell."

"That alone has kept me from drawin' on Leavitt."

"Wal, it's aboot all cleared up in my mind. Thet's the status of one Kalispel Emerson. . . . How'd you come to fetch Blair an' his daughter in heah? I heahed talk aboot thet, too—not to yore credit."

"I happened to meet them in Salmon. Pritchard an' his outfit had got on the scent. An' Borden got after the girl. He busted into her room an' I threw him out. Wal, I got acquainted with the Blairs. They jumped at the idea of goin' with me to my gold prospect. So I fetched them—an' fell good an' deep in love with Sydney—the girl—on the way in. On gettin' here I was so wild to find a stampede on, an' Leavitt holdin' our claim, that I busted loose. Shot Selback an' got drunk. When I came to, Leavitt had played up to the Blairs an' ruined my chance of winnin' back Sydney's confidence."

"So thet's the story? . . . Did the girl care for you?"

"Yes, she did. I reckon she might have loved me in time," replied Kalispel, sadly. "But things have gone from bad to worse. Leavitt has it all his way now. She might be damn fool enough to marry him—unless I——"

"You've shore split on Leavitt," interposed Masters. "Stands to yore credit thet you haven't bored him."

"I've shore wanted to."

"Wait, youngster. . . . Heah's an idee. Suppose we work some slick deal on the town. For a spell you an' me will become open enemies, apparently, always lookin' to meet an' shoot it oot. Only we won't. I'll furnish you some bags of gold dust. An' you start roarin' around camp, pretendin' to be drunk, thet you struck a big claim. Anythin' to show the gold an' brag. Then bandits will trail you up, if they think you're drunk enough. But you hold them up. An' thet way we might round up these robbers."

"Ha! We might round up more'n you gamble on. Masters, I'm your man."

101

"Good! I'll slip up heah after dark tonight. . . . Suppose you point out the Blair cabin. I'll drop in on them."

Kalispel did so, and experienced again that blade in his heart, for Sydney was on the porch.

"There's Sydney now. She'll see you've been here."

"Wal, I'll tell her I was makin' a missionary call on you, but all in vain. Thet you cussed me oot, swore you'd draw on me at sight, thet you are a discouraged boy goin' to hell."

"Aw!" groaned Kalispel, flinching.

"Youngster, the way I'll say it ought to wring tears from thet girl."

"All right. If you can wring her heart, I'll die for you. . . . An' say, Masters, while you're callin' on people don't pass up Dick Sloan an' Nugget. You'll love them, by gosh! Inquire down by the bridge, on the other side."

Next day Kalispel took Jake with him to the big high basin over the south slope and packed down the meat of two elk. A herd of several hundred had come into the basin, which evidently was their winter abode.

"Jake, I got a great idee," announced Kalispel.

"Idees are great when they are great," replied Jake, non-committal.

"Soon as it gets cold enough to freeze meat hard we'll come up here an' slaughter a hundred of these elk, drag them over to the rim above the valley, an' hang them up in that heavy growth of firs. Meat-market for the winter."

Jake did not express any rapture over this very creditable plan; however, when Kalispel confided the ruse Masters had suggested as a clever means to identify the bandits and possibly to learn something more, then Jake showed how sparks could be struck from flint.

That afternoon Kalispel strolled down to Sloan's tent. Before he mounted the steps of the spacious, canvas-topped dwelling he heard Dick's deep, pleasant voice and Nugget's silvery laughter. Both rang sweetly in Kalispel's ears.

"Hey," he called, "I'm invitin' myself to supper."

"Come in, you life-savin' hombre," called Dick, gladly.

"Oh, it's Kal," cried a high treble voice, in wild welcome. And Kalispel found himself being leaped upon and kissed by what appeared to be a lovely, little, rosy-faced, golden-haired boy in blue jeans. "Where *have* you been for so long?"

"Folks, I've been plottin' murder," replied Kalispel, with a voice and smile that made him a prevaricator.

"We been hearin' things. I was goin' to hunt you up

tonight. But thet d—— new sheriff dropped in yesterday afternoon. He was darned nice to me an' Ruth, but he shook his buzzard head doubtful about you."

"Kal, we hated him for that," added Nugget, who was clinging to his vest and gazing up with troubled, appealing eyes. "Have they put him against you?"

"Say—dog-gone! You look just like peaches an' cream," rejoined Kalispel, suddenly realizing the girl's wonderful improvement. Her face had lost its pallor; the hollow cheeks had filled out; the red lips that had been bitter were now sweet; the blue eyes no more the windows of havoc. She was happy. It seemed incredible. But Kalispel accepted what his keen scrutiny revealed.

"Nugget, you always was pretty, but, gosh!— Why, now you're lovely!"

"Not Nugget any more, not even to you. Ruth."

"All right, then it's Ruth. Dog-gone! If I'd had a hunch you was goin' to turn out happy an' beautiful like this, I'd shore grabbed you for myself."

"Kal!" cried the girl, startled.

"I shore love you heaps, Ruth."

"Hey, stop makin' up to my girl," ordered Sloan, gayly. "She likes you too darn much already. An' we're not married yet."

"I shall always—love him, Dick," she said, earnestly.

"Wal, don't be scared my heart will break again," rejoined Kalispel, with pathos.

"Kalispel, how is it with you and Sydney?" she asked, presently, watching him with a woman's eyes.

"It's not atall."

"I'm going to call on that girl some day," declared Ruth, with a spirit that boded trouble for Miss Blair.

"I see her with Leavitt," interposed Dick, gravely. "Doesn't strike me right."

"It's rotten, if you ask me," burst out Ruth. "Won't somebody tell her the truth about Rand Leavitt?"

"That's up to one of us. Nobody but you an' me an' Kal know. An' tellin' her what Leavitt really is—if she believes—will be damn serious for us. He an' Borden have gotten thick."

"Don't you kids worry any more. Sydney Blair will find out some day, probably too late," returned Kalispel, darkly.

"Kal, Cliff Borden has been here to see me twice, while Dick was out on his claim," said Ruth.

"Ah-huh. Wal, what of it?"

103

"First time he tried being persuasive. He wanted me back. Made me extravagant offers. Seemed to be struck with the change in me. Tried to make love to me— He laughed when I told him Dick and I were not living together. And he got sore when I told him I intended to marry Dick. He stamped out, saying he'd see me soon. Day before yesterday he came again. He was different. He threatened me. I called him every bad name I ever heard and drove him out. But I am worried, Kalispel."

"What'll we do?" queried Sloan, anxiously. "If my claim wasn't pannin' out so rich I'd take Ruth an' rustle away. But that'd be throwin' away money enough to start us for life."

"I reckon you better leave it to me," replied Kalispel.

"Then I won't worry," declared Ruth. "This Thunder City is not the bloodiest camp I ever saw, by far. But it's low-down and mean. I can't cope with these men. Neither can Dick. But *you* can, Kalispel. And I, who haven't prayed since I was little, am thanking God for you. That's all. You talk with Dick while I get supper."

Kalispel went outside with Sloan, where they walked up and down.

"Ruth saw through Masters," said Sloan. "He's not as unfriendly toward you as he wants it to look."

"Dick, that Texan is a man to tie to. I should smile he is not unfriendly. But you an' Nug—Ruth keep this to yourselves. Masters wants me to make a bluff at bein' drunk, an' go round flushed with gold—which he staked me to—an' get some of these bandits to hold me up."

"You don't say!" exclaimed Sloan, amazed and concerned. "Will you risk it?"

"Shore looks good to me."

"I'll bet none of these two-bit robbers will hold you up in a hurry. Whoever they are, they are miners, workin' claims or prospectin', an' they know you."

"Wal, it won't hurt to try."

"It'll hurt you with Sydney Blair."

"I couldn't be hurt no worse with her."

"Ruth seems to think you've got a chance there. Don't ruin it by becomin' a rowdy."

"Sort of tickles me. She's goin' to be the fooledest girl some day."

"Kal, you can't let her marry that cheat of a Leavitt," declared Sloan, hotly. "Even if you didn't love her! Ruth told me. An' if I was a shootin'-man, believe me, I'd go after Leavitt."

104

"Take care you don't shoot off your chin," advised Kalispel. "Ruth knows too much an' talks too much. She's got nerve. But Borden an' Leavitt have a strangle hold on this camp. They can ruin you. An' if I kill them before I can show them up, two-thirds of the diggin's will rise up to hang me. An' I'll lose my chance to find out if Leavitt really made 'way with Sam."

"You bet he did," cracked out Dick. "Ruth told me. She swears it."

"Hell you say!"

"Yes, the hell I say. She knows, but she can't prove it."

"How could she know an' *not* be able to prove it?"

"She says it's a little of what she heard an' a lot that she felt."

"Wal, that wouldn't go far in a court, unless what she heard was important."

"We take her word. I'll bet Masters would, too. But nobody else would take stock in what a dance-hall girl swore to. That's the weakness of the case."

Kalispel admitted it. Leavitt had Boise mining-men interested in the quartz lode. To get possession of the property by force seemed impossible; and any other way began to loom as a forlorn hope. Kalispel divined that the day was not far distant when he would abandon that hope. In this event all he wanted was a short pregnant meeting with Rand Leavitt.

That night Kalispel went on his pretended spree. He staggered into every saloon on the street, smelling of rum, inviting all idlers to drink with him, yet contriving not to drink himself. Everywhere he displayed a big bag of gold nuggets. The invitations to gamble were as numerous as the gamblers.

"Ump-umm. No time—gamble," he would reply. "Wanta drink—an' shoot thish town up. I'm bad hombre—I am—an' lookin' fer trouble. Gonna shoot daylights outa dansh-shall fellar—an' lousy claim-jumper."

He created a sensation everywhere. Word flew from lip to lip. "Kalispel Emerson on the rampage!" The roar subsided when he entered, pale-faced, maudlin, staggering, with a bag of gold in his left hand; the chairs scraped or fell over or the players left them; the crowded bars turned a sea of faces; the throng split to let him through; and mixed together again to follow him out into the street. He broke up the dance at Borden's hall and shot out the lights. Lastly he weaved from side to side up the center of the street, singing a range drinking-song, and thus on outside of town. But that

105

night the ruse did not work, and he arrived at his cabin tired out and disgusted.

Next morning he saw the sunrise from the rim of the south slope.

Kalispel's bad moods might start out with him, or like giants stalk behind him on the trail, but they never lasted. When, on this day, he gained real solitude, his morbid thoughts began, one by one, to drop away like scales. The labor of climbing high, the smell of pine and fir, the intimacy of the old gray cliffs, the melancholy twittering of birds on their way south, and the low song of insects bewailing the death of summer, the color and wildness of the ledges, the freedom of the heights, the wild life that ranged before his gaze—these and all the phases of nature, increasingly more satisfying as the days multiplied, began to soften defeat and heartbreak, and the evil of the sordid greedy camp below.

The valley was now a hideous blot in the wilderness, a checkered hive of toiling bees, an evidence of how white men despoiled nature in their madness for gold.

From Kalispel's lookout he could see the whole of the mountain that loomed over the mining camp. In bulk it dwarfed the area of the valley. He never gazed at this mile-long slant of denuded, soft earth that he did not feel its forbidding aspect. It hung there precariously. The faint rumble that resembled thunder and which sounded at infrequent times, the gloomy face of the great slide, its ghastly, naked, mobile nature—these to a mountaineer were fraught with catastrophe.

But in other directions the views were superb, a sea of choppy jagged waves of rock, peaked and curled and frosted, suggesting the purple depths of canyons between, and the brawling streams deep down.

Kalispel led his pack burros back to the edge of the basin, where he hunted, and tying them to saplings, he began his stalk.

Chapter Ten

Late that night in the fitful glare of Kalispel's camp fire, Blair appeared like a man who was afraid of his shadow.

"Say, Blair, it's right dangerous to come sneakin' up on

me," warned Kalispel. "I can't tell for shore who my friends are in the dark. An' Lord knows my enemies multiply."

"Never thought—of that. Excuse me—Kal," panted Blair, finding a seat. He was sober, but apparently laboring under great stress. "Leavitt and Sydney—have been haranguing me. Made my life—hell—lately. I didn't want them to see me—coming here—so waited till dark."

"It's long after dark, old scout," replied Kalispel, scrutinizing the other's haggard face. "I got in late. Had a heavy pack of meat. . . . What's on your chest?"

"I'm a ruined man."

"Wal, that's nothin'. I've been ruined a lot of times."

"You're young and you don't care a damn for anything or anybody."

"Shore. But you can do like me. Get up an' go on!"

"I can't. This gold-digging was all right for me when I had some results and didn't work too hard. But that's finished. The gambling is worse. I'm a fool. I had twenty thousand dollars when we got here. All gone!"

"Whew!— Twenty thousand? My Gawd! man, you have drank an' gambled all that away?"

"No, not by any means. I bought two claims, you know. Then I had ten thousand hidden in the cabin. . . . The rest went for our living, and my——"

"Wal, that's different," interrupted Kalispel. "You're not ruined if you've got ten thousand."

"I haven't got it. Stolen out of the cabin! It was in a big leather wallet, hidden in a chink between two logs, high up where I thought nobody could locate it. But somebody did. Sydney left the cabin open. She went downtown with Leavitt. That was the night you got drunk and went raving around town."

"Yeah, I did sort of slop over," drawled Kalispel. "If Sydney went downtown I reckon she saw me."

"Did she?— Well, I guess she did. She quarreled with Leavitt. And later with me she was in a passion. It struck me she was madder about your break than she was at the loss of our money."

"Humph!" ejaculated Kalispel, in a quandary. "I reckon you're barkin' up the wrong tree, Blair."

"I always have done that," returned the older man, plaintively. "But I still have ears. I can hear. And I heard Sydney lacing it into Leavitt about *you*. Evidently he had been blackguarding you, and she, like a woman, roasted him for it when it was true. Later she did the same to me. I haven't

107

any tact. I'm testy, anyway, these days. And when I said: 'If you cared so much about Kal, why in hell did you let him go to the dogs?' I thought she was going to tear my hair out."

"Wal, I'm a son-of-a-gun!" exclaimed Kalispel, utterly floored.

"Sydney ended it by swearing she despised you—that if I ever spoke to you again she'd leave me—and that for her you were dead."

Kalispel sat mute. His consciousness could not get beyond the query— "Did she care so much for me?"

"But to come back to the money," went on Blair. "I didn't dare mention to Sydney that I wouldn't put it beyond Leavitt to steal. I haven't a leg to stand on, Kal. And I ought to be ashamed. All the same, I'll be damned if I don't believe he might have stolen it. No one else has been there—at least indoors."

"Wal, there are two more men in camp who'd back you up. Jake an' me," declared Kalispel. "But that's far-fetched, Blair."

"Maybe. I'm finding out a good deal. . . . Leavitt has only a quarter share in that quartz mine. He had to give the other shares to mining-men of Boise to back the deal. He told Sydney that they had taken out about three hundred thousand dollars. Also that lately the vein panned out on solid granite. The engineer who was here claimed they'd strike the quartz again, but it would be necessary to pack in and install a hundred-ton stamp-mill. At enormous expense. Leavitt doesn't believe the mine is worth it. And he confided further to Sydney that he'd be leaving Thunder City by spring. Wants her to go out with him and marry him. . . . All of which he asked her to keep strictly secret."

"Queer deal from the start," muttered Kalispel, as if he were alone. "But Leavitt is a deep lyin' hombre."

"Why would he want it kept secret? That about the quartz vein failing in solid granite is bound to leak out."

"I reckon these minin'-men are all close-mouthed. Maybe Leavitt has other irons in the fire here. For instance, he's a pardner of Borden in that saloon an' dance-hall."

"That's news indeed. Wonder what Sydney will say."

"Aw, she won't believe it if she's hipped about the fellow."

"She's strange these days. I'm afraid coming here has ruined her as well as it has me."

"Blair, if that isn't shore yet, it soon will be, unless I can find some good reason to kill Leavitt."

"I should think you have reason enough."

"Ump-umm! If I could force him to an even break where we had witnesses—that'd be fine. I'll try it next time I meet him. But if he can't dodge the meetin' he'll shore dodge the fight. An' you see, if I kill him anyway, this gang of his will hang me."

"Well, it's a sickening mess. I have failed, my girl is drifting, and you have gone back to your old habits. You'll break out presently and get shot or hanged. Then we won't have a friend."

"Wal, you could count on Leavitt," replied Kalispel, with a sarcasm he was far from feeling.

"I've fallen low enough without accepting charity from him."

"Hell, man! He sold you worthless claims—planted claims—at enormous prices. Borrow from him."

"You said that about planted claims before. You mean he had gold dust stuffed in the sand and gravel so that it'd look like a natural deposit?"

"Shore, that trick is as old as minin' gold."

"There have been several other claims which panned out the same way, and every single one of them was bought by men who didn't get here early in the stampede."

"More damnin' evidence."

"Then—there's no redress," said Blair, with finality.

"Nothin' but red blood," replied Kalispel.

Blair got up to slink away, bent and plodding, like a man overburdened.

"Tell Sydney I'll be droppin' in on you pronto," called Kalispel. "An' don't *you* be surprised at anythin'."

"Better not come. Sydney will— And what do you mean?"

"Wal, wait an' see. An', Blair, if you got any sense atall try to figure things out."

Blair went on mumbling to himself. Then Kalispel set about making himself as dishevelled and drunken-looking as was possible, in accordance with the part he had to act. He meant to make the best of it, and thought that if he did get to see Sydney, it would be an adventure.

"Dog-gone!" he soliloquized, as he started out. "I been this way so often that actin' it is just sorta natural. Gotta be extra good for Sydney!"

The porch of the Blair cabin was dark and the door was closed. Kalispel espied a crack of light, and stumbled up the steps, puffing like a porpoise, and staggered to the door.

"Ushed be—door round someplash," he grumbled. After fumbling around he knocked loudly. The door opened swiftly enough to make him suspicious that Sydney, who opened it, had heard him before he knocked. She looked like an outraged queen, yet intensely curious. Kalispel lunged in, pushing her aside. The room was bright with lamp and fire, very colorful and cosy. Blair sat staring at this intruder in astonishment.

"Howdee, Blair," said Kalispel, wiping his nose sheepishly. "Where is that lovely dotter of yours?"

"She let you in," replied Blair, and suddenly he averted his face to hide a smile.

"Ish that you, Syd?" asked Kalispel, turning to the girl.

"Get out of here," she ordered, anger, disgust, and sorrow expressive in face and voice.

"Jush wanta tell you—ain't gonna drink no more . . . turnin' over new leaf. . . . An' I'm comin' back to you."

"You are not."

"Aw, Syd, be reasonable," he begged, reaching for her with unsteady hands. She avoided him, as if his person was contaminated. "You ushed to be—turrible fond of me."

"Yes, to my shame and regret," she retorted, hotly. Yet he fascinated her.

Suddenly Kalispel ventured a dramatic transformation.

"Say, girl . . . this talk buzzin' round. . . . You ain't lettin' this fellar Leavitt make up to you?"

"That's none of your business, Mr. Emerson. But I am."

"Should think you'd be ashamed."

"Well, I'm not. Why should I be? Rand Leavitt is—is all that you are not."

"By Gawd, Lady, you shore said it! Haw! Haw! Bad hombre as I am I wouldn't be lowdown enough to make love to you—an' then go straight to them dance-hall girls," exclaimed Kalispel, passionately, forgetting the part he was playing. But all she got was the content of his words, not their delivery.

"Oh, you liar! . . . Get out! I will not listen to your insulting him in my own home."

"I'm gonna *kill* him!" hissed Kalispel.

"Maybe you are," she returned, bravely, though she shrank visibly. "I am not so scared about that as I was. You're pretty much of a blowhard. And if what I hear is true, you will be arrested before you can do this mischief."

That flayed Kalispel. There was no sense in acting with this girl. You had to stand for what you actually were, or be made out a fool. He wiped his wet face and brushed up

110

his dishevelled hair, and swiftly dropping his rôle, he trans-fixed her with a gaze no drunken man could have managed.

"Miss Blair," he said, in a voice like a bell, and made her a mocking bow. "I am shore indebted to a little trick to find out just what you think of me. An' I'll say that I'm as disappointed in you as you are in me. I thought you a won-derful fine girl, too wise to be made a fool of, too loyal to go back on your friends. But you're just ordinary, after all. You've been easy for this lyin' villain, Leavitt. It'd serve you right if I let him go on an' ruin you as he has ruined your father. Maybe I will. . . . An' as for insult, you can take *this* for yours to me."

And he slapped her face, not brutally, nor yet gently. She gasped and swayed back, her hand going to the red mark across cheek and mouth, and her eyes widening with horror, fury, and utter incredulous amaze.

Kalispel stepped out, slamming the door behind him. In all his life he had never known such passion as had just waved over him.

"Oh, Daddy—he—he wasn't drunk!" Sydney cried, wildly, inside the cabin. "He wasn't *drunk!* Yet he struck me. . . . I don't understand. There's something—wrong—terribly wrong! . . . Oh, his eyes!— He will kill Rand! He will. I saw that. . . . What can I do?"

"Daughter, it strikes me you can't do anything," Kalispel heard Blair answer. "Least of all save that rotten Leavitt's life. Not from this Kalispel boy! And I wouldn't raise my finger to avert it."

"Oh, it'd be awful—if they hanged him!"

Kalispel passed down the steps out of hearing. What he had heard blew out his passion like a storm-wind a candle, and he went out in the open. . . .

For a long time he sat on a log in the darkness. The upshot of his pondering was that Sydney's amazing reaction to his denunciation of her seemed to be a divided fear that he would kill Leavitt and get hanged for doing it. Kalispel regretted his impulsive play-acting. His jealousy and his habit of trying to rouse her one way or another always got him into hot water. This last madness left him in torture. She still cared something for him or felt herself involved or responsible in some degree.

At length Kalispel, mindful of Masters' game, passed on into the town. The familiar lights and sounds, the raw atmo-sphere in the street and smell of rum, smoke, and sawdust, the loud-voiced, rough-garbed, bearded miners and the pale, hawk-eyed gamblers all seemed to pall on Kalispel this night. Having resolved not to overdo his part, he probably underdid it this time. At any rate, he must have created the impression that he was out gunning for some man. Which, he reflected, was close to the truth. Borden he wanted particularly, and he certainly felt that he would go to extremes to make that individual fight. But as to Leavitt, there was always Sydney's influence. She inhibited him. Like as not, he fumed, his absurd reluctance to increase her disgust for him would result in his letting Leavitt go entirely or getting shot himself.

For that night, at least, Kalispel gave up, and thought more of his growing idea of trying to work less obtrusively to gain the same end. He returned to his cabin and changed his boots for crude moccasins he had recently made. Passing by Blair's cabin, he listened under the lighted windows. Some one was moving about within, but evidently the Blairs did not have company.

Kalispel decided upon a venture he had long cogitated—and that was to track Leavitt relentlessly, like an Indian bent upon revenge. He knew that there was always a guard on duty at the quartz mine, the shafted opening of which was only a step from Leavitt's cabin. If occasion required, Kalispel could overpower the guard, but what he wanted was to act with caution until he would be rewarded by something to substantiate his suspicion that Leavitt was leaning toward the career of Henry Plummer, who, most notorious of all prominent officials of a frontier mining-town, had all the time been the leader of the most desperate and murderous band ever hanged on the frontier.

Kalispel confessed that he was a bull-headed cowboy who would never give up on a trail, if he had seen the slightest signs of tracks. In this instance the only track he had was the masked, hard brilliance of Leavitt's eyes.

He made his way across the boulder-strewn bench to the edge of the bare slope. Once again he sustained a trenchant sense of what all the gold-mad inhabitants of Thunder City seemed to be blind to—that this vast mountain was actively threatening. The town lay directly in its way. Kalispel's cabin, and many of the habitations along the stream to the east were out of line of even a tremendous avalanche. But the fact which came revealingly to Kalispel then was that if or when Thunder Mountain slipped, Thunder City would be destroyed and Thunder Valley would become an inland lake. The faint seep of sliding sand, the faint rolling of pebbles, always to be heard here in a quiet hour, attested to the instability of the mountain, and were indeed warning whispers of catastrophe.

Lights in the gloom marked the location of the mine, but the mill and adjacent buildings, and Leavitt's cabin, could not be detected until Kalispel was right upon them. This sort of work was not new to him. Much of a cowboy's labor had to be done at night, so that he learned to see in the dark like a cat. Moreover, Kalispel had himself been a fugitive more than once; and many times, alone and with posses, he had tracked rustlers. It was a familiar thing for Kalispel, this slow vigilance, this peering through the blackness, this listening with the ears of a deer. And now it became a deep-seated, exciting passion, prompted by suspicion and fostered by jealousy.

Step by step he proceeded until stopped by a high barbed-wire fence which surrounded Leavitt's claim. The slanting shaft and the shacks on the slope loomed above him. He could not see the lights that had attracted him. Following the fence, Kalispel rounded the corner. Huge piles of boulders, cleared off the claim, afforded ample cover for him to approach the cabin. At length he passed the claim fence and faced the open. Leavitt's big cabin sat apart, with bright flares streaming from door and window. Slow footfalls sounded on the porch; voices came from inside; the black shadow of a man barred the light.

Kalispel sank behind a boulder to listen and watch and decide upon further action. He could not distinguish what was being said inside that cabin. It would be necessary for him to get a position under the window. That seemed impossible in view of the fact that the guard patrolled the porch and the space in front of the claim. Kalispel watched for a long time, during which the guard left the porch twice to pass between Kalispel and the fence. It would have been easy enough to waylay him at the extreme limit of his beat, but that seemed of no importance at the moment and eventually would lead to making Leavitt aware he was being watched.

Waiting until the guard passed a third time, Kalispel crawled from his covert and wormed his way across the open ground. It was ticklish work, a risk very different from being on his feet, ready for any emergency. Still, he knew he could not be seen and would have to be stumbled over. He had just crossed the space when by one of the chances that rule events the guard turned back off the porch. Kalispel sank, silently flattening himself to the earth. He held his breath, his hand on his gun. The guard was smoking. He was talking

113

to himself. He passed within ten feet of where Kalispel lay, and went on toward the end of his beat. Kalispel glided to the cabin and a point under the lighted window. When he got beyond the outflaring ray of lamplight he cautiously rose to his feet, with a sense of relief. He had the situation in hand.

"Mac," came in Leavitt's voice, "tell Leslie to keep off the porch."

Heavy footsteps followed this order.

"Cliff, I don't like this man Masters. To hell with Texans, anyway," went on Leavitt, pounding a table with his fist.

Kalispel quivered. Borden and Leavitt together there in the cabin!

"Well, he's after that damned meddling gun-slinger," replied Borden.

"Bah! How much is he after him?" retorted Leavitt. "Masters is like the rest—afraid."

"The miners say Masters is a real, sure-enough Texan of the old school."

"Too much so, for us. If he isn't afraid, why doesn't he arrest Emerson?"

"I asked him," replied Borden irritably. "He said, 'Wal, I reckon I ain't had reason yet.' I said, 'How about the rumpus he made in my place the other night?' And he replied: 'Borden, if I arrested Kalispel Emerson on a charge like thet, I couldn't keep him jailed forever, an' when he got out he'd shoot you shore.'"

"Like as not. The infernal cowboy has got us all buffaloed. It was he who took Nugget away. I'll bet as much for his own pleasure as for that fellow, Sloan. Have you seen Nugget again?"

"Yes. No good. She's brimstone and steel, that kid. Once off the drink, she can't be handled."

"Well, let her go," returned Leavitt, roughly. "I'm through. Sydney has said a couple of queer things to me lately. She's heard gossip. Or maybe Emerson put something in Blair's head. He's got leary of me."

"All the better. You can't be saddled with him, girl or no girl. I'll gamble there's no more to be squeezed from him."

"We'd better let Nugget alone," rejoined Leavitt, evasively. "I'm through. And if you know when you're well off, you'll do the same."

"Hell! . . . Rand, the fact is I didn't know I was stuck on the girl. Maybe I wasn't till she left. But you should see her now. She's got your proud, dark-eyed beauty beaten to a frazzle. And I'm going to get her back to the place."

"Look here. It's not good business. I'm reminding you that I have a half share in your place. No kick coming as to returns. It's a gold mine. But don't press this case of yours over Nugget."

"I'll have her back," clipped out Borden.

"How?"

"I've thought of a way, all right."

"Risky. You've not a safe man to deal with, Borden. You might do away with Emerson without risk. But if you did the same by Sloan, it'd stir up the miners. They've stood for the hold-ups pretty reasonable. Plenty of gold dust. If you go to killing some of them, though, you look out."

"I won't take your advice," replied Borden, sullenly.

"Why not? I certainly have more brains than you. And I *tell* you, damn your stupidity, that Emerson will kill you. Lowrie told me you had clashed with Emerson before and only got off because of Sydney. The cowboy was crazy over her. And she had a soft place for him, believe me. . . . Why won't you listen to me?"

"You run your own affairs. I'll run mine."

"I see. We're not making as good a team as I thought we'd make."

"Leavitt, excuse me for being blunt," returned the other, hotly. "But you seem to be whole hog or none. I had a hunch you were head of this hold-up gang and——"

"Don't talk so loud, you damned fool!" rejoined Leavitt, in a voice like the clink of cold metal. "You've hinted that before. Don't do it again."

"Well, here are the cards on the table," returned Borden, insolently. "You are pretty smart, but you don't know it all. Your right-hand man, Charlie March, loosens up a bit in his cups. And he told Sadie and Sadie told me."

There followed a pregnant silence. Kalispel heard the soft tapping of pencil or some hard instrument on the table inside.

"What?" asked Leavitt, coolly.

"That your quartz vein was done. That you're sore because your partners got most of the gold dug. That talk of a hundred-ton stamp mill was a bluff. That you meant to clean up here by spring and then leave."

"All of which is true, Borden. This place will soon be played out. I got a—rather unsafe start for me. I'm sorry, because there's plenty of placer gold yet, and no doubt more quartz veins to be opened."

"Thanks," returned Borden, gruffly.

At this juncture Kalispel heard men talking in front. They were walking up and down, directly across the only avenue by which he could escape. The cabin stood against the slope, which could not be scaled.

"Borden, you're skating on thinner ice here than any man in the camp. Once more I *tell* you. Don't trust this Masters. Lay off Nugget. Keep out of Emerson's way."

It appeared to be Borden's turn to be silent. In the ensuing stillness Kalispel fought something almost too strong to be resisted, and that was a fierce impulse to confront Borden and Leavitt. He discarded this for the old reason that he could not prove sufficient motive to insure his safety from the large contingent of miners whom Leavitt influenced.

"Suppose I won't take your advice?" queried Borden, presently.

"Then we split. Amicably, of course. You can pay me what you think square for my interest in your place."

"All right, I'll think it over," concluded Borden, and stamped out. Kalispel heard his heavy boots crunching the gravel. Then came the scrape of Leavitt's chair and the measured tread of a man locked in thought. This continued until the cabin was entered again, as it turned out to be, by the man who had gone out to see the guard.

"Mac, shut the door," ordered Leavitt, suddenly.

"Boss, what's up?" inquired the other, complying with the order. "Borden's went off cussin' mad. An' you look kinda pale behind the gills."

"March has been gabbing."

"You don't—say!" gasped Mac, in a sibilant whisper.

"I always distrusted Charlie where a combination of woman and liquor could get to him."

"Wal, he has been runnin' thet girl Sadie pretty strong."

"He has talked to her and she told Borden. We can't risk any more, Mac."

"Hell no!"

"Where will he be now?"

"With the girl, shore."

"All right. You and Struthers slip round to Borden's by the back way. Hide by that side door. It's dark there, you know. When he comes out, let him have it. And rob him! . . . Savvy?— Everybody knows he's my right-hand man."

"I savvy, boss. Not a bad idee," replied the other, in a hoarse whisper, and he left the room and cabin with no uncertain steps.

Kalispel leaned sweating and shaking against the cabin

wall. He had the thing in a nutshell. How raw and simple, after all! But what to do? He battled again with a temptation to hold up Leavitt and take him down to Masters. This idea was not tenable. Suddenly it occurred to him to intercept Leavitt's men before they accomplished their work, and better, to get to Charlie March first. If he could convince March of this plot against him, he might make an ally out of that worthy. Kalispel decided on the attempt.

When it came to getting away unseen, however, Kalispel encountered difficulty. The guard hung close to the cabin. And another, who came to relieve him, offered no opportunity until Leavitt called the man in. Whereupon Kalispel was divided between his new project and a desire to hear more from Leavitt. Quickly he decided on the former and glided away in the darkness.

Once on the noisy, glaring street he strode rapidly downtown. The roar of Thunder City was in full blast—that sinister sound of revel which attended the pleasure and business of gold-miners in a bonanza camp.

A crowd of unusually large proportion stood in front of Borden's resort. Kalispel had not before beheld so many persons grouped in that attitude of singular suggestiveness, but he had seen many a knot of somber men, heads together, talking low, with that unmistakable air of fatality about them.

"What's happened?" queried Kalispel of the nearest men.

"Some fellar shot, comin' out of the bird-cage," was the reply.

"Killed?"

"Yes, an' robbed, too."

"Who was he?"

"Nobody seems to know."

Kalispel mingled with the crowd and was not long in discerning the quality of its temper.

"Men, thet's carryin' this hold-up game too far," said one.

"First shootin', an' ought to be the last," replied another.

"Hell, if this keeps on it won't be safe to come out after dark."

"Thunder City ain't nothin'. I was in both the Bannock an' Alder Creek gold rushes. Plummer's gang murdered a hundred miners before he was found out."

"Wal, what we want hyar is a vigilante."

Masters came out of the hall with several men.

"Sheriff, did you identify him?" asked a bystander.

"Yes. It's Charlie March, foreman at Leavitt's mine."

117

"March!— That'll shore make Leavitt hoppin' mad."

"Reckon he didn't know thet March was hell on likker an' wimmen."

Masters, moving into the less-crowded street, encountered Kalispel.

"Howdy thar, cowboy," he called in a voice markedly louder than his usual drawl. "Was you heah-aboots when this shootin' came off?"

"Just got here, Sheriff," replied Kalispel, not amiably. He did not relish attention being focused upon him at that moment.

"I heahed you was always around where there was dancin' an' fightin'—an' hold-ups."

Kalispel was dumbfounded at this caustic, significant speech, and unable to understand it, or accept it in any way as friendly.

"Wal, Sheriff," he retorted, bitingly, "when I am around such—usually the right man gets shot."

Chapter Eleven

The crisp cool weather gave place to a warm threatening spell that according to Jake would end sooner or later in the equinoctial storms. The wholesale killing of elk for meat storage was not advisable until frost came again.

Discouraged and defeated gold-seekers took advantage of the mild days to leave the valley. The winding trail was now seldom vacant of pack-animals and plodding men, leaving without regret the El Dorado that had not glittered for them.

Kalispel noted, however, that none of the parasites left the valley. They would stay on, intensifying their leechlike endeavors upon the diminishing throng of miners. The next phase of Thunder City, therefore, could be expected to increase the activity of those who preyed upon the diggers.

Blair made it known to Kalispel that he had tried in vain to sell his claims back to Leavitt, for merely enough to hire some freighter to pack him and Sydney out of the valley.

Kalispel made no comment.

"How are you fixed for supplies?" asked Blair, as if forced.

"Can let you have flour, bacon, coffee, salt, some tinned fruit, but no sugar," replied Kalispel.

"Help me pack it down to my cabin. There'll be hell," went on Blair, desperately. "I swore I'd starve before I'd eat any food that came through Leavitt. And Sydney swears she'll leave me if I get any from you."

"Ah-huh. Where would she go?"

"Once she said she'd go to Leavitt. And again that she'd become a dance-hall girl."

"Bluff. Let's call her."

Wherewith they packed the supplies down to Blair's cabin. Sydney stood silent upon the porch, watching them carry in the goods. She had grown thinner; her bloom had faded; and her large eyes were all the more wonderful for their tragic pride and scorn. Kalispel felt his heart soften. If she had only really loved him, only a little, he could have forgiven her incomprehensible affair with Leavitt.

"Sydney, do you want to leave here?" he asked, abruptly, as always carried away by her presence.

"Yes."

"I'll get some money somewhere."

"Somewhere!" she echoed, scornfully.

"By gamblin' or borrowin' from Nugget or even holdin' up a miner," replied Kalispel, with passion, driven to strengthen her miserable estimate of him.

She gazed at him in horror and wonder. Her woman's intuition detected some insincerity about him, something baffling that repelled as well as fascinated her.

"My Gawd! Lady, I wouldn't have as much to beg forgiveness for as you have—not for a million," he mocked.

"Oh, is that so?"

"I reckon. But once more, Sydney, an' the last time, so help me Gawd! For your father's sake, for yours—for your honor an' more than life—give up this man Leavitt."

"Why?" she asked, as if leading him on.

"He's not what he seems."

"Are you?"

"No. But that's no matter. I've lost power to influence you."

"All men are liars."

"Ump-umm. Not me, Sydney Blair. I might lie to tease you or keep you from bein' hurt, but I wouldn't tell you a black lie to save my life."

"You lied about your little Nugget," she returned, in a hot passion that would have betrayed jealousy but for his hopelessness. "You rescued her for your friend—from the vile dance-hall. How noble! How chivalrous! . . . Yes. But to share her with——"

"Shut up! . . . If you don't close your catty lips I might—or you might say somethin' no man could ever forgive."

"You prate that word forgive," she went on, furiously. "Why, you conceited, stupid cowboy——"

"Never mind more of that. One word about Leavitt. Yes or No."

"No," she cried, violently. "And if you come here tonight a little before eight—and conceal yourself there—you shall see him kiss me."

"Sydney!— Don't—don't say you ever let him——"

"I have not yet. But tonight I shall. That will end this farce. Brutal as you are, you could hardly murder him in my arms."

"I'll come—I'll be here," whispered Kalispel, spent and shaking. "An' if you let that villain have you—Gawd help him—an' Gawd help me!"

Kalispel, long before the appointed hour, hid in the dark shadow of the large rock upon which one end of the Blair porch rested. He leaned there, sick, desperate, his faith in Sydney fighting against utter hopelessness. It seemed he had never believed in an irrevocable step on her part. But to go so far as she had threatened—that would be staggering. Leavitt was a thief, a bandit, one of the frontier's greatest criminals. Nevertheless, it was manifest that he was fascinating to women. Kalispel had seen a little of the magnetic influence exercised by complex men of dual nature, combining virile and physical force with suave and attractive personality. He did not imagine that he belonged to such a class. Kalispel had been in love often, once or twice so seriously that he knew he would never recover.

He had not only recovered, but lived to fall more deeply than ever—in this case, with Sydney Blair. The affair had turned out unhappily, and what hurt Kalispel so terribly was not Sydney's failure in affection—for, after all, she really had cared—but her shallowness, her readiness to believe the worst said about him, or the slightest circumstantial evidence against him. Were she the loveliest and sweetest girl in the world—and she might be no longer conceded this point—he would not want her if she had no lasting ineradicable faith.

Blair left the cabin early, grumbling as usual, and disappeared in the blackness. Clouds obscured the stars and the air was warm. Nighthawks swept overhead, uttering melancholy cries; a wolf mourned from the heights; and the stream murmured on as if weary of its endless task. Miners strolled by on the trail, going down to the town, to drink and dance and gamble. Kalispel wondered over the fact that he had no desire to go with them. He felt no more need of that kind of expression. He did not feel old, yet he had changed and seemed to be weighed upon by long experience. Something waited for him, and it was not like anything he remembered. But it did resemble that mysterious, looming mountain, waiting there for the great hour of its existence, and surely its dissolution. Kalispel had no illusions about the brevity of life. He had seen too many accidents. Death might be lurking downtown for him at this very moment. For himself, all he asked was what his kind called an even break. For those he chose to serve, however, he demanded more—time and opportunity and luck. This Thunder City was undermined by deceit and intrigue and evil that struck straight at the hearts of the few people Kalispel loved.

His sensitive ear caught the beat of rapid footsteps coming along the trail. They sounded like the steps of a formidable man who would be hard to turn aside. And they came direct for Blair's cabin.

Kalispel leaned out to see a tall dark form leap up on the porch. Leavitt! Kalispel sank back into the shadow. It was coming. The hot passion that leaped through his veins did not wholly drown the sick revolt of his soul.

"Hello, Sydney," called Leavitt, in a low, eager voice as he knocked at the open door.

"Rand! . . . There you are. Late again!" replied Sydney. "It is after eight."

Kalispel gaped in amaze. Sydney's reply did not seem natural. But, he corrected, what did he know about the many sides of a woman?

"I'm—sorry," replied Leavitt, breathing fast. "I took time while my man was away at supper—to hide some more gold. You see, I'm growing stingy. I want a lot of gold for you to help me spend."

Sydney laughed—a curious little laugh without mirth. "Don't come in. It's cool outside. . . . Now, Rand! . . . I get so tired resisting your advances."

"Stop then! You'll never have any peace until you do," he responded, with the ardor of a lover.

Kalispel saw the upper part of their forms silhouetted black against the frame of yellow light of the doorway. Leavitt had his arm around her waist. They walked out of the flare,

121

and presently appeared at the porch rail, side by side, their faces indistinct in the gloom.

"You are always talking about gold," she said. "If I were ever to—to care for you, I'd be jealous of your gold."

"Ever!— Don't you care now?"

"I'm afraid not—in the way you want.— Speaking of gold, father said you offered to lend him some today."

"Yes. He refused it. Your dad has changed toward me in some unaccountable way. I'll have to buy back his claims to help him. And I'll be glad to do it. I always regretted these claims failed to pan out. But they looked as good as any."

"Thank you, Rand," she murmured, gratefully. "Where do you hide your gold? Aren't you afraid it will be stolen?"

"I hide mine under the floor of my cabin. A section of log slips out—it fits so perfectly that it could never be detected. Underneath there's a space hollowed out in the base log. . . . There! I have trusted *you*. The only person I would trust."

"Take care I don't steal your riches, sir," she retorted. Then in a grave voice: "Father thought he had a safe hiding-place for his money. But he would soon have gambled it away."

"Emerson stole that money," declared Leavitt.

"So you have said before. I should imagine it would be embarrassing to tell *him*. . . . Why do you think he took it?"

"Well, he has been seen with considerable gold lately. It is known he seldom pans for gold. And it is hinted that he is one of the bandits who are taking toll of us miners, more and more."

"Better safeguard your own, then."

"I seldom leave my cabin, except to come here. Then I have guards who patrol my claim. . . . I'm more afraid of a landslide than robbery."

"Rand, are you not afraid of Kalispel Emerson?" she asked.

"No. But why should I risk gun-play with a notorious cowboy?" he replied, somewhat coldly. "I'm surprised that you ask."

"Father said you and Borden were deathly afraid of the fellow."

"That is not true, of me, at least. He has threatened me, I know. But there's nothing for me to gain by fighting Emerson, and everything to lose. . . . *You!*"

"But how about your Western code of honor? As I understand it, when a man has an enemy and accuses him of something—and dares him to come out—if he fails to do so he is branded a coward."

"That is true. Still, it can scarcely apply in my case. I am a man of affairs, with a future. Kalispel Emerson is a wild cowpuncher, a drinking gamester, a bully, proud of his gun record—and if he doesn't get shot he'll hang."

"I understand. But still there it is—the man-to-man thing."

"Sydney, you could not possibly want me to meet this gunman in a street fight?" demanded Leavitt, in great or pretended concern.

"No, I hate fighting. This blood-letting sickens me. A little more will send me back home. . . . Still, I'm a woman—and curious."

"Indeed you are a woman—and glorious," he replied, passionately, throwing his arms around her. "Sydney, I'm hungry for you."

"Then you are a cannibal, too," she rejoined, laughing.

"Darling, this is the first time you have let me embrace you!" he exclaimed, in a transport.

"Why, so it is! You should not have told me." And she drew away from him. Suddenly he grew bolder and snatched her to his breast.

"Sydney, don't you love me?" he implored.

"I don't think—I do," she returned, faintly. "I'm afraid you fascinate me. But you should wait. . . . Oh!"

He had kissed her. Kalispel's suffocating ears registered the soft contact of the man's lips. Then for an instant Sydney's pale face gleamed against his dark shoulder, and she drew away.

Kalispel staggered like a drunken man from his covert, and made his way round the corner of the cabin to the other side, where he headed for the open bench.

"Take your medicine, Kal," he whispered, huskily. "It's over—an' not so tough! . . . Gawd! these women! They're like snakes. . . . Yet in her heart she despises him."

Suddenly into the hot hate and agony of the moment there flashed an idea that effected almost instant transformation of his feelings. He remembered Sydney's strange luring from Leavitt the secret of the hiding-place of his gold. What had been Sydney's motive—knowing Kalispel heard there in the shadow? Was it just woman's deviltry? Whatever it was, Kalispel responded to it without doubt or hesitation.

He ran across the bench to the slope. He glided along that to the fence which inclosed Leavitt's claim. There he rested, regaining his breath, listening, peering for the guard. There was no sound, no moving object. He slipped among the boulders and stealthily made his way to the point almost opposite the cabin. A light shone from Leavitt's window. The door was closed. Footfalls attracted his attention. They were coming. Soon a dark form appeared. It grew blacker, took the shape of a man. He passed by close to the fence. When he was out of sight, Kalispel crossed the open space and hid behind the corner of the fence. He drew his gun and knew his course of action. If he bungled, he would have to kill the guard; this he did not want to do unless compelled.

Presently the guard returned. He passed the corner scarcely a yard away. Kalispel took one quick step and struck the man a hard blow on the head with the butt of his heavy gun. The fellow dropped like a log, his rifle clattering to the ground. Kalispel knelt and rolled him over on his back, intending to bind his mouth and hands. But he had no scarf, and Kaispel did not want to leave a clue by using his own. Rising, he ran to the porch, leaped up to try the door. Barred! Listening a moment more, he sheathed his gun and hurried round to the window. It took but a moment to force it and climb into the cabin.

He turned up the lamp and cast a swift, keen gaze round the room, scrutinizing the lowest log of the wall. In several places that log was hidden by bed, bench, chest, table. Kalispel dragged away the bed and felt with scrupulous care, searching for a joint. He did this all around that side and then the other. Each log ran the whole length of the wall. Behind Leavitt's table and under a canvas curtain where he hung his clothes Kalispel found what he was seeking.

His sharp fingernails halted at a smooth, scarcely perceptible joint. About four feet to the left of it he found another. With powerful hands he pressed the section of log, which slid out upon the floor, disclosing a dark hollow in the base log beneath.

Then as Kalispel bent over, the first object with which his eager hand came in contact was a large, long, leather wallet. It felt full of money. Kalispel could have yelled his glee. Blair's wallet!

The wallet was too large for Kalispel's pocket. It took but a moment for him to snatch a blanket from the bed. This he spread by the aperture in the log, and dropped the wallet upon it. Then he lifted out bag after bag of gold of various sizes—some canvas, but mostly buckskin. He did not desist until he had a pile of them that would have filled a bushel basket. Where, he thought with grim irony, had Leavitt got all the gold? Next he twisted the ends of the blanket and carried it to the window. He peered out. All quiet! It took all his strength to lower the heavy load down to the ground. Then he leaped out.

When he swung that improvised pack over his shoulder he calculated there was in excess of a hundred pounds of gold in it. He wanted to make the welkin ring with his triumph. But never had he been more vigilant. He stepped on the grass and on stones, out to the hard trail. The guard lay where he had fallen. Kalispel passed him and gained the boulders. Sheering to the left, he soon reached the base of the slope.

Only then did he relax, to exult and revel. He had done it. He had recovered Blair's money and he had taken what rightfully belonged to Sam Emerson.

"Gosh!" whispered Kalispel, halting to rest his burden on a convenient boulder. "Even if we'd never made this strike, I'd turned robber once, just to get even with this two-bit thief."

Of all the considerable feats Kalispel had ever achieved, this one gave him the most exultation. He was safe. He could never be apprehended. And nothing was any surer than that he could hide and keep this gold, which, added to what he had hidden, would make a fortune. He reverted to the youth that had dreamed of romance, adventure, daring feats, to the day he ran away from home to seek the pot of gold at the foot of the rainbow. He had unearthed the pot, but the bright face of the rainbow had faded.

He toiled on in short stages, careful each time to listen, to peer ahead, to make certain of his direction and safety. At last he reached his cabin, hot and wet, with bursting veins and throbbing heart, exhausted from over-excitement and exertion, but full of a satisfaction that made up for the irrevocable loss of Sydney Blair.

When he got ready he would return her father's money to him, with a few caustic words to Sydney anent where he had found it. And possibly some of the gold the miners had lost could be identified and returned to them. Then he had Jake to think of and plan for, to establish in life, and also Nugget and Sloan, and lastly himself. Somehow thought of the ranch, certain to be his if he lived, did not rouse the old joy.

Kalispel, all the while with whirling thoughts, concealed his treasure, assured that his hiding-place could not be discovered without long and painstaking search.

The hour was late and he took advantage of this to burn the blanket.

"I reckon my high-minded Sydney would figure me out a thief," he soliloquized. "My heaven! If she cared for that hombre, what a jar she'll get!

"But," he puzzled again, "why did she persuade him to tell where the gold was hidden, when she knew I was there?"

He went to bed without disturbing Jake, who slept like a log, and he lay there wide-eyed until the gray dawn.

That day Kalispel remained in camp, restless and watchful, working at small tasks, expecting any moment a posse of miners with Leavitt at their head. His loaded Winchester leaned against the door of the cabin, and he had an extra gun in his belt. He felt capable of holding off even a determined band of men.

But afternoon came without any untoward event. Then when he espied Leavitt on Sydney's porch, apparently no more excited than usual, he concluded that the loss of the gold had not been discovered. Kalispel pondered over this amazing aspect of the situation. No doubt that guard knew how Charlie March had come to his untimely end. He might have recovered consciousness without it becoming known that he had been assaulted, and then in the interest of self-preservation he had chosen to keep his mouth shut. Kalispel reflected that he had left Leavitt's room as he had found it, except for the purloining of the blanket. This loss, too, might not have been noticed.

Leavitt made a lengthy call upon the young woman he was wooing, most certainly too long for a man who had lost a fortune. In this Kalispel had positive proof that Leavitt did not yet know of his great loss.

"Dog-gone!" ejaculated Kalispel, rubbing his hands in glee. "My luck has changed. I'll play it to the limit."

About midafternoon Kalispel, watching, saw Rand Leavitt rise to make his departure. Either he wanted Sydney to accompany him downtown or she wanted him to stay there. In any event, they idled some moments at the head of the steps, in plain view of Kalispel—which was assuredly known to both—and at length Leavitt leisurely left. Kalispel watched him take the trail to town instead of the one across the bench toward his cabin.

Jake had keener observation than Kalispel had credited him with.

"Brother, you're on edge today, like a stiff wire in a cold wind," remarked Jake. "When are you goin' to kill him?"

126

"Him!— Say, Jake, are you dotty? What's eatin' you?"

"Nothin'. I been watchin' you watchin' Leavitt down there sparkin' yore girl. An' I wouldn't give two bits for his life."

"Hell! Am I that easy? . . . Wal, Jake, jealousy is pretty tough, an' what's more it's new to me."

"Has Leavitt added outrage to theft?" queried Jake, his big eyes flaring.

"He shore helped queer me with Sydney, but I reckon I was most to blame. I was responsible for bringin' the Blairs here. It has been ruin for them. Blair has gone to the bad. Sydney hates drink. An' altogether she's had too much of wild West an' Kalispel Emerson mixed."

"Not a sweet drink, I'll admit," growled Jake. "But, hell, hasn't she got any guts? If she is as tenderfooty as she looks she wouldn't do for you. Reckon it's just as well. When you go to ranchin' you'll want a husky girl who can cook, sweep, sew, milk, an' look after a flock of kids, an'——"

"Hey!" interrupted Kalispel, red in the face. "Do you take me for a Mormon?"

"Are you still keen about the ranch?"

"Keen? I'm worse than ever. If I didn't have a couple of scores to keep here I'd leave pronto."

"But, Kal, you can't buy that Salmon River ranch on credit."

"Wal, I've got enough saved up for a payment. Forgot to tell you."

"Thet's different," rejoined Jake, brightening. "An' I'm offerin' myself as cowboy, milkman, farmer, or any other help you'll need. . . . Just for a home, Kal. I'm sick of this gold fever. Sam is dead. I feel it. An' I don't want any more prospectin' without him."

"Same here, Jake," replied Kalispel, feelingly. "I'm takin' you up, Jake. But I won't give you a job an' wages. You'll be my partner. . . . Dog-gone, but that cheers me! It's just fine of you, Jake, an' we'll shore——"

"Who's thet goin' up on Blair's steps?" interrupted Jake.

Kalispel wheeled as on a point. A slight-statured boy in blue jeans had just mounted to Blair's porch. But when the sun, that had peeped out late, caught a glint of golden hair, Kalispel realized with a start that the boy was not a boy.

"Nugget!— Wal, I'll be damned! She swore she'd do it," ejaculated Kalispel.

"Do it? What? An' who's Nugget?"

"She's Dick Sloan's girl, an' she's callin' on Sydney Blair. Struck me funny, that's all."

127

"Lots of funny things happenin'. . . . Kal, do you know thet they're hintin' you could tell a lot about these hold-ups?"

"*Could I?*— My Gawd! man, believe me I could—an' I will when I'm ready," cried Kalispel, so fiercely that Jake stared aghast, and then resumed his camp tasks.

Kalispel riveted his gaze upon the Blair home. He made out Nugget standing outside the open door for some minutes before she was admitted. If she had decided to acquaint Sydney Blair with some revealing facts, it would require nothing less than force to prevent her. Kalispel grimly recognized that Sydney Blair was in for some bad moments. Nugget could convince a wooden image of Leavitt's guilt, if she chose to. Probably she was mostly concerned with proving Kalispel's innocence and honesty; nevertheless, in the process of explaining this she would hardly spare Leavitt.

Nugget did not come out. The minutes dragged. She was making a lengthy call. Somehow Kalispel's sympathy was with Nugget, and, strangely, for the balance of the endless hour that the girl stayed there, Kalispel's thought was of her, not Sydney.

Finally she came out, to trip down the steps, to run gracefully away, her hair shining in the sunlight. She did not take to the trail, but sheered off to disappear among the tents along the stream.

Scarcely had she gone out of sight when Sydney appeared on her porch, hesitatingly advanced to the rail, and clung to it as if for support. For a moment she appeared bowed and shaken. Then she raised her head to gaze toward Kalispel's cabin.

She saw him sitting on his bench before the door. She waved her scarf, dropping it a moment, then waved again. Next she beckoned for Kalispel to come, and her action was urgent, appealing. The imploring gesture that followed was almost a holding out of her arms.

"Ump-umm, Lady! Not me," Kalispel was muttering, feeling his heart in a cold vise. "Not after last night!— You can walk on me—an' spit on me—an' insult me scandalous, but, by Gawd! when you gave that hombre what I yearned for an' never had—I was through!"

Sydney edged along the rail. Plainly she was gathering courage or strength to come to him. When she got as far as the porch post she clung to that and watched him, her posture and demeanor most expressive of trouble and weakness. At length she gave up and went into the cabin.

Kalispel seemed released from the vise. He gazed around

in inexpressible relief. The sun had set, yet fan-shaped rays shot up toward the zenith and down into the valley. The broken clouds of purple and gold appeared edged with fire. And for a moment longer a marvelous color bathed the fringed peaks. Then it faded, and that fading of the exquisite glow appeared to resemble what had happened in Kalispel's heart.

That Sydney should wave to him, beckon for him, almost hold out her arms! That was as incredible as his strange callousness to her entreaty. Too late! He understood that. Not that she had failed him so often, but that she had lightly given what he had regarded sacred! He would have killed men and moved mountains for her kisses.

Twilight fell and dusk mantled the valley floor. Jake called him to supper. Kalispel went in, shaking himself as if to throw off fetters. He ate without his usual gusto. Jake talked of the ranching plan, growing enthusiastic, but Kalispel scarcely heard. Then came a timid knock on the cabin door.

"Somebody knockin'," whispered Jake.

Kalispel stared at the door. Another knock, fainter, brought him to his feet on fire within and cold without. Slowly he swung open the door. The broad flare of lamplight shone upon Sydney Blair. Kalispel grasped the manifestations of her passionate trouble before a sense of her beauty waved over him.

"Come in," he said, and as she entered he indicated Jake, who stood staring as if at an apparition. "My brother Jake— Miss Blair."

"Glad to meet you, miss," replied Jake.

Sydney bowed. Then her wide dark eyes traveled back to Kalispel. "I must see you alone."

"Jake, will you leave us?" said Kalispel, tensely, and it was as if he girded up his loins for battle. Jake went out. Kalispel turned up the lamp to increase the light. "Sydney, you look shaky. Please sit down."

She made no move to take the chair he offered.

"Why did you not come?"

"Do you need to ask that?" he countered.

"You saw me wave and beckon and—hold out my hands to you, like a drowning woman?"

"Yes, I saw you. An' I reckoned I'd spare you some pain— an' myself hell, if I didn't go."

"Then you *were* there last night!" she affirmed, tragically, and sinking on the couch she covered her face with her hands. "I couldn't tell. Oh, I was mad!"

"Shore you were mad," he agreed. "Yes, I was there . . . an' when he kissed you somethin' in me cracked. I sneaked away then."

"That—was nothing," she whispered, revealing her shamed face. "He pulled me back to the hammock—made violent love to me. I forgot you. I—I thought I was in love with him. . . . And I promised—to—marry him."

Kalispel's laugh was not harsh, but she flinched at it. "Ah-huh. An' after Nugget got through with you, Mr. Leavitt didn't rate such a good bargain, eh?"

Humbly she shook her head.

"An' what you thought last night you don't think now?"

"I loathe him!"

"Wal, Sydney, that gives me back a little of my respect for you. I reckon you got off easy. A few words of love, a hug or two, an' some kisses—they probably go terrible against the grain for so proud a girl as you. But there's no harm done. An' if you despise him—why, that ends it."

"Ends it, yes. But not my shame."

"That will wear away, Sydney. I reckon you felt the same when I mauled an' kissed you so scandalous."

"No. I was furious, but not ashamed."

"Wal, nothin' much can be done about it. I remember when I was a kid an' learned cuss words my mother used to wash my mouth with lye soap. You might try that. I have a piece here somewhere."

"Don't jest!" she importuned.

"All right," he retorted, harshly. "An' *now* you want me to kill Leavitt?"

"Oh no, Kalispel, no!" she cried. "I don't care what he has done—what he *is*. But it'd be horrible to kill him. An' you cannot forever escape yourself!"

"Humph! You'd care a hell of a lot, wouldn't you?" he exclaimed, unable to resist that gibe.

"Yes, I would care," she replied, steadily, with unfathomable eyes on his.

"Wal, that doesn't matter atall. Ever since I first saw Leavitt an' read in his eyes that he'd done away with my brother, I've intended to kill him. An' I'm goin' to do it!"

" 'Vengeance is mine,' saith the Lord. 'I will repay,' " she quoted, solemnly.

"Beautiful words, Sydney. But they don't go out here. . . . What did Nugget tell you?"

With a little cry of distress, Sydney again covered her face.

130

"Never mind, if it hurts," he added, relenting. "I reckon I can guess."

"I *will* tell you," she cried, poignantly, "if it kills me."

When Kalispel did not reply, she went on:

"She came. She stood in the door. She said, 'I want to tell you something.'— And I asked how she dared address me. 'I'm sorry you're like that,' she said. 'I'm wondering where Kalispel will get off.' I was amazed at her. She stood there white and cool, with the sweetest face, the bluest eyes—the very prettiest girl I ever saw. Then she came in and shut the door.

" 'You've given Kal Emerson a rotten deal,' she went on. 'And I'm here to call you for it. . . . He was a wild cowboy, a bad hombre, as they say in the South. One way and another he has been driven to defend his name, his life, or some one who needed a friend, until he became notorious. He's what the West calls a gunman, a killer. But all the same he's a better, finer, truer man because of that. The West has to have such men. Don't *I* know? Good God! How many drunks, bums, thieves, adventurers, gamblers—how many lowdown men do you guess I've seen shot in the street or dragged out of dance-halls?—Yes, and I've seen good boys like Kalispel go down—worse luck. . . . You are to get it into your head, Miss Blair, that this Kal Emerson is a better man than your father, a better boy than your brother, if you have one. He was so clean an' straight—so true to *you*—that he could dance with me, be my friend, with never a word that you could not have been glad to hear. I loved him! . . . He brought a boy to see me, Dick Sloan, and that boy, too, was clean and fine. He loved me. I treated him badly. I did all I could to make him despise me. I couldn't. . . . Then Kal came for me—dragged me out of Borden's hall—scared me stiff because I thought he meant to beat me—and I can't stand that. . . . Dick wanted to marry me and Kal made me promise. . . . I'm living in Dick's tent now. And I might be his sister! We will be married as soon as it's possible. I'm free. I'd be—happy if—I could forget.' "

Sydney's husky, failing voice trailed off. For several moments there was silence.

"She fascinated me," went on Sydney. "And then she changed somehow. The scorn—the earnestness—the sweetness all fled. 'Now for your new lover, Leavitt,' she began, with a terrible look at me. 'I'll make short work of him—and the rest of this job. . . . Rand Leavitt is two-faced, and one of his faces—the one *I* know—is that of a dog. I know

131

he made way with Kalispel's brother and jumped his claim. But I can't prove it. He sold your father two worthless claims, which I *can* prove. If your father has been robbed, as I've heard, one of Leavitt's men did it. But *that* side of Leavitt is the least vile. All this time that he's been making love to you he's been trying to get me. Oh, you needn't glare at me!—I can prove that, if you need proof. Any of the girls at Borden's will corroborate my statement. . . . Leavitt played the gallant lover to you. He vilified poor Kal and talked marriage to you. To *me* he showed the beast. In many ways you couldn't understand if I told you. But you'll understand this. He beat me when he couldn't get the best of me. He has beaten other of the girls. He likes to beat women.' "

Sydney panted in her agitation, and for a moment could not continue.

"She saw I was faint," she presently went on. " 'I could tell you more, Miss Blair,' she continued. 'But unless you are mad indeed I've told enough. That is the kind of man Rand Leavitt is.' . . . She left me without another word."

Kalispel paced to and fro in the confined space of the cabin, and tried to avert his face from his visitor. He divined that the most trying part of this interview might yet come.

"I have told you—about all," said the girl, haltingly.

"Shore. An' it's been hard on you."

"Can you—forgive me?"

He was silent and stared fixedly at the smouldering fire. The wind outside moaned under the eaves and roared hollowly down the chimney.

"I was a proud, egotistical, conceited thing," she went on, humbly. "And out here only a tenderfoot. I love the beauty of this wilderness. But I hate the raw, the crude, the toil, the blood. I thought I could stand it. I fear now I never can. . . . Please forgive me!"

"I reckon. . . . All except last night. That I can't forget. . . . Maybe in time."

"Kalispel, I do not know myself. I am weak or crazy—or both. I *was* jealous of that girl Nugget. I despised myself. But I was. And yesterday I grew furious at you. I wanted to hurt you, drive you insane with jealousy. I *had* loved you. I thought you'd killed it. . . . And in the end all I did was—promise to marry—Rand Leavitt."

"There was one thing I didn't understand, Sydney," queried Kalispel. "Why did you get Leavitt to tell you where he hid his gold, knowing I might be there to hear? You didn't think Leavitt was a thief then."

132

Sydney's face flamed scarlet. "I don't know, Kalispel. It was just part of my madness. Maybe I had an idea it might prove to me if you were a bandit. I wanted to believe the worst of you. Can't you understand? Or maybe I just wanted to show you how much Leavitt cared for me—to tell me where he hid his fortune. Oh, I don't know what it was—I was just out of my head."

Kalispel nodded. "I guess—I understand, Sydney," he said, slowly. Then, "Sydney, what will you do?" he queried, as if suddenly released.

"Is there nothing—for you—and me?" she faltered.

"Hopeless," he burst out, with dry lips. "I am a gunman, a killer. I mean to do for Leavitt an' Borden before I leave here. . . . You are a lady, far above me, too fine for this bloody West. . . . Wherever I go my name will follow me. If you—you married me you'd be a pioneer's wife. You'd have to pitch hay, bake bread, cut off the turkey's head, milk the cows—an', as Jake said, look after a brood of kids. . . . You see it isn't a pleasin' prospect."

"It would be if I were woman enough," she replied, and rising faced him with eloquent eyes that made him weak. Then she moved toward the door.

"Aw!—I'll see you home, Sydney," he replied, hurriedly, and followed her out.

The night was dark and windy, with storm in the warm air. He led the way for her among the boulders, and once had to take her hand. She clung to his a moment and then let go. They reached her porch without speaking again. She started up, then turned to him, so that her face gleamed pale, with shadowy eyes.

"No woman like me could ever love you like that girl does. No other woman could ever have such cause. . . . It was a revelation to me."

"Aw, Sydney, you exaggerate. Nugget is grateful, of course, but——"

"She blazed with it," interrupted Sydney. "And out of this ghastly lesson I'll get most from that."

"I'm awful glad you see the kid fair an' straight now. She never was bad!"

"Thank God you saved her!" returned Sydney, with deep emotion. "Good night, Kalispel."

He bade her good night and wended a thoughtful and sad way among the boulders, while the old black mountain rumbled its low thunder.

133

Chapter Twelve

There had been humility, remorse, and scorn of self in Sydney's capitulation. Like a pendulum she had swung over to the other extreme. She had all but killed something beautiful and wonderful in Kalispel, and now it struggled to rise again and live. Under the dark and threatening sky, where he walked his beat, he was to find that love did not die so easily. His survived, and he was glad that was so, for he hated hate. Sydney still cared for him, in some degree, enough to sue for his forgiveness and his allegiance.

But in the light of all her vacillation Kalispel realized that he was not the man to make her happy. One wild hope shook him to the core—to take her and his gold, and go back where she belonged, where his fateful gun-play would never be called upon again. This idea, however, was untenable. He belonged to the West. They were incompatible. The biggest thing he could do for Sydney was to conquer his longing for her, to renounce her beauty, and to let her go to a better and more suitable mate. He succeeded, but it was the bitterest victory of his life.

It did not leave him peace. The long strife wore his nerves raw. What seemed left was a stern duty to expel these softer emotions which had made him weak, and get back to the grim and hard passion that had obsessed him before this upheaval.

Jake returned to the cabin late, to find Kalispel burning the midnight oil.

"Hello!" he said. "I allowed I'd let you have plenty of time with your lady-love."

"Wal, I had plenty, believe me," replied Kalispel, gruffly.

"Peaches an' cream, thet girl, an' sweet on you, Kal, or I'm a born fool."

"You are a born fool, Jake."

"Reckon I better change the subject or get bored. . . . Lots of talk downtown."

"What about?"

"Masters an' Leavitt have locked horns, it seems. You know Leavitt has been sore about Masters' election. Wal, they're at odds now about a vigilante committee. Masters wants one elected by the miners, with him, of course, at the head. An' Leavitt holds that he has power to appoint the vigilantes."

"Whew!—That'll make a hell of a mess.—Jake, keep this under your hat. Leavitt is the boss of these bandits."

"Thunderation an' damnation!—Is it possible? But I'd believe anythin' of thet man. . . . Are you shore, Kal?"

"Absolutely positive."

"Can you prove it?"

"I could to honest, fair-minded men. Not to Leavitt's crowd."

"An' that's the rub.—Son, look here. If Leavitt organizes a band of vigilantes to catch an' hang his own outfit—that will be a hell of a mess."

"Worse. They'd hang me."

"I wish you'd bored thet——long ago," declared Jake, thoughtfully. "What're we goin' to do?"

"Hang on an' see what comes off. But I'm bound to say, if this news of yours isn't just camp gossip, it's gettin' sort of hot around here."

"I should smile it is."

"An' I'm at the end of my rope."

"Wal, thet's good. Just so long as you'll not be at the end of their rope!"

"How's the weather?" asked Kalispel, as he began to pull off his boots.

"Mistin' a little. But clouds breakin' some. It'll rain shore, sooner or later. Then it'll turn off cold an' winter will set in colder'n blue blazes."

Kalispel lay awake for a long while, and then slept late, far into the morning. Upon arising he shaved and then partook of a belated breakfast which Jake threatened he would not keep hot any longer. Kalispel did not waste words that morning. From the open door he saw that the storm still held aloof. Securing Blair's wallet, he wrapped the bulky thing in a burlap sack and set out.

"Mind camp," he said to Jake. "From now on one of us must be here all day."

The hour was about noon. He found the kitchen door of Blair's cabin open. Father and daughter were at lunch. "Howdy! Excuse me, but this is sort of ticklish," said Kalispel, as he went in and closed the door.

Blair's greeting was cordial and curious. Sydney had been weeping. Her smile was something to conjure with.

"Can you be trusted—now?" he asked Sydney, with strong emphasis on the last word.

135

Sydney submerged the old outraged dignity, but it took an effort. Kalispel unwrapped the burlap sack and laid the wallet on the table.

"Can you be trusted to take care of this yourself?" demanded Kalispel.

Blair leaped up in great excitement. "For the land's sake!— My wallet! . . . Let me feel—let me look!"

"No, I will," declared Sydney, after a gulp, and she snatched the wallet away from Blair's clutching hands. She opened it. "Yes—yes—the money appears to be all here. Oh, how glad I am! . . . Kalispel, where did you get this wallet?"

"Where do you suppose?" he launched at her, keenly.

She flushed. "I—I did not mean anything. . . . But where?"

"I stole it from Leavitt."

Blair betrayed his excitement by cursing prodigiously.

"Sydney, it's not likely Leavitt will suspect you or search your house," said Kalispel. "But hide the wallet in your bed or on your person. An' never forget it. Pack your belongin's an' plan to leave the valley with one of these freighters as soon as this storm is over. I wouldn't advise it till then. You might get caught up on top. An' that'd shore not be any fun."

"Pack! . . . Are you leaving, too?" she inquired, tremulously.

"No. Not unless I get chased out."

"Oh!" she exclaimed, and dropped her tell-tale eyes. "Come back and let me thank you."

"Kal, I just noticed you're wearing two guns," said Blair, his eyes popping. "Must be going to a prayer-meeting."

"Ornamental, that's all, Blair. So long," drawled Kalispel, and cautiously opening the door, he saw that the coast was clear and went out.

Once at the gateway of the town it seemed to Kalispel that he was entering Laramie or Medicine Bow or Butte or Kalispel. It was not a happy nor an easy mood. Thunder City did not look as if it had lost half of its inhabitants, for the thoroughfare was as crowded, as loud, as bustling as usual. But the fact was that at least half of the miners had decided against being snowed in on a bonanza diggings the bright bubble of which had burst.

Kalispel had no particular objective just then except to ascertain the facts about the Masters-Leavitt controversy. If the argument developed into a dispute, that would be favorable to Kalispel. He went into one place after another. The business of buying, selling, freighting, eating, drinking, gambling, gossiping, prevailed as always. Kalispel received his meed of greetings and avoidances. Far ahead he espied Haskell and Selby, the latter still with his arm in a sling, standing in front of the Dead Eye Saloon. They crossed the wide street, obviously to let Kalispel pass.

At length he ran straight into Masters, who emerged from his office with no other than Borden.

"Hello! Just the man I'm lookin' for," ejaculated the sheriff.

"Wal, if you want anythin' short of arrestin' me you got to keep better company," replied Kalispel, curtly.

Borden broke out of his rigidity; his swarthy face paled, his jaw bulged, his big eyes dilated, and with an imprecation he strode swiftly away up the street. Kalispel turned deliberately to watch him.

"Chip on yore shoulder, eh? An' packin' double hardware?" drawled Masters. "Will you come in an' have a little talk?"

Kalispel followed him into the little board shack without troubling to reply. The room contained a rude table piled high with papers, two boxes for seats, a sawed-off shotgun, and a rifle.

"I needn't tell you that walls have ears," warned Masters, dryly, as he fastened his searching, eagle eyes upon his guest. "Our little plan to locate the bandits didn't work, eh?"

"Not yet. An' I reckon I'll lay off that," replied Kalispel.

"Just as wal. It might have turned out embarrassin' for me."

"Masters, I don't need to make bluffs to get a line on the bandits," declared Kalispel, pointedly, as he sized up his man. "Do you want to know who's their chief?"

"Emerson, I'm not so damn keen as I was," drawled the sheriff.

"Gettin' cold feet?" queried Kalispel, just a little sarcastic.

"No. My feet air always warm an' they stay on the ground. I'm leary, Emerson. I want to find out more before I act."

"More about what—or who?"

"I reckon you could tell me, Emerson."

"I reckon I could. But it looks like I'm playin' a lone hand."

"You mean I've got to show my hand, heah? Declare myself for Kalispel Emerson or against him?"

"You savvy."

"Wal, I'll do that. I'd stack yore friendship against the

137

enmity of Borden an' Leavitt any day. They're the men buckin' me heah."

"Straight talk from a Texan," returned Kalispel. "Shore you've heard this low-down hint about me bein' a bandit?"

"Yes. I've been asked to arrest you."

"Wal, I reckon if you go hobnobbin' all over town with me it'll offset thet talk."

"Yes, an' raise a hell of a lot more. But I'll do it."

"All right. Now what's this vigilante deal?"

"Wal, it's the queerest deal I ever stacked up against," declared the Texan, dragging at his mustache. "I proposed to elect a vigilante committee. Judge Leavitt overruled me an' appointed the men himself."

"Has he already done it?"

"Shore. This mawnin'."

"How many?"

"I don't know. He didn't say. Borden, who I had in heah pumpin', didn't know, either. An' he didn't care a damn. He's out with Leavitt."

"Take a hunch from me, Masters," rejoined Kalispel, impressively. "Appoint another vigilante committee from the miners you know an' do it pronto."

"Youngster, I hadn't thought of thet. You got the jump on me. . . . What you drivin' at?"

"Masters, I'm not ready to come clean yet with all I know."

"Wal, you've made one thing damn plain," declared the sheriff, gravely. "If I cain't trust Leavitt's vigilante committee, I cain't trust Judge Rand Leavitt."

"Take it as you like," said Kalispel, coolly. "Come out now an' make good your friendliness for me."

"Son, I'll do thet little thing with genuine pleasure."

They went out together, and Kalispel was about to lead his companion up the street when a young, heavy-booted miner halted to accost him.

"Ha, Emerson—hyar you—are," he panted. He was livid of face and sweating. Kalispel recognized one of Sloan's friends and sensed calamity.

"What's come off?"

"Sloan!—He's been beat—and knifed. Bad shape—I'm awful worried. . . . Nugget sent me. I—run all—way to your cabin. Come."

"Holy—!" Kalispel leaped as one under the leash. "Masters, trail in on this. . . ."

They had almost to run to keep up with the young miner, whose incoherent tongue worked as fast as his legs.

"Get yore breath—an' then talk," suggested the Texan, brusquely.

By the time they reached the log bridge over the stream the miner had recovered sufficiently to be understood.

"I got it—this way," he said. "Sloan had a new claim—over in the brush. He laid off workin' it—an' this mornin' when he went there—it had been jumped by three men. Argument ended in a fight. Sloan was hurt serious. He crawled till he got help. They took him home—did all thet was possible for him. But we reckon he'll cash from the lung stab alone."

"Ah-huh," breathed Kalispel, as if a weight were on his chest.

"Did Sloan recognize his assailants?" asked the practical Masters.

"I didn't hear thet."

They turned up the trail which ran between tents and cabins and the stream. A knot of miners stood outside Sloan's cabin.

"You go in, Emerson," said the sheriff. "I'll talk to these men heah."

Kalispel entered. Besides Nugget, and Sloan, who lay on the bed, there were two others present—a neighbor miner whom Kalispel knew by sight, and a serious-faced woman, evidently his wife.

"Kal!—It took you so long," said Nugget. "He wanted you so badly. And he's sinking now."

"I'm shore sorry," replied Kalispel, not wanting to face her then. "I was downtown."

He approached the bed. Sloan lay dressed, except for his boots, and his boyish face was ghastly of hue. Kalispel had seen the shade of death too many times not to recognize it here. But prepared as he was for the worst, the actual presence of fatality, the pity of it, the raw evil, sent the freezing cold to his marrow.

"Pard," whispered Sloan, faintly. "Ruth—will—tell you."

Kalispel took the boy's limp, clammy hand.

"Dick, it shore breaks my heart to see you this way," returned Kalispel, huskily. "But don't give up. You might pull through."

Sloan's singularly intense blue eyes appeared to burn with a fire not for himself. Kalispel found them shockingly sad to gaze into.

"Kal, would it be—askin' too much of you—to take care of Ruth?"

"It shore would not."

"She has no—other friend. . . . You saved her. . . ."

"I'll take care of her, Dick," interrupted Kalispel, squeezing the cold hand

"Thanks, pard," Sloan said, more clearly, with passionate gratitude. "Thet was makin'—me hold on. . . ."

"Don't talk. Only give me a hunch. You told Ruth all you know?"

"Yes," replied Sloan, appearing to rally as he reached weakly for the girl. Quickly she took his hand in hers, and kneeling pressed it to her breast. "Ruth—thet horrible fear—is gone. . . . Kal will look after you. . . . Some day. . . ."

"Dick, I would never have gone back," she interposed, softly. "You must not talk so much. It'd bring on another hemorrhage. . . . Rest, and fight the thing, Dick. While there's hope."

He smiled faintly, as one who knew and was relieved, and closed his eyes wearily. A trace of blood appeared at the corner of his mouth. Ruth wiped it away. He lay still, breathing slowly.

After a few moments Ruth released his hand and stood up. Kalispel found that Dick had let go of him. Then Kalispel drew the girl away. At that juncture Masters entered and went up to Sloan's bed to gaze silently down, shaking his lean head. He turned then to whisper:

"We cain't do nothin'. Shore you got his deposition?"

"Ruth did. Masters, you take these folks out an' leave me alone with her."

When the Texan had complied, Kalispel turned to Ruth. She was pale but composed, and outside of a hunted expression in her blue eyes betrayed no other marked evidence of emotion. As he looked down upon her, however, she took hold of his gun-sheath and clung to it, a wholly unconscious action.

"Nug—Ruth, are you up to talkin' now?" he asked, earnestly.

"Yes."

"Who do you think is back of it?"

"Borden."

"Why?"

"Two days straight running he has been here. Last time I had to fight to keep him from packing me off. I kicked and bit and screamed. He went out to run into our neighbors,

140

who'd heard me. When I heard him lie to them I went out, too, and told the truth. Called him I don't know what, right before them. Then he left, white with rage. . . . I *know* he is behind this attack on poor Dick."

"Yet he might not be."

"I feel it. A woman *never* makes a mistake when she feels that way."

"I feel it, too. But, Ruth, we must have facts. These miners are in an ugly mood. Did you know Leavitt has organized a vigilante band of his own, with himself as leader?"

"No. I hadn't heard."

"Wal, it's true. An' it's bad news. I reckoned he an' Borden had split. But so far as I'm concerned he'd take Borden's side. I must have facts."

"Kal, I have facts as to Dick's assailants, but I can't connect Borden with them."

"Uh-huh. All right, you might as well tell me now."

"Dick left early this morning," she began, swiftly and intelligently, "to work his new claim. He hired Presbry, a neighbor miner, to work this claim here, on shares. It is about panned out. Dick's new claim is way across the valley, up high, among the rocks and brush. I've been there. It is hard to get to. . . . Well, I don't know how long ago—two hours, maybe, men came packing Dick in here, all bloody and dirty, terrible to see. He had been stabbed in the back and beaten over the head. While we worked over him as best we could he talked. . . . He found that his new claim had been jumped. There were three men, one of them digging. Dick had seen him before, but did not know him. They seemed friendly at first, as if he ought to take it for granted they had a right to jump his claim. But as Dick had visited that claim every day, he did not agree with them. They argued, and finally Dick got sore. He jumped in the hole to throw the man out. Then began a fight, in which the other men joined. In the scuffle one of them called out: 'Don't shoot! You might hit Mac!' . . . This man in the hole, then, was the one named Mac. Dick said he had a stubby red beard and a bloody patch pasted over a recent wound just above his ear. One of the two above stabbed Dick in the back. The blade went clear through in front. Then they beat him over the head. When Dick came to he was alone. They had no doubt left him for dead. He walked and crawled within call of the miners who carried him home—and that's all, I think."

"Did they rob him?"

"Oh, I forgot. Yes, his watch, gun, money, everything was taken. And his pockets turned inside out."

"Pretty slick. Robbery motive, eh? Wal, we know enough. Ruth, that fellow Mac is one of Leavitt's trusted guards. An' *I* made that wound on his head. . . . Why in hell didn't I kill him while I was about it?"

"Let him go, Kal. . . . Let them all go!" she begged, suddenly changing from the calm, cold girl who had related Sloan's story. Her eyes turned a darker, stranger blue. Nervous hands pulled at the lapels of Kalispel's vest.

"Ruth, you ask that?" he queried, in surprise.

"Yes. I implore it."

"I reckoned you knew me."

"I do. But it's too late to save Dick. And even if you *are* Kalispel Emerson you might get killed."

"Shore. Only that's not the way to meet this situation. If I showed yellow I'd stand a heap more chance of cashin'. Besides, Borden would get you shore."

"Not alive!" she flashed.

"Ah-huh. There you're admittin' the weakness of your argument to let these skunks off. Can't you see that, girl?"

"We could leave Thunder City as soon—as—" she faltered. "Kal, can't *you* see something, too?"

"I see a lot, Ruth. An' the biggest thing is for me to go on the rampage. Borden an' Leavitt are white livered, an' their men are not the real stuff. They shoot in the dark an' knife in the back. I'm goin' to wipe out some of them an' scare the rest of them stiffer'n a crowbar. That, with the proofs I have, will wake up these miners. Masters is on our side. He's a crafty Texan an' he shore smells a rat."

"Oh, Kal—suppose—" she choked, and after one terrible gaze into his face she sank against him, quivering.

Kalispel held her, suddenly troubled with the memory of Sydney's statement about this girl. That was scarcely credible. Yet— Ruth drew away from him. To his surprise and admiration, all trace of weakness had vanished. She was of different caliber from Sydney Blair, not built of the same stuff.

"You know best, Kal," she said, with composure. "It is not for me to try to stay your hand. . . . Go—and don't worry about me."

"That's the way to talk, Ruth," he rejoined, hiding his own feeling. "Looks like Dick is unconscious. Reckon he won't come to again. An' that's just as well, seein' he's done for. . . . Ruth, don't worry now about me."

142

"I'd hate to be in Borden's boots," she replied, lightly, and went to Sloan's bedside.

Kalispel strode out slowly, gazing back at Ruth. There was a girl who understood a man. Once out of the door, he was himself again. Masters stood outside, talking to the couple. The crowd, except for a few groups, had dispersed.

"Folks, go inside an' stay with Ruth," begged Kalispel. "Masters, you come with me."

They had crossed the bridge and reached the main street when the Texan broke the strained silence.

"Youngster, you're aimin' to play a lone hand?"

"I reckon."

"Wal, I calculate I'd back you up," returned the other, deliberately.

"Masters, I'd be most damned glad to have you line up with me on this deal," said Kalispel, forcefully, as he gratefully squeezed the sheriff's arm. "But if I got in deep an' dragged you in, why, you might not be left to look after your friends. An' believe me, if we got bored, they'd shore need it."

"Emerson, you're hintin' of a Henry Plummer outfit. An' I reckon thet's far-fetched. Neither Leavitt or Borden air Plummer's caliber. An' the rest of this gang air four-flushers."

"My idea, too. But this gang may be bigger than I've figured."

"No matter. Without leaders they'd wilt like yellow paper in a blaze. I've sized up every man in this camp. An' you're the only hombre heah I'd be leary of. It wasn't because I was afraid of you that I offered to back you."

"Fine. That's like a stiff drink, which I needed. The only thing I'm leary about is bein' picked from some door or window."

"Wal, thet's not liable to happen if I hang close to you. At the same time it'll show this outfit thet there's something damned onsartin' in the wind."

They had halted just short of the corner to conclude this conversation.

"Look for a stocky man with a stubby red beard an' a bloody patch over his ear. . . . An' let me see. It'd be his right ear, thet's shore."

"Must have put thet patch there yourself," was the deduction of the shrewd sheriff.

"They call him Mac," said Kalispel. "I can't describe him, more'n that. But I'll shore know his shape when I spot it."

In the town there was no indication that the killing of Sloan had become the latest news. But talking and walking miners, and other inhabitants of Thunder City, were not slow to take cognizance of Bruce Masters and Kalispel stalking up the street.

"Hey!" called one excited observer. "Looks like Sheriff Masters has arrested thet gunman."

"Not to me, it doesn't," replied another.

They entered the Dead Eye Saloon. It was blue with smoke and noisy with voices.

"Say, crowd," shouted Kalispel, piercingly, and when the hum ceased and all faces turned, he continued: "I'm lookin' hard for a man with a stubby red beard an' a patch over his right ear where he got slugged recently. He answers to the name Mac."

Every man present, even the card-players, looked at his neighbors. Then a bartender set down a glass with a nervous clang.

"Boss, nobody in hyar who answers to thet," he called.

Kalispel led the way out, and he heard the buzz that arose behind him.

"Reminds me of bein' in Texas," drawled Masters, with a chuckle.

"What does?"

"Why you, boy."

Kalispel merely glanced into the stores. But he went into the Gold Dust Saloon, the Elk, the Bonanza, the Thunder Boom, all the resorts on the right side of the street, in each of which he interrupted gayety to spread silence and consternation. But he did not find his man. By this time a crowd followed at a respectful distance and the whole tenor of the main street had changed as if by magic.

"Wal, Kalispel," said the Texan, as they crossed the street at the extreme east end of town, "nobody figgerin' now thet you air under arrest."

"Reckon we have them guessin'."

"None of these men will meet you for an even break."

"Don't expect it, Masters."

"Looks like you'd have to hole them up. An' when you're outside of a barricaded cabin, up ag'in' shotguns an' rifles, it gets testier'n hell. As a Ranger I had a lot of thet."

They faced downstreet on the right side, passing the blacksmith shop, some closed tents, and a merchandise store. As far down as Kalispel could see men were gazing in his direction, and not a few of their number were taking to the middle of the street. In the Red Likker Saloon Kalispel's ringing challenge elicited a reply from some one in the crowd.

"What you want Mac fer?"

"He an' his pards jumped Dick Sloan's claim."

"Wal, thet ain't sayin' what you want," replied the gruff voice.

"Sloan's dyin'!"

Kalispel advanced upon the group before the bar and ordered them to spread out. His swift scrutiny failed to locate a man with a stubby red beard. He backed out of the saloon, keenly aware of hostile looks. On down the street he went, searching in the places where miners congregated. Opposite the Dead Eye Saloon Kalispel espied a tall bearded man who strode across in a manner to excite a second glance. Kalispel knew him as a friend, a neighbor of Blair's.

"Shore you're lookin' at this fellar?" inquired Masters.

The miner came on without slacking his pace or betraying any sign that he recognized Kalispel. But as he passed he shot out low-voiced: "Your man's been tipped off. . . . Dead Eye Saloon!"

Kalispel halted.

"Heah thet?" queried Masters, sharply. "I reckon I'll stand aside now, Emerson."

It was a hundred long steps or more diagonally across the street to the Dead Eye Saloon. When the Texan moved on a little way and then faced about, it appeared to be a signal for every man in sight of Kalispel to halt. Various comments carried to Kalispel's sensitive ears.

"There! Masters has shied away," said one, in hoarse excitement.

"He ain't drunk *this* time, shore."

"Who's he after?"

"He's watching the Dead Eye."

"Gentlemen, the ball is about to open."

"We'll be duckin' lead pronto."

For these observers the stage had been set for the familiar street-scene drama of the frontier. But in Thunder City there had been few indeed of these duels.

Kalispel cupped his hands around his mouth and yelled, "Somebody tell Sneed to drive Mac an' his pards out—or I'll burn 'em out."

A man shouted into the door of the Dead Eye. If Sneed did not comply, Kalispel would take his failure as inimical to himself. He counted, however, on the fact that the creed of the West was for men to meet in the open and decide their disputes without risk to spectators.

Bill Sneed appeared, opening wide the swinging doors of his saloon.

"Git out!" he bellowed. "I ain't harborin' ye, by Gawd!"

Two white-faced men sneaked out, followed by a third, whose sombrero, pulled low, failed to hide the betraying red beard. The first slipped like an eel into the backing throng. The others dashed into the street, sheering widely to the left.

"Stop!" yelled Kalispel, and he shot at the foremost runner. The bullet kicked up the dust beyond and whined away. But it had hit the runner, for there was a violent break in his swift action. Kalispel's second shot, aimed low, brought the last man down in the middle of the street. He screamed with pain and terror. Like a crippled fowl he flopped, attempted to get to his feet again, but fell, screaming all the time. Then as Kalispel leaped forward into the street the man raised himself from the hips and pulled his gun, to fire rapidly. The bullets splintered glass and thudded on wood, and caused a rush of onlookers to get out of range. Kalispel plunged to a halt and shot to kill. His adversary spun around and went down, while his gun slid in the dust. Again Kalispel leaped forward to his prostrate foe, glad to find him alive. The second bullet had taken him high up in the breast, from which the blood was pouring.

"Howdy, Mac," called Kalispel, grimly, as he stood over him with smoking gun. The black sombrero lay in the dust and Kalispel had needed no more to recognize his man.

"Masters, come here an' bring somebody," yelled Kalispel to the sheriff. Then he bent his gaze upon the claim-jumper. "Sloan marked you, Mac."

"Is he—daid?" queried Mac, hoarsely. His eyes rolled furtively.

"I reckon, by this time."

"Don't kill me—Emerson. . . . I'll talk."

Masters came hurriedly up, accompanied by two miners. "Winged, eh?— Make him squeal, Kal," he said, stridently.

"Mac, I reckon you won't cash if you don't get bored again," added Kalispel, deliberately aligning his gun at the fallen man's heart. "Talk—or I'll bore you again!"

"Fer Gawd's sake, Emerson! . . . I didn't knife Sloan— or slug him, either. . . . I was for robbin' an' kidnappin' him —so Borden could get—Nugget!"

Chapter Thirteen

Like wildfire the news spread up and down the main street of Thunder City that Macabe, one of Leavitt's guards, had confessed having been forced by Borden to put young Sloan out of the way. Rumor ran as fast as men could walk and their tongues could wag. The motive for the crime—to waylay and kill an honest young miner for the purpose of dragging his sweetheart to the dance-hall den, and to a life of drink and violence—that inflamed the populace to an increasingly dangerous degree.

Kalispel patrolled the center of the wide street, the cynosure of all eyes. The tide had turned his way. The creed of the frontier would force Borden to meet him.

Sunset was still several hours away. Kalispel's beat covered the lower end of town, just out of rifle-range from Borden's place. Borden had been located at once and informed of Macabe's confession, and that there was a man waiting for him out in the street.

Toward midafternoon business, except that of drinking, ceased for the day. Everybody wanted to see the encounter between Kalispel and Borden. If there were exceptions, they were Leavitt and his men up at the mine. They had been told. And later the news flashed around, from the very messengers who carried it, that Leavitt had refused to protect Borden from Emerson. "Tell the girl-snatcher to go out and take his medicine!" was Leavitt's coarse reply to that appeal. Gossip quickly added the fact of Leavitt's half interest in Borden's property, and that the mine-owner would not be unhappy to take over Borden's half. The lower end of the street was deserted except for Kalispel's solitary form, pacing to and fro, or standing motionless and menacing. The throng, drinking more and more, gradually succumbed to the mob feeling, so easily aroused in crude men at such an hour. Kalispel's status rose to that of a chivalrous and admirable man, while Borden was labeled a trafficker in women.

Dick Sloan's neighbor, the young miner, detached himself from the crowd and hurriedly strode out to Kalispel.

"Better give me elbow room," warned Kalispel, somberly.

But the young fellow came on unheeding.

"Emerson, it's over," he said, hoarsely, his face pale and set. "Sloan died without comin' to."

"No surprise to me. I gave him up. . . . An' how'd Ruth take it?"

"Game as they come. She's with me. We was huntin' you."

"Hang on to her an' get her home."

"I'll hang, all right, but I'll never get her off the street," declared the young man. "She's goin' to see it!"

"Let the crowd know that Sloan's dead."

"I've already sprung it. . . . They're with you, Kal."

It did not take a long while for the tragic death of Nugget's champion and would-be husband to become known to all. It flowed from lip to lip. And it was the last spark that precipitated an unprecedented explosion. Mutterings and curses augmented direct calls to Kalispel.

"We're with you, old Montana!" yelled a miner.

"Bore him low down, Kal!"

"Go in after the yellow dog!"

"If you want us to rout him out—say the word!"

Such outspoken ejaculations served to unleash the passion of the mob. Men would shout to Kalispel and then go into a saloon for another drink. That Borden did not appear wore on the unruly miners. The raw good humor of the many subtly changed. They merged closer and closer to Kalispel, forming a dense circle behind him across the street. And gradually they edged him foot by foot toward Borden's hall. This largest building in the town was the last upon the street, and presented for once a lonely aspect. Doors and windows appeared like dark, vacant eyes. It stood isolated, apparently deserted.

The impatient mob, thirsty for blood, switched its vociferous acclaim of Kalispel to a sinister call for Borden.

"Come out, Borden!"

"Hyar, you skunk! Mac has squealed an' Sloan is dead! Come on!"

"Borden, we all want to see you!"

"Borden, it's your only chance!"

"You're done in Thunder City!"

"Walk out like a man, you —— —— —— ——!"

"An' let us see daylight through yore gizzard! Haw! Haw!"

"Come out, Borden, or get run out!"

A leather-lunged miner bawled: "Smoke him out!"

A roar attested to the mood of the watchers.

"Burn him out!"

And when they stopped to catch their breath the stentorian-voiced miner rent the pregnant air.

"Borden come out an' fight—or we'll lynch you!"

The cry, "Lynch him!" was caught up and carried along like a wave, until Masters ran out to confront the crowd. He held his hands high to quiet them.

"Steady, men," he yelled, authoritatively. "Give Emerson time!— We don't want a lynchin'. An' fire might destroy the town. . . . I'll guarantee to fetch Borden out!"

Above the murmuring roar cut out a sharp high voice:

"All right, Sheriff. But no arrest goes hyar. We want to see Borden shot or swing!"

Masters sped swiftly to confront Kalispel.

"Thet gang's in an ugly mood," he said, with a gleam in his gray eyes. "They might set fire to Borden's place. An' thet'd be hell. These shacks would burn like tinder. . . . Emerson, you better let me go in after Borden."

"He's hid in there," warned Kalispel. "He might shoot you."

"I'll take thet risk. An' if I get to him, I'll make him see thet shore as Gawd made little apples this mob will burn him out an' hang him. An' I'll agree to protect him from them if he kills you. Thet'll fetch him. It's his only chance."

"Suppose he bobs up with a rifle?" queried Kalispel, darkly.

"Wal, if he's thet much of a cheat I'll bore him myself," replied the Texan.

"Masters, I don't like the deal. It's plumb good of you. But it'll queer you with Leavitt. An' Leavitt is strong—we don't savvy how strong."

"To hell with Leavitt. One at a time! . . . Do I go?"

"Shore. An' thanks, old-timer."

Masters swung away, pulling out a white handkerchief which he began to wave. The crowd yelled both encouragingly and derisively. They did not wholly trust this action of the sheriff's.

It was more than two hundred yards from where Kalispel stood to the dance-hall. Masters slowed his pace. When he got halfway there he shouted, and went on. He had nerve, but undoubtedly he calculated that Borden would see him and grasp at anything to avert a meeting with Kalispel. Masters then increased his gait, as if the suspense was less insupportable than the risk. He still waved the white handkerchief. And when he got within a hundred feet of the hall,

149

Borden suddenly appeared in the doorway with a leveled rifle.

"Halt!" he yelled.

Masters lowered his flag of truce with suggestive violence. His clear voice rang even to Kalispel.

"Air you drunk or crazy? Drop yore rifle. The mob back there will burn you alive or hang you, shore."

"What you want?" yelled Borden, stridently, and lowered the weapon. Masters went forward then, talking fast, but Kalispel could not distinguish what he said. Masters approached to within thirty steps of Borden, who still held his rifle threateningly. The Texan might wisely halt there and deliver his proposition and leave, thought Kalispel. Masters' posture did not lose dignity, but his few gestures were singularly expressive of the finality of a cold ultimatum. He whirled on his heel, and swerving out of line to the left, he strode rapidly up the street toward the crowd.

Kalispel watched that rifle, and if it had started for a level he meant to leap aside for cover. He would not take any chances with a hound like Borden. The crowd seemed locked in suspense, waiting, with eyes on the two principals. Into this oppressive lull the leather-lunged miner projected his raw yell:

"Take your choice, Borden! . . ."

And the shout that burst from the crowd proclaimed that every watcher divined what the choice was—to drop the long-range rifle and come out like a man, or use it and swing by the neck. Certainly Borden understood, for the echo of that taunting decree had not ceased, when he lifted the rifle high to fling it down. The metallic crash of its contact with the flagstones came plainly to the listening ears.

Even at that distance Borden's swarthy visage gleamed.

"Wal, Emerson, he's comin' an' we're gamblin' you'll bore him low down in the middle," yelled the wag from the crowd.

Borden whipped out two guns, and lowering his head, like a bull about to charge, he leaped out of the doorway.

"Spread out everybody!" boomed the miner with the clarion voice. "The ball's opened!"

Kalispel started to stride forward, drawing his gun. Borden gained the center of the street and, like a man propelled by irresistible force from behind, came lurching on. He threw forward the gun in his left hand and fired. The ball whizzed by Kalispel, glanced on the gravel behind, and brought a shrill yell from some person in the crowd. Shouts and trample of feet attested to the splitting of the mob to both sides of the street.

Kalispel kept on swiftly. Borden halted. His gun flamed red and cracked. Another bullet hissed uncomfortably close to Kalispel's body. Far beyond it struck up dust and ricocheted along the street. Again Borden strode on and again his big gun boomed. Then bang! bang! bang! he emptied the gun in his left hand, as if driven to be free of it. He flung it aside and raised the one in his right.

Kalispel stopped to turn his side toward his adversary, upon whom he brought his gun to bear. The distance was far over a hundred yards. Kalispel froze in his aim and pulled trigger.

Everybody heard the sudden impact of that bullet. It had the soft, thudding sound of lead entering flesh. Borden's hurried stride appeared blocked as if by a battering-ram. He uttered a choking cry, but he strung like a whipcord and began to shoot. Deliberate and cold, Kalispel took time, well knowing that this was no game for snap-shooting, and aimed as at a target, while Borden's first and second bullets passed whistling by Kalispel, one on each side. Kalispel shot. And Borden was knocked flat, as if by a hard fist. In frenzied action he sprang up like a bent willow released, and shot wildly. But something about Kalispel's posture, his statue-like immobility, his dark, terrible calm, pierced Borden's chaotic brain. He essayed to take his cue from his adversary. Dropping on one knee he rested his elbow on the other, and steadying his gun, took slow and careful aim.

A suspended breath seemed to wait in the onlookers. A woman screamed as if she could not stand the deliberation for which Kalispel was famed.

The silence burst to the ringing crack of his gun. Borden's rigidity underwent a break. His gun fell to explode. And simultaneously he appeared to be batted to one side, as by an invisible force. On hands and knees, his back to the crowd, he wrestled himself almost erect, then suddenly plunged down on his face to kick the dust and lie still.

Standing alone in the street, with the breathless crowd beginning to stir, Kalispel stood over his prostrate enemy to watch him die. It was one of the prerogatives of gunmen, to be in at the death, and owed its origin to the incentive to make sure that the enemy did die. In Kalispel's case it was an ordeal, where ruthlessness gave way to a sickening remorse.

Borden lay beyond his last convulsion, conscious.

"Nugget?" he tried to articulate. She was his last thought, one seemingly divorced from the hard motive that had brought him to this pass. It might have been a revelation of love.

"I'll look after her," replied Kalispel. And Borden died with something like relief on his ghastly face.

Kalispel hurried down the street to avoid the surging crowd. He made his way out of town and down the stream to the bend, and up to the sage slope where he had often gone. It seemed almost a physical action to dismiss Borden from his consciousness. Then he was solely concerned with the revolt in heart and brain, the battle of returning normalcy with the primeval instinct of self-preservation, which was to kill or be killed. He had to make slow shift of that here, because there was Ruth to think of. And his first thought of her was that the name Nugget died with Borden.

The hour was past sunset, crimson and gold, tranquil and sad. The relentlessness of man, with his love, his hate, his avarice, did not intrude here. The stream murmured on, unmindful of the little lives of men, and the great walls frowned broodingly down. The shadows came and deepened to purple. High up on the rugged slope a wolf wailed his wild note of loneliness. Nature had been a panacea for Kalispel's ills, from the old recovery after a cowboy debauch to the heartbreak he had sustained recently, and now to the repetition of the cruel retrogression of blood-lust.

Dusk fell. He could tarry no longer. A chill air floated down the canyon. Nighthawks and bats were fluttering. He left the fragrant sage bench and retracing his steps, crossed the bridge to Sloan's tent. Several miners, and Barnes, the kindly partner of Sloan, met Kalispel and informed him that they had just buried Sloan on his own claim, in the deep hole where he had dug for gold and had found a grave.

"Barnes, I'll be takin' the girl up to my cabin," said Kalispel. "Sloan's claims an' tools are yours. . . . An' I won't forget your friendship for him—an' your goodness to her."

"Aw—thet's nothin'," replied Barnes, haltingly. He, like the others was, for the moment, inhibited by Kalispel's presence.

Kalispel went into the tent. The interior was almost too dark to discern objects.

"Ruth," he called, "where are you?"

"Kal!" she cried, gladly, and her light feet pattered on

the floor. He made out her pale form against the gloom. Then she was clinging to him, with her head pressed against his breast.

"Wal? . . . Don't shake so, child," he said, gently, as he held her. "Brace up. You've seen a lot of hard doin's, though not so close to home. . . . Barnes told me they'd buried Dick right here. I reckon that was the thing—to get it over."

"Yes. I told them to," she replied.

"Can't you stand on your feet?" he asked, finding that he had to hold her.

"My legs are—shaky."

"But, Ruth—you're the gamest kid. This is gold-diggin's life, you know. Shore it is awful tough, your losin' Dick— but it's done—it's over, an' you got to brace."

"Kal, I'm terribly sorry about Dick," she whispered, and then suddenly she clutched him, "but—but it was your fight with Borden—that knocked me out."

"Aw!— Didn't Barnes drag you off the street?"

"I stayed. I seemed possessed of a thousand devils while you waited for Borden. . . . Oh, how I wanted you to kill him! And I knew you would. I gloated over the thought. The crowd was for you and that thrilled me. . . . But when Borden plunged out, like a mad bull—then I went to pieces. I suddenly realized—he might kill you, too. And I nearly died of terror. . . . I saw it all. . . . Then I collapsed."

"Ah-huh. . . . Wal!" ejaculated Kalispel, strangely affected by her poignant words and clinging hands. She was only a child, this dance-hall girl, and he was her only friend. "Ruth," he got out, at length, "I'm takin' you up to my cabin."

"Kal!— I'm glad, but I can't walk."

"I'll carry you." He lifted her and swung her around comfortably against his shoulder, and edged sideways through the door.

"Barnes," he said to the waiting miner, "would you be good enough to have your wife pack up all Ruth's clothes an' things, an' bring them up to my cabin?"

"Shore'll be glad to," was the reply.

Kalispel took the trail up the stream. For the most part it was dark, though he could readily see the pale path winding between the shacks and the creek. Here and there lamps cast a yellow glow through doors or canvas, and camp fires flickered, silhouetting burly, red-shirted miners at their evening meal.

"Kal, I'll walk now," said Ruth, after they had gone a long way.

"You might stumble in the dark."

"How strong you are!— But I am heavy, and you must be tired."

"Wal, you were like thistle down at first. An' I'm bound to admit you're not quite as light as that now. But I can pack you."

When Kalispel passed the Blair cabin, almost under its high porch, he saw a light and heard Sydney's contralto voice. How strange to pass by Sydney this way in the darkness with a girl in his arms—a girl whose life and happiness henceforth must be his care! He tightened his hold on the slender form in his arms. And he was unable for the moment to straighten out his labyrinthine thoughts or comprehend his conflicting emotions.

They passed the last shack. Far across the bench flickered a camp fire that was Jake's. Kalispel had been increasingly aware that Ruth's head had slipped from his shoulder closer and closer until her cheek rested against his neck. It felt warm and moist. She was crying.

Jake was stirring around a camp fire outside the cabin. He heard Kalispel's footsteps and straightened up to peer out into the darkness.

"It's, me, Jake."

"Aw!— Shore glad, son. I saw your meetin' with Borden. All same Kalispel Montana!— Suited me fine. . . . Hey! what you packin'?"

"What you think? A sack of flour?"

"My Gawd—a girl!— If you don't beat the Dutch!"

"Shut up, an' light the lamp in the cabin."

Jake knocked things over in his hurry to execute that order. He stared with rolling ox eyes at the white-faced, golden-haired girl Kalispel laid on the couch. Ruth sat up.

"I'm not an invalid," she said, with a wan smile. "Howdy, Jake. Your brother has packed me up here."

"I see," replied Jake, with a broad grin. Ruth's looks quickly found the hearts of men. "I reckon you're the gurl ——"

"Ruth," interrupted Kalispel, shortly. "Jake, put a canvas up outside the cabin. An' take your bed out. You an' me will bunk together."

"So our family's increased permanent?" rejoined Jake, beamingly.

154

"Our family's shore increased permanent," drawled Kalispel. "Rustle now, an' get some supper first."

When Jake went out, whistling, Kalispel turned to the girl, sensing full well that he was in for what he knew not. He caught the recession of a vivid blush which left her face white, and accentuated the cornflower blue of her eyes. He had never met such an earnest, lovely light in a human's gaze.

"Kal, let's have it out now," she said.

"Out! Have what out?" he queried, blankly.

"This deal."

"Gosh, child——"

"Don't call me child. I am a woman, Kal."

"How old?" asked Kalispel, sparring for time.

"Eighteen in years—but years are nothing."

"So old? You're short huntin' Methuselem. . . . An' what deal is this you're rarin' about? Fetchin' you to my cabin? What else could I do? Just because Borden has gone to join the angels is no reason to believe you'd be safe alone."

"No. I heard what you promised Dick."

"Wal?"

"You said, 'I'll take care of her, Dick'! . . . What did you mean by that?"

"I meant what I said," declared Kalispel, bluntly, as if his word had been questioned.

"You'll be my friend—my brother—as Dick was?"

"No. I reckon I didn't mean that."

"What then?"

"Didn't Dick intend to marry you?"

"Yes."

"Wal, that's what I meant."

"You'd *marry* me—Kal?" she cried.

"Why, shore! What kind of a hombre do you take me for?"

"You are the most wonderful . . . But, Kal, you're in love with Sydney Blair!"

"I reckon I was, tolerable. But when she dared me to come over an' see her in Leavitt's arms—an' I took that dare— Wal, it all died, pronto."

"Oh, Kal, *she* wouldn't—she couldn't do such a thing."

"The hell she wouldn't," flashed Kalispel, stung by the memory. "She did do it. I saw Leavitt kiss her."

"Oh, she must have been driven."

"Wal, I don't care a whoop whether she was or not," de-

155

clared Kalispel, bitterly. "It hurt. An' it showed me a lot. You'll oblige me, Ruth, by not alludin' to that again."

"Forgive me. I never will. . . . But, Kal, do you think Dick meant for you to marry me?"

"Shore he did. How else could a man take care of you?"

"Very well, then," she replied, with a dangerous softness. "I won't marry you."

"Why not?"

"I won't, that's all," she rejoined, and averted her agitated face.

"Ah-huh. Wal, shore I'm no match for Sydney Blair or for *you,* either.—No honest, fine, young fellow like Dick!"

"Kal Emerson!" she flashed, and turned with an angry blaze of eyes.

"Shore. Kal Emerson! Bad hombre! Tough cowboy! Rustler! Gun-slinger! All-around desperado who no woman atall would be wife to!" ejaculated Kalispel, in sincere scorn of himself. This emotion, no doubt, was a partial regurgitation to the sickening aftermath of a fatal gun-fight.

"Don't lie that way about yourself," she retorted. "You're Western and you're great, Kal Emerson. I won't have you demean yourself to me."

"Never mind my promise to Dick. I'd have asked you to marry me, anyhow."

"Oh, Kal!— Don't!— God knows it's hard to refuse——"

"Wal, why won't you?"

"Because I love you," she cried, passionately.

"Ruth!— You mean same as you did Dick?"

"No. I didn't love him."

"But, child, how come you to love me? . . . Aw, it's just gratitude, Ruth. An' you're awful upset."

"Don't ask *any* woman, good or bad, how she came to love. It can't be explained. It happens."

"Wal, then, if—if you do—why that's all the more reason for you to be my wife."

"It is not."

"Ruth, we're off the trail," he said, soberly. "When I thought of marryin' you it wasn't just to get a wife—a woman. I had only a wonderful feelin' for you—the kid who's had such a rotten deal from life. An' I meant to take care of you always as I would of my own sister. But when you say you love me, why that makes me think and remember. I always wanted a real home, a wife to keep me straight, an' kids——"

"Hush!" she sobbed, and put her hand to his lips. "I love

you, Kal. . . . I love you as I never loved anyone, even my mother. I will live with you, be faithful till my dying breath, work my fingers to the bone for you, but I will not marry you!"

He took her hand in his and kissed it. For a while, neither spoke.

"I'm distressin' you, Ruth," he said, finally. "But, one more word. If you won't marry me you can't be my real wife. Savvy, dear?"

"Yes, I savvy," she whispered, sagging against him.

"An' I'll keep my promise to Dick just the same," he went on, eagerly. "An' I reckon you'll be my salvation, just the same. . . . Forget it now, Ruth. . . . There's so much to think of. To plan for! An' I've much to do before we leave here."

"*Leavitt!*" she cried lifting eyes he could not gaze into.

"Yes. I meant to kill him. I ought to."

"Kal, it's not for me to—to stop you. Not to serve *him*, of all men! . . . Only—today! . . . Can I stand that again?"

"Wal, don't worry, maybe Masters will take care of him."

Jake opened the door a half-inch. "Hey, Romeo an' Juliet! Will you have supper served in the drawin'-room or out on the balcony?"

Chapter Fourteen

During the night the long-deferred equinoctial storm broke.

Jake got up to reinforce his end of the improvised shelter. "Hey, Kal, is it wet over where you are?" he called.

"Ump-umm," replied Kalispel, sleepily.

"Wal, it's wetter'n hell over hyar," growled Jake. "Thet storm finally busted an' I'll bet it'll be a humdinger. Might as wal wake up an' get ready to be washed away."

"What time is it?"

"Wal, it was somewhere's near mornin', but I don't know what it is now . . . Whew! Blazes an' brimstone! Kal, I wish we was safe out of this hole."

"So do I," replied Kalispel, sitting up. A blue-white blaze filled the valley with weird light and a ripping thunderbolt rent the heavens. And before the booming echoes ceased reverberating, another flash of lightning streaked the inky blackness and a mighty sound as of mountains rolling down

157

deafened Kalispel. Soon the intervals between the illuminating flashes appeared to be mere glimmerings and the thunder mingled continuously. Rain fell in torrents.

Kalispel and Jake huddled close to the cabin wall, and by covering themselves and blankets with a tarpaulin managed to keep dry. Toward dawn the violence of the storm subsided and the rain slackened. Morning broke dreary and gray.

The stream was roaring. Kalispel went over to look at it. Miners all along, as far down as he could see, were trying to rescue rocks, flumes, boxes, tools from the yellow flood. It was bank-full and rising rapidly. Many of the claims would be flooded. Even those above high water could not be worked, for all the holes were filled.

Thunder City would continue to roar, but not with labor. The saloons and halls and dens would reap a harvest.

As always, Kalispel swept an appreciative gaze across to the bare slope. This morning it presented a furrowed front. Thin yellow streams were running down its face, flattening out on the level to triangular areas of mud and silt. It presented an ugly sight. Far up, the peak was obscured in gray cloud. Kalispel calculated that it would be snowing up there; and he conceived the idea that it would be well to get ready to leave the valley as soon as the storm was over. He returned to the cabin. Jake was fanning a refractory camp fire which he had started under the shelter.

"I reckon it'd be a good idea to wrangle our burros an' horses," Kalispel remarked, thoughtfully, to Jake.

"Shore would, an' grain 'em good before thet drill out."

"All right, let's rustle breakfast," replied Kalispel, brightening with the definite decision. Something dragged darkly at him, holding him back, a cold grim passion hard to relinquish. "Then you go downtown an' buy a sack of grain, a pair of alfagos—I want two new strong ones—an' let's see. I'll figure on it. . . . I'll rustle the stock."

"Kal, hadn't you better stay in camp an' let me do the rustlin'?" queried Jake, gruffly. "You got the girl hyar, an' our cabin is shore strong built. With them two rifles you could keep off——"

"Hell!" ejaculated Kalispel. "I reckon I had. But after yesterday, wouldn't you figure Leavitt to lay low an' let me shake the dust of Thunder City?"

"You mean mud, son," replied Jake. "My idea, Kal, is that when you think, you shore get those deals right. But you had hell yesterday an' you ain't thinkin'. I've a hunch Leavitt had somethin' up his sleeve organizin' them vigilantes."

"Ah-huh. Wal, I'll think," snapped Kalispel, between his teeth. "An' I'm thinkin' I'd better see Masters pronto."

"I'll send him up hyar," replied Jake, hurriedly, with a speculative glance at his brother. "After we eat I'll rustle. An' you get to packin'. This storm will let up today, an' in a couple of days we can be on the move."

Later Kalispel knocked on the cabin door.

"Come in," replied Ruth.

Kalispel entered to find her in bed, with the red blanket tucked up under her chin.

"Wal, ain't you ashamed, you sleepy-head?" was his greeting as he stepped close to look down upon her with a queer sensation of possessiveness.

"Is it late?" she asked, smiling up at him.

"No. I was just foolin'. Can I fetch in a pan of hot water? An' after that some rice, bacon, coffee, an' a biscuit? You don't need to get up. It's a rotten day. Did you hear the storm?"

"Storm? No, I didn't."

"Dead to the world! Gosh! if you didn't hear the thunder, you should have heard Jake cussin'. He woke up in a puddle. . . . All right, I'll fetch things in. Reckon I might as well get used to bein' your maid."

"It'll be the other way around."

"Say, what's all this?"

"My bags. Barnes brought them last night."

"Lady, you'll require a whole pack-train. Gosh! Ruth, we only got six burros."

"We'll burn my dance-hall clothes."

"All except that skimpy blue thing you had on the first time I saw you in Salmon. You shore caught my eye, kid!"

"We'll burn that, too, darling."

Kalispel beat a hasty retreat, presently to carry in a pan of water and her breakfast on top of a box. She sat up like a delighted child.

"Kalispel Montana, my maid and cook!" she exclaimed. "Who would believe it? . . . Put the box here and give me the pan on my lap. And hand me that small bag. . . . Oh, don't go, Kal—unless you're busy."

"I'm shore busy," replied Kalispel, lamely, and he went out. He had been struck with something new and sweet in the intimacy of that moment, in the girl's beauty, in the blue eyes that appeared glad for his presence. He sensed a problem to be contended with in the future. But he dismissed disturbing reflections and set to work at the many tasks.

Jake returned to report that Masters had been flooded out, like many others who had tents and shacks close to the treacherous slope of silt. Masters would call on him later in the day. But the busy hours passed by without the sheriff putting in an appearance. Jake finally rounded up all the stock, and with them in the corral, Kalispel began to have visions of the long winding trail down to the Salmon. Suddenly, then, he remembered the ranch he had coveted so dearly; and with a sense of exultation, he realized that he had the gold to buy and improve and stock a dozen such ranches. Ruth must be his wife. He resolved not to distress her now, but when they got to Challis he would insist on marriage in name at least. It was the only way he could really protect her and silence gossip for good and all.

It had rained on and off until midafternoon, when the clouds broke, showing a bit of blue sky and a gleam of sun. Ruth emerged to stretch her legs, she said, and she wandered around among the huge boulders, going as far as the stream, which was now a torrent. She came back to tell how the miners were moving back off their claims. All at once the sun shone out strong, and as if in happy augury of the future, it appeared to strike a bright glory from Ruth's golden head.

"Oh, there is Miss Blair—watching us!" cried Ruth suddenly, and then, with scarlet face she went indoors.

Kalispel did not look in the direction of the Blair cabin. His great pity went out to Ruth; but still, if Sydney was hurt, as it seemed she was, he felt an unavailing sorrow.

Kalispel had hidden his bags of gold dust and nuggets under the flat hearthstone in front of the open fireplace. Beneath this was a hollow boulder, the opening of which he had discovered by accident and which would not be easily detected. For the present he did not want either Jake or Ruth to learn about his treasure.

That night while Ruth slept and Jake worked outside, Kalispel packed the gold in two alfagos and hid them under the pile of firewood in the corner of the cabin.

When at length he went out to go to bed, Jake remarked with great satisfaction, "It's clearin' off cold." The stars were shining white, and a nipping wind blew down from the heights. Before Kalispel went to sleep, he had decided that it would be sensible to try to avoid trouble with Leavitt. If anything happened to him, Ruth might be left alone. When he analyzed this deduction he found that life had become singularly and incomprehensibly sweet. This for a cowboy whose heart had been broken was thought-provoking.

The day dawned frosty and bright. Miners were astir early, and two pack-trains left while Jake was getting breakfast.

"They're beginnin' to drift out," said Jake. "An' I'll have all our pack-saddles an' harness mended today."

"Brother, I reckon you're not in any hurry atall to shake the gold dust of Thunder City," drawled Kalispel.

"Kal, one of my hunches is workin'," nodded Jake, somberly.

"Which one?"

"Wal, two hunches, in fact."

"You an' your hunches!"

"Hell, man! Tell me one thet never worked out."

"Forced to think of them, Jake, I'll be darned if I can remember one that didn't. . . . Oh yes, you were wrong about old Thunder Mountain."

"How so?"

"Why, you always croaked about old Thunder Mountain slidin' down on us."

"Wal, she ain't yet, thet's true," admitted Jake, morosely.

Ruth came out to interrupt the gloomy conversation. She wore a gray woolen dress, and with some color in her cheeks this morning, she made a picture from which Kalispel found it difficult to keep his eyes. She extended her small hands to the fire. "Gee! it's cold," she said, merrily. "I don't see that you gentlemen have proceeded far with breakfast."

"My land! gurl, we jest got up," retorted Jake, who had taken a decided liking to Ruth and delighted to serve her. "An' you're springin' somethin' on us this mornin'."

"Ruth, do you like cold weather?" asked Kalispel, thoughtfully.

"Love it. I came from Wisconsin, you know."

"Ump-umm, I didn't know. An' can you ride a horse?" he went on, eyeing her slim lithe figure.

"Can I ride a horse! Listen to him, Jake. . . . Can a duck swim?"

"Say, kid, where'd you ever ride?" queried Kalispel, hopefully.

"Kal, you'll be tickled when I tell you that I was a regular cowgirl once."

"No!"

"Honest Injun."

"Wal, I'll be dog-goned!" ejaculated Kalispel, radiantly. "Where an' when?"

"My dad moved to Wyoming when I was twelve," Ruth answered, subtly changing. "He bought out a rancher near Chadron——"

"Chadron! . . . Why, Ruth, that's near Cheyenne. I rode there, myself."

"Must have been before my time," she went on, while Jack drank in her words. "You see, I left there only three years ago. Dad did well for a while—until the rustlers cleaned him out. He never got over that. It killed him. . . . I was left to the tender mercy of a stepmother . . . and well— I was sixteen when I came to Cliff Borden's dance-hall. . . ."

Kalispel's sudden transition from keen delight to bitterness left him speechless.

"Don't look so—so terrible, Kal," she said. "I had to work or starve—and Borden lied to me about the job. But it's all over now. Oh, Kal! . . . I know I've been such a trouble for you all along. Worrying and fighting over me!— But just realize, if you can, how blessed good you've been for *me*. . . . And, Kal, when we're away from this madhole we'll forget. Then I'll make it up to you."

"Let's get away pronto," replied Kalispel, with one of his flashes of passion. "This afternoon or tomorrow, shore. Jake, rustle breakfast. Then pack. Put Ruth's bags in the canvas packs. An' you, young lady, get into your blue jeans. Keep out a warm coat, gloves, boots. It'll be a tough ride for a couple of days. Soon as I eat a bite I'll rustle down to see Masters. He's been pretty decent, or I wouldn't go at all. I want to tip him off. An' I reckon—that'll let me out here."

"You reckon? Aren't you sure, Kal?" queried Ruth, a doubt edging into her face.

"Gosh! you can't be shore of anythin' except death."

"Promise me you won't look up Leavitt," she entreated.

"Wal, that's easy. I promise. . . . But if I meet him . . ."

"Bore him an' rustle back here to tell me," interrupted Jake, coolly. "An' then I'll show you some real packin'."

Soon Kalispel sallied forth on his last visit to Thunder City. At Blair's cabin two packers were busy assorting and weighing packs. Burros, not yet saddled, stood haltered to the porch. Blair waved cheerfully to Kalispel: "We're leaving today." And Kalispel replied just as cheerfully: "So are we. Hope we see you on the trail." Sydney appeared in the rider's garb in which Kalispel had admired her so exceedingly. He suffered a divided pang—one of regret and the other of relief. Those proud dark eyes were not destined to shine

162

upon him. They watched him pass by, intent and haunting as ever. But she made no motion.

The sun had just come up bright over the eastern mountain-top, to shine down upon the flooded valley. Thin skins of ice glistened on the ponds; white frost burned like diamonds on the roofs of the shacks; blue columns of smoke curled upward; and the swollen stream brawled on its swift, noisy way toward the canyon.

On the hillsides and high parts of the benches the miners had returned to their blasting, digging, panning. But two miles of flooded claims along the stream had left hundreds of men idle. Therefore the main street of Thunder City presented the spectacle of a circus day in a small town.

Kalispel hoped to escape notice in the crowd, and succeeded to some extent. He found Masters in his half-demolished shack, a pondering and somber man.

"Howdy, Kal," he drawled, with those penetrating gray eyes hard on his visitor. "You look fine for a hombre who's just added another notch to his gun."

"Aw, I'm fine as silk. Leavin' today, Masters."

"Good. Did your brother give you my message?"

"All he said was that you'd be up to see me."

"Nix. I told him no—an' for you to rustle out of heah quick."

"Wal, he didn't tell me, the son-of-a-gun. What's up, old-timer?"

"Reckon I cain't find out all thet's doin' in this heah gold-camp, but the little I know is shore enough."

"Uh-huh— Wal, if it's enough for an old Texas steer like you, it'll be more'n enough for Kal Emerson. But come on with it."

"Leavitt took over Borden's property, on half shares an' debts, he claims. My show of friendship for you 'pears to have riled the judge. He politely sent me word to turn over my office an' my badge."

"The hell he did! Wal, of all the gall!— Masters, you wouldn't think of that?"

"Wal, ordinarily I wouldn't. But I didn't seek this job. My friends shoved it on me. An' now most of them have packed an' gone. The bottom is droppin' out of this boom, Kal. I reckon I couldn't locate a dozen men who'd back me in any deal against Leavitt. So what is there in it for me?"

"Damn little, if you're askin'," replied Kalispel, shortly. "But are you goin' to let Leavitt bluff you?"

"No man ever bluffed a Texan Ranger," drawled Masters.

"I'm just sore enough to resign, pack, an' get ready to leave with my friends—then call on Leavitt to leave my caird."

"Your card?— Ah-huh, I savvy," rejoined Kalispel, with a cool ring in his voice. "By thunder! I'd like to do that. But I promised Ruth I'd not look Leavitt up."

"Square of you. Thet girl is deservin', Kal. An' about the prettiest one I've seen since I left Santone."

"Old-timer, I'd shore feel better if I knew *you* was goin' to present my compliments to Leavitt. . . . Listen, this is what I came down to tell you. Leavitt is at the head of this bandit gang, an' he's runnin' it shore slick."

"Emerson, are you sure?" queried the Texan, leaning forward like a striking hawk.

"Hell, yes!" whispered Kalispel. "I stood under Leavitt's window an' heard him betray himself. It was I who put that scar over Macabe's ear. Macabe, Leslie, Struthers, all right-hand men of Leavitt's. An' it's somethin' to figure on that Macabe implicated only Borden in the Sloan case. Leavitt can run men of that caliber. But he's also a common, low-down, two-bit thief, a second-hand murderer, an' a slick-tongued deceiver of women."

"An' don't forget he's a leader of Thunder Mountain's vigilantes!"

"Masters, has he really carried it as far as that?"

"Rumors are flyin' thick as autumn leaves. I don't know what is true an' what's false. But now I'll bet my guns thet Leavitt has gone through with it. He hasn't been seen downtown since you shot Borden. Nobody knows what's up, an' everybody's figgerin'. But for me you've about cleared it up."

"Ah-huh. You get my hunch. If Leavitt has organized a vigilante committee you can bet your last dollar the men in it are his hold-up gang."

"Precisely. A damn slick dodge! We underrated this man Leavitt. . . . An' now, Kal, my advice to you is rustle out of heah hell for leather!"

Kalispel got up with a cool little laugh and a sharp hitch of his belt.

"Shake. An' that's my advice to you."

"I'll trail you up street a ways."

Kalispel did not like the suspense in the Texan's mien and voice. There was something in the wind. The instant Kalispel got outside, he was amazed to find that the street that had been noisy and animated a few minutes before was now silent, empty except at the extreme lower end. There strung across from Borden's hall to the Last Chance Saloon stood five masked men, armed with rifles.

Kalispel cursed as a fiery current ran along his veins. Vigilantes! He could not see the upper end of the street, because it curved slightly. His thoughts centered around the query—did the presence of those vigilantes have to do with his visit to town? He decided to cut through the first alley between buildings to make the creek trail. Once back at his cabin, he and Jake could hold off any reasonable number of men.

There were no alleys near. He must go through a store or saloon. Faces appeared in doors across the street. Everybody in town knew——

"Hands up, Emerson!"

The rough, deadly voice, nervous in its timbre, carried threat of instant death. Kalispel had heard that note before. Freezing in his tracks, he elevated his arms high above his head.

"Up they are!" he ejaculated, damning himself for overconfidence.

"Keep 'em thar." Cautious, heavy steps sounded with that voice. "Frisk him, Dan."

Rude hands jerked his guns from his belt. He heard the click of a hammer being raised, then felt the hard prod of a gun-barrel against his back.

"March!"

Kalispel strode up the middle of the street, with his heavy-booted captors close behind. And he heard the slam of doors, the buzz of voices, shouts and trampling of feet. As he turned the slight bend, he saw far at the upper end of this trap, five more masked vigilantes on guard. Cold fury possessed Kalispel, and for a moment he saw red. In the power of the vigilantes! That meant Leavitt. Instantly he realized the grave nature of the predicament. He had been in close quarters before, but never in a situation so perilous as this. A sensation of futility and despair assailed him. Leavitt had hatched some plot to capture and execute him. Probably he had discovered the loss of Blair's money and the gold, and had connected Kalispel with its disappearance. Possibly Sydney had betrayed him. Suddenly Kalispel remembered Ruth, and then indeed life became significant for him. A rush of tremendous spirit banished his fears. He would get out of this. There would be a way.

"What's the deal, boss?" he asked.

"It's a straight hand, Emerson, without cards to you," came the reply.

Kalispel was marched up the street, where, at the end, the five masked vigilantes led the way toward Leavitt's cabin and mill. Judging from the increasing hum and trample in the rear, all of Thunder City was in attendance. It seemed a long walk to Kalispel, and he had to muster all his nerve to dam emotions that might militate against his readiness to seize any opportunity.

"Halt!" ordered Kalispel's captor, when the procession had approached to within twenty paces of Leavitt's cabin.

"I'm kinda tired holdin' my arms up," complained Kalispel, as he halted, and slowly lowered them.

The five vigilantes in the lead lined up to one side. Kalispel heard the others stop behind. And from far back came the increasing roar of the trailing mob.

"Captain Leavitt," shouted the spokesman, "we have your man!"

The cabin door stood wide open. A table and chairs on the porch had a business-like look. Presently two miners came out, followed by Leavitt. He was white of face and stern. His flaring gaze leaped upon Kalispel standing motionless in the open square, and then swept over the vigilantes and to the approaching crowd, then back to the prisoner.

"Leavitt, what's the meanin' of this outrage?" demanded Kalispel, his voice carrying far. He might as well not have made a sound, for all the attention Leavitt paid to him.

"Let the crowd come close enough to hear the proceedings," ordered Leavitt.

The trampling of many feet slowed up behind Kalispel and spread in a half-circle, until it was possible for him to see the people on both sides. This swerving of his gaze brought into his line of vision a scaffold newly erected. Kalispel sustained his last shock, for with a realizing shudder that this instrument of frontier justice had been erected for him he became a man of iron. Leavitt would never hang him.

"That's close enough," called out Leavitt, and then he appeared to fix his flaring eyes upon some man whose slow steps could be heard. "Masters, that applies to you, too."

"Wal, I reckon I'm sheriff of Thunder City," drawled the cool, easy voice of the Texan. It warmed Kalispel's heart. It meant something for him to grasp.

"Yes, and a damn poor sheriff you are," retorted Leavitt. "Flaunting your friendship for this desperado in the face of the whole town!"

"Leavitt, I back my actions. Thet's why I'm heah. We might disagree as to Emerson's status. An' if this heah deal

166

is a trial, as I reckon it is, you'll want it to stand the test of public opinion."

"Certainly. There's nothing secret about this trial. Emerson is before the vigilantes of Thunder City."

"Wal, in thet case somebody must represent him, an' I'll make thet my last official duty, after which I'll resign."

"Very well. We accept your stand for Emerson, and also your resignation."

Masters slowly came into the line of Kalispel's vision. Sight of the cool Texan flooded Kalispel's grim soul with gratitude. Whatever Masters meant, it seemed unreadable to anyone there, except Kalispel, who grasped the nerve of the man, the intention to befriend. But how he was to do it seemed inscrutable.

The Texan turned to Kalispel with slow, casual steps.

"Am I acceptable to you, Emerson?" he queried. "Looks like a high-handed procedure to me. But if these vigilantes mean to put you on trial I'm heah to see it's fair."

"Thanks, Masters," returned Kalispel. The Texan's words were potent, but negligible compared with the wonderful power and meaning of his gray eyes. Kalispel was swift to read that gaze. There could be no question of a fair trial here. Masters' action was merely a ruse to permit him to come forward, gradually to edge closer and closer to Kalispel, until, when the situation reached its climax, he would be near enough for Kalispel to leap and jerk free Masters' two big guns and shoot his way to death or freedom. Leavitt in his suppressed deep passion was as good as dead at that very moment.

"Judge, before you make a charge against the prisoner, may I ask what constitutes yore right to this procedure?" queried Masters, deliberately.

"I am captain of these vigilantes," replied Leavitt, curtly.

"Wal, thet won't stand before the law. You were not elected. You appointed yoreself."

"But I was elected judge of this mining-camp," parried Leavitt, with composure. "If you know the laws of gold-diggings you will agree that I have absolute authority."

"Wal shore, aboot all claims, arguments, sales an' exchange, an' all thet. But hardly to make arrests an' build scaffolds. That ought to be my job."

"Masters, we won't split hairs over that," declared Leavitt, with cold finality. "Emerson is on trial, and I'm his judge."

"Air you puttin' him on trial for gun-play?"

"There is no law on the frontier against even breaks."

"Wal, then, what's Emerson's offense?" demanded the Texan, sharply.

Judge Leavitt seated himself at his table and arranged papers before he replied.

"Emerson is a bandit."

Masters wheeled to take a long stride toward Kalispel.

"You heah thet?" he called.

"I'm not deaf, Masters."

"Wal, what you got to say about it?"

"Leavitt is a damned liar."

Again Masters faced the porch. Kalispel felt like a tiger about to leap. The Texan stood a little to the left, a good long jump distant, and his black guns hung in plain sight, as easy to draw as if they had been on Kalispel himself.

"Judge, I've heahed yore accusation. An' I heard Emerson's denial. I mean no offense when I say thet his word before the court is as good as yores. You'll have to furnish proof."

"That is what we propose to do," rejoined Leavitt, loudly. "Keep quiet there in the crowd. This is a trial. . . . Jones, step forward."

The smaller of the two men who had come out of the cabin with Leavitt strode forward to face the Vigilantes. He looked like any other middle-aged miner.

"State your evidence against this prisoner," ordered Leavitt.

"He robbed me," returned Jones, in resonant, frank voice. "It happened at night, two weeks ago come Wednesday, just after six o'clock. I was comin' from my claim in the dark. Just off one of them deserted tents down the crick a man stepped out behind me an' jabbed a gun in my back. He asked for my dust. I had bags, one dust an' the other nuggets. I gave them up."

"Did you recognize Emerson?" asked the Judge.

"No, thet is, not his person. But I shore did his voice. I'd heard thet often."

Masters turned to take another step in Kalispel's direction.

"What you say to thet?"

"Sheriff, it's another rotten lie," called Kalispel, piercingly. "An' Jones couldn't look at me with it, unless he knew I'd never get out of this alive."

"Matthews, step forward," ordered the Judge, to the second man, who was tall, pale-visaged, and less convincing. "State your case against the prisoner."

"Emerson held me up, Jedge," replied Matthews. "It was last Saturday night, at about half after eight. It was right in town. An' he stepped out of the shadow of Spence's store.

He had a scarf over his face, but it slipped down a ways when he was friskin' me. An' I recognized him easy. He took my gold, watch, an' guns."

"Matthews, you say this occurred last Saturday night at half-past eight, and that you recognized Emerson perfectly?" queried the Judge.

"Yes, sir."

Leavitt waived the witness aside and again attended to the sheriff. "Masters, that seems conclusive to me. There's no doubt in my mind Emerson is guilty of all these hold-ups, and shootings, too. . . . I'll put it to a vote."

"Never mind havin' yore vigilantes vote yet," returned Masters, with sarcasm. "The trial ain't over."

He faced around to Kalispel, the third time with unobtrusive step.

"Kalispel, you heahed?"

"Yes."

"An' I reckon thet's another lie?"

"It shore is."

"Wal, it sounded fishy to me," replied the Texan. "An' if you can recall shore jest where you was on Saturday night at half-past eight, I'll take yore word for it."

"I was—" began Kalispel, readily, when suddenly he remembered that on the hour in question Sydney Blair was alone with him in his cabin.

"Wal, speak up, an' make it plain to this listenin' crowd," said Masters, impatiently.

Kalispel let out a hard laugh. It did not make any difference to Leavitt and his Vigilantes whether he cleared himself or not. And in another moment he would be leaping for Masters' guns.

"Sorry, old-timer," his voice rang out. "I reckon I can't remember."

"There," flashed Leavitt, his hand extended shaking. "Condemned by his own lips!"

The crowd stirred to restless shifting of feet and sibilant whispers. Then Kalispel was transfixed at sight of Sydney Blair running in to face Leavitt.

"Rand Leavitt," she cried, in her high tones that pierced to every listening ear in the multitude, "Your tool, Matthews, has not condemned Emerson, but himself as a liar—and *you* as a worse one!"

"*What?*" hissed Leavitt, leaping up, to lean forward with purpling face. The surprise had penetrated his armor.

"Kalispel Emerson absolutely could not have robbed

169

Matthews last Saturday night, at half-past eight," rang Sydney's voice, vibrant with righteous anger.

"And why not?" shouted Leavitt, furiously.

"Because he was with me—in his cabin!"

It was then that the jealous lover took precedence over the presiding judge.

"In his cabin . . . alone?"

"Yes, alone."

"Sydney Blair!— *You?* . . . My promised wife! . . . What —why were you there?"

"I went there to tell him what a villain you are—to tell him I had broken my engagement with you . . . to beg him to—to forgive me and take me back again!"

The transformation that swift, poignant speech wrought in Leavitt was monstrous to behold. The suave gentleman, the confident mining-boss, the cold, grim judge went into eclipse. And a malignant, mouthing, passion-ridden devil leaped off the porch.

"Look there, woman!" he shouted, strident with hate, as he pointed with quivering finger at the scaffold. "You shall see your lover hanged!"

This seemed to Kalispel to be the moment for him to leap for Masters' guns, kill the maddened Leavitt, and then turn loose his fire upon his captors. But Sydney stood in the way. There would be other shooting beside his, a wild tumult, pandemonium. He dared not risk harm to her. Masters edged back toward him. There was time. He would wait.

"Men! Seize him," yelled Leavitt. "By God! he hangs!"

The answer was a woman's piercing cry, whether Sydney's or another's Kalispel never knew. And at the same instant the solid ground shook under his feet.

"Hell's fire!" shrieked a vigilante, suddenly gone crazy. "The mountain! The mountain! . . . *Run for your lives!"*

Chapter Fifteen

Every spectator looked. The vast slope was waving like a sea. And on the instant a groaning, straining rumble came from the depths. Far up, a whole bare ridge began to slide.

"Avalanche!"

"A slide—a slide!"

170

These pregnant cries were drowned in the united yell of the crowd. And this was lost in a terrific thunder that came unmistakably from a mountain mass in movement.

Terror clapped on Kalispel, but when he saw Sydney sway and fall he leaped out of his paralysis to snatch her up in his arms and back away from the awesome spectacle.

The vigilantes were in full flight with the rest of the crowd. Masters passed Kalispel, yelling words that could not be heard. Leavitt had run from the lee of the cabin to look up and see the slow, waving descent of sections of slope, of ridges and mounds. The earth seemed shaken to its core. Thunder that was not thunder filled the air.

Leavitt seemed suddenly bereft of his senses. He dashed a few steps after the crowd only to whirl and dash back. No sense of escape actuated him. He bounded up on the porch and into the cabin.

What had been rumble and thunder died in a crash as if the earth were rent asunder. A great slide piled down on Leavitt's mill, crushing, shoving, covering the chutes, and at last, as if by magic, obliterating the mill. Out of the thick rolling mass of mud huge balls of dry earth broke to let out puffs of dust.

The mill was gone and with it went the splintering crash. Hoarse shouts of men, sounding far away, pierced Kalispel's ears. He backed against a boulder, still holding the girl, who appeared to be regaining consciousness. Masters stood by him, holding his arm, shouting Kalispel knew not what. The spectacle fascinated them, and when Leavitt appeared in the door of his cabin, acting like a man bereft of his senses, they were rooted to the spot.

His frenzy, his wringing hands, his voiceless yells were eloquent of something that was gone! gone! gone! Kalispel understood then that not until this tragic moment of catastrophe had Leavitt known of the loss of his gold.

His pale face vanished from the dark doorway. And that instant, with a rumble and a shake the mass of slope let loose in a landslide to move down upon the cabin. The roof caved in, and earth poured down like water into a vessel.

Leavitt appeared at the door and then was felled by a falling rafter. He went down, his head outside the door. And there, wrenching and lunging, like an animal caught by its hind feet in a trap, he raised his body and flung his arms. In each hand he held a bag of gold. His face was a gray blotch, his strained action terrible.

The sliding silt filled the cabin and began to pour out of the door over Leavitt. Still he struggled. Like a waterfall the earth rushed off the roof on each side, leaving a slowly-closing, fan-shaped aperture through which the doomed man could be seen. Then came a sliding roar, a cloud of dust—and the cabin disappeared.

As if in mockery of the littleness of man, nature pealed out the doom which the wise old beaver and the savage chief had foreseen. No sound before had ever equaled that thundering travail of the mountain yielding its might, its bulk, its stability to the stupendous force of gravitation. For ages its foundation had groaned warnings. And now the hour of descent had come.

The slope was a billowy sea on end. Far up the trees were aslant, falling, wagging, piling up and sliding down. The hollows filled, the scant thickets rode the avalanche, the ridges rose like waves and sank in furrows. Majestic and awful, the mile-high face of the mountain moved down. Gradually the movement slowed and as gradually the rumbling thunder diminished. The shouts of men could be heard. Once more the sound of the stream penetrated the valley.

Blair approached Kalispel and Sydney, who had recovered from her faint.

"My God! Kal—isn't it awful?" gasped Blair, taking hold of Sydney.

"Shore came in the nick of time for me," replied Kalispel, hoarsely. "Pack an' rustle, Blair."

Masters appeared, approaching the edge of the slide, which had moved out some distance on the bench. He stopped for a while to watch it.

Sydney seized Kalispel's hand.

"Look! The place where—I fell—is covered," she whispered, with a glance Kalispel would never forget.

Presently Masters held up his hand and bellowed to the watching crowd.

"She's movin' three feet a minute. . . . Thunder City is doomed. . . . Run an' tell everybody. Grab yore gold, some grub, a blanket, an' rustle out of heah!"

Kalispel ran toward his cabin, every few moments halting to look back at the extraordinary spectacle. It was as great and as strange as had been his deliverance. Every rod that he progressed away from the sliding slope changed its perspective; the farther he got away the more he could see. Three feet a minute! It would not be long until the encroaching landslide must reach the edge of the long, one-streeted town. Miners were running like red-jacketed ants in every direction.

Jake's gloomy visage lightened at sight of Kalispel.

"About time you got back! Didn't I tell you I had a hunch?"

"Don't rub it in. . . . Where's—Ruth?"

"Poor kid, she's scared 'most damn near to death," replied Jake, indicating that the girl was inside the cabin.

Ruth lay on the couch with her face covered. But Kalispel saw the heaving of her breast.

"Ruth!" he panted as he sat down beside her and tore her hands and scarf from her face. "I'm here."

She leaped up to clasp him in her arms, and the horror faded from her eyes as she kissed him wildly, unconscious of all save his return.

"Why—kid—don't take on so!" he said, huskily, but her clinging hands and lips were sweet to him.

"I saw the vigilantes march you up to Leavitt," she whispered. "Jake held me back. He swore you'd come through. . . . But, oh, I nearly went mad!"

"Closest shave I—ever had," replied Kalispel, breathing hard. He beckoned for Jake to come in the open door. Then he recounted to them the pregnant events of the last hour.

"Kal, there must be a God," said Ruth, solemnly, when he had finished.

"I'll never doubt it again," replied Kalispel, fervently.

They did not remain longer in the cabin. Outside again, they gazed spellbound at the unparalleled scene. Shacks and tents were riding up-ended at the base of the moving mountain, splintering sounds came clearly across the distance; the sinister inexorable landslide crept toward the town.

But if the spectacle low down was fascinating, that high up on the slope was indescribably so. The movement seemed more visible there and it was monstrous. Over the ridge back of the center of the town hove in sight a moving forest that ordinarily had been hidden from view. With firs and pines uprooted, upflung, upended, a section of slope slid down with slow and terrible precision. Far at the end of the town, where the valley narrowed in its approach to the canyon, the landslide had made more progress. Borden's huge dance-hall stood in line for almost instant annihilation.

"Oh, I hope the girls are safe!" cried Ruth.

"Never fear. They've had plenty of time. If only they had sense enough to get their clothes an' grub. It'll be bad if they don't."

"Kal, that landslide will wipe Thunder City out, dam the valley, an' make a lake where we're standin' now," declared Jake. "Aw no! I never had a hunch—not atall."

"Wal, what hunch is eatin' you now?" queried Kalispel.

"I'll tell when I get one. . . . Wow! hear thet smash! Borden's dance-hall dancin' to its grave! Ain't thet a queer sight? It jest ain't real, folks."

"Jake, rustle to your packin'," ordered Kalispel, remembering the issue at hand. "We want to get out ahead of the mob."

"I reckon the exodus won't begin till tomorrow," returned Jake. "Most of these gold-hawgs will hang on till the end."

"Ruth, rustle into warm things an' overalls. It'll be tough sleddin' on the pass. But we'll get over before night an' camp below the snow line."

"Listen! Oh, listen to the thunder!" cried Ruth, her eyes shining with excitement, her golden hair flying in the wind.

They packed feverishly for a while and then stopped to breathe and gaze again at the phenomenon. The Blairs rode by behind the freighters and a train of pack-animals. Far across the stream miners could be seen in droves, moving their effects up on the high bench. Fire broke out in one of the overturned buildings, sending forth flames and volumes of yellow smoke. The grinding of boulders went on, the cracking of walls, the thudding of trees, and the incessant shouting of excited men.

Kalispel selected the best burro to pack the alfagos which carried his gold. Over this pack he strapped his bed. Then he haltered the burro close at hand. The grimness of the hour did not prevent a singing of his heart. Ruth came out dressed to ride, and when he saw her he did not fear that the picture of Sydney Blair in riding-garb would ever haunt him again. By this time Jake had packed the other two burros.

"If you pack my saddle-horse, Jake, I'll walk. I reckon that'll take the outfit," said Kalispel.

"Oh, look!" cried Ruth.

A mile of the face of the landslide had crept upon the long line of the buildings on the north side of the main street. Three feet a minute! Yet it might have been a tidal wave, for the crashing and rending, the smashing and rolling, the collapsing and upheaving of tents, shacks, cabins, stores, and saloons, gave the impression of swiftly-advancing havoc and ruin. The landslide seemed relentless. It had waited long; it had faithfully warned this mushroom city; and now it was fulfilling its augury.

Thunder again! The ground shook beneath Kalispel's feet, and Ruth reached for him with eager hands and parted lips. Only a huge slide of earth from far above, pouring over the lower strata like lava over an old slow-moving stream! Rocks heaved out of the moving silt to roll, to be buried again, to appear once more, to slide and gather momentum until they were hurtling down to leap the boulders on the bench and crack as if exploding, or were thudding soddenly into the piling earth around the houses. One half the city seemed alive, writhing and crunching in the maw of the avalanche, while the other half waited apprehensively the approach of the cataclysm.

"Ruth, fork your horse," ordered Kalispel, driven to tear his gaze from the spectacle. "Jake, move 'em along. We're late now."

He watched the girl, keen even in that moment to see if she could make good her boast of horsemanship. Ruth never thought of it. She stepped up and swung into her saddle with a lithe ease and grace which could come only from long practice. Somehow the sight enhanced her value and suddenly gave her a charm he had not appreciated till then.

"Wal, you win, Calamity Jane. Ride on," he called. And then he untied his burro, and with rifle in hand stepped out upon the trail.

At the bend of the stream, where the trail turned, Kalispel had his last close view of Thunder City and the juggernaut which was destroying it.

That Ruth did not look back seemed strange. Kalispel turned even after he could see no more. But he could still hear the detonations like sodden blows. Far up the trail a train of pack-mules zigzagged toward the summit of the pass. The stream, bank-full, and yellow in hue, roared hurriedly down, as if sensing an hour when no escape from the valley would be possible. And the sun, westering, had begun to gild the white clouds over the western wall.

Kalispel marveled at his deliverance. There had been a moment when he had given up and prayed only to get his hands on a pair of guns. This vengeance had not been meant for him. A higher power had settled the score with Leavitt.

The trail grew steep and began its zigzag course. Jake, always a careful leader, often held the burros to rest. Kalispel climbed behind Ruth's horse. She did not talk nor did she look back. Kalispel anticipated the moment when from the summit of the pass he would view the unparalleled scene of his life.

The air grew cold, with a hint of snow in its breath. Jake toiled on, his wide shoulders bowed. The lop-eared burros plodded on behind him. Kalispel never let go of the halter of his burro, a procedure which the wise animal regarded with disfavor. Jenny did not realize the preciousness of the treasure which burdened her. Nor was Kalispel able to make himself believe it.

The melodious roar of the stream ceased to thrum in Kalispel's ears. It died gradually away. Sharp cold wind rustled the sagebrush on the slope. The rush of a bird of prey sounded above his head. And the patter of tiny hoofs went on.

At last Jake halted on the first level of the pass, where patches of snow spotted the gray. His ruddy face, almost as red as his shirt, turned down toward the valley. His mouth gaped, his jaw dropped, his eyes popped, and he threw up one long arm in a voiceless salutation of something awe-inspiring.

Ruth must have seen him, she must have understood. But she bowed her head over the neck of her horse and did not turn. Kalispel's lips had opened to call her, to have her share with him this last and unforgettable view of Thunder City. But suddenly he understood. Ruth had the strength not to look back. She had forever bidden farewell to that sordid gold-camp and to the life she had led there. She wanted no transcendant beauty of scene, no terrible convulsion of nature, limned on her memory.

But Kalispel gazed back and was stunned.

The long valley lay at his feet, under slanting rays and veils of golden light, and through its center meandered a shining stream of fire, which ended in a broad, shield-shaped, blazing lake.

The farthest end of the landslide had dammed the stream. Houses, half-submerged, like sinking boats, floated upon its surface. Men like ants toiled along its farther shore. Kalispel looked in vain for what had been the long, narrow gray-walled, white-tented town, for the long, wide street with its teeming life.

Chaos reigned down in that valley, transcendantly beautiful in its sunset hues and curtains, terrible with its naked destructive forces of earth and rock.

Kalispel had to gaze over and over again and readjust his perspective to make clear what he really did see. And when Jake and Ruth had gone on up the trail, and the sun sank behind the western wall, Kalispel had painted forever on his memory the grandeur of the slide of Thunder Mountain into the valley.

To his right and far above gleamed the stark, smooth, glistening slant of solid rock from which the mountain of earth had finally detached itself. Through the years it had moaned this intention. Halfway down and more, the avalanche had slid; and now even high up, its gradual subsiding was perceptible to the awe-struck watcher. It was moving to its rest. A wide belt of bare, dark earth slanted down from the naked rock. But this smooth slope gradually roughened down to the boulder-strewn, tree-spiked, hummocky middle of the landslide. Here began the chaotic evidences of the devastating nature of the element earth when once released from its confines. The slow, processional, downward trend had an awful solemnity. By steps and crevasses and bulges, all working, heaving, swelling, caving in, the great unstable bulk crept irresistibly down, and always down, growing wilder and raggeder, until it fell into the terraces that had moved like slow swells of the sea to wipe away the town.

What was left of Thunder City rode the avalanche, or was shoved ahead of the sliding wall out into the blazing lake.

These long uneven terraces of debris fascinated Kalispel. From this viewpoint he could grasp all, as an eagle could when it leaned wide wings against the wind. From below Kalispel had not had any conception of this monstrous defacement of a mountain and the destruction of habitations of thousands of men. What struck him most was the relentless, slow descent. Every phase of this austere motion had in it the illimitable power that had doomed Leavitt. Watching there, Kalispel had a strange thought that the landslide had waited there for Leavitt.

Beyond all and above all shone forth its appalling and ghastly and sublime beauty. The triangular side of the mountain, the rock face, gleamed with the gold of the sunset; and the dark earth grew rich in purple and lilac; the rolling terraces caught the tints of the sun like oncoming billows of surf burning with gold fire on their crests; the tilted houses, ghosts of edifices where mirth and greed and hate had abided, moved on under down-dropping curtains of rose light, while others floated on the lake, gray-sailed barks that grotesquely rode the shimmering water.

Mountain and valley had existed there side by side, the one looming grandly over the other, for untold ages. Then, one amber-veiled afternoon, the mountain had begun its slide, and the valley was filling with debris and water. Death had stalked there. And only a step away the throng of intrepid miners, undaunted by this cataclysm, had pitched camp on the high bench beyond, there to watch it out, to remain behind for the precious gold, or to take the long trail, defeated but not despairing.

Kalispel wrenched himself from the scene, and profoundly grateful and humbled and troubled, he led his burro up the pass into the snow. The trail had been made and packed by those who had gone before. And on the descent beyond, the cold white mantle thinned out and failed. As twilight fell Kalispel plodded down into a sheltered grove of aspens where a bright fire blazed and Jake whistled at his tasks. Ruth sat before the fire, her face rosy and sweet, with no trace of grief, her small bare hands extended to the heat.

"We're over the hill!" said Kalispel, as he gazed down upon his charge, and he meant vastly more than the surmounting of the snowy pass.

The Middle Fork presented Kalispel's next problem. If it was in flood, there would be many miners camping at the ford. Kalispel desired to avoid contacts. The river itself did not worry him. He would wait until the flood subsided or build a raft and ferry his packs over on that. Ruth was at home in a saddle, and this surprising fact gave Kalispel unending satisfaction.

Trailing downhill was easy on burros and men. The ford of the Middle Fork was reached in the late afternoon of the third day out from the valley. The river was high, but not so high as to hold back the miners who had turned their backs upon the Saw Tooths. Kalispel ordered camp and busied himself constructing a raft.

"What'n hell do we want a raft fer?" snorted Jake.

"Keep your shirt on, brother. I'm buildin' it, you see."

"But what's it fer?"

"Reckon to freight Ruth's fine togs safely across."

"Kal, I burned them!" exclaimed Ruth.

"Aw, wal! . . . I'll pack mine over on it, then. Hate to wet my clothes an' bed."

Next morning disclosed his wisdom. Jake had a ducking in the icy water and one of the burros was rolled by the swift current. Kalispel dragged his improvised raft up stream a hundred yards and crossed on it with his alfagos without a hitch. Ruth handled her horse like a cowboy.

"Yip-yip!" yelled Kalispel, unable to subdue exuberant feelings.

Chapter Sixteen

Kalispel made noonday halt in a grove of cottonwoods on the bank of the Salmon River below Challis.

He wanted to give that congested town a wide berth. But he sent Jake in to fetch back some very necessary fresh supplies, and upon a mission he did not confide to Ruth until his brother was out of sight.

"Say, kid," he began, hesitatingly, as he felt his cheeks grow hot, "Jake is goin' to fetch back the—the parson."

"The—*what?*" flamed Ruth, starting up.

They sat resting in the shade of the cottonwoods some distance from the road, and screened by willows from passers-by. It was a pretty spot. Leaves of gold and green fluttering over them and carpeting the ground, blue sky and white clouds, warm sunshine and the amber river rolling on with its deep, gurgling, sonorous note—these seemed to encourage Kalispel in his delicate task.

"I sent for the parson," he replied, after a pause. "I shore hate to make you feel bad, but, wal, it's terrible important."

"Kal Emerson, you're going to stick to that promise to Dick?"

"I'd forgotten about him, but not about marrying you. I shore intend to do that."

"I won't," she declared.

"You will," he returned.

"A woman has to swear to—to love, honor, and obey a man, doesn't she, before it's binding?"

"Why, I reckon. But you can cut out the obey if you want."

"You know every little wish of yours would be law to me," she said, passionately.

"Ruth, I didn't know that, but fine—fine! My wish is for you to be my wife."

"Why?" she asked, her face paling.

"Wal, for a number of reasons, most particular of which is that I want to take care of you an' make you happy."

"But you don't have to *marry* me—to do that. I'll be happier than I ever was in my life—just to be with you, work for you."

179

"Maybe you could. An' that would be all right with me," he rejoined, earnestly. "Only, our story will be known. . . . An' wal, I won't have it any other way."

"I can jump in the river," said Ruth, tragically. "I always wanted to. Those deep green pools always fascinated me."

She rose to her feet, her face white, her eyes dark with pain, but with something rebellious in them that persuaded Kalispel she would not naturally go so far.

"Aw, Ruth, you wouldn't," he replied. Nevertheless, he laid a strong hand on the nearest blue-jean leg.

"I would rather than disgrace you," she asserted.

"But, you little dunce, if you won't marry me, you will disgrace me."

"I—I thought I'd settled it," she faltered, miserably.

"If you cry I'll—I'll spank you," he declared, threateningly.

"I'd forgotten everything—and I was happy."

"Ah-huh. An' now you're unhappy just because I'm determined to make you Mrs. Lee Emerson? . . . Gosh! It's shore flatterin' to my vanity."

"Kal, I'm not like other girls—for instance, Sydney Blair."

"Yes you are, an' a darn sight nicer."

"Oh!— Oh! If you only—*only* had met me—when I was sixteen!" she sobbed, and broke down.

Kalispel almost took her into his arms. He surely wanted to, and choked up with his feeling, but he was afraid of hurting her further. After a while, when she grew composed once more, he said: "Ruth, it's only for appearance's sake. I told you that. . . . You'll not be my wife, really. So there'll be nothin' for you to be ashamed of. An' I'll have you to take care of—an' you'll have me."

"Very well. I will marry you," she replied, in faint and sober tone.

Kalispel left her alone then and walked under the cottonwoods realizing that he did not understand himself very well. But he felt greatly relieved and glad of her decision. Presently he heard a clip-clop of hoofs and the crunch of wheels on the gravel road. The vehicle proved to be a light spring-wagon which turned off toward the cottonwood grove. Soon Kalispel saw that the driver's garb betokened him to be a minister and that the other occupant of the wagon was Jake.

"Kal, this is Parson Weeks," announced Jake as they came to a stop. "I commissioned him to pack our fresh supplies out. An' he's offered to sell the hoss an' wagon cheap. So I reckon, when he winds up by hitchin' you an' Ruth, thet it'll be a right pert day for him."

180

"Howdy, Parson. I'm Lee Emerson, called Kalispel by some, an' I'm shore glad to meet you," drawled Kalispel, offering his hand, as the gray-haired, blue-eyed, brown-faced little man alighted.

"The pleasure is mine, Emerson. I've heard of you and I'm glad to shake this good right hand of yours."

"Come an' meet the lady."

Ruth rose from her log seat as they approached, and Kalispel's fears were unfounded. She showed no trace of distress and met them with a smile and brave, sweet eyes.

"Ruth, this is Parson Weeks," announced Kalispel. The meeting came off to Kalispel's keen pleasure.

"Parson, I have promised to marry him," said Ruth, presently, with lovely, troubled eyes uplifted. "I will—but I ought not."

"And goodness me! why not, if you care for him?" exclaimed Weeks, kindly.

"Oh, I do love him, but I was a dance-hall girl and I can never live down the bad name that gave me."

"Suppose you were," he replied, slowly. "That is nothing if he wants you." He turned to Kalispel.

"Yes, I do!" interrupted Kalispel, with passion. "Parson, I took her out of a dance-hall, but that doesn't say she was bad. An' I'm goin' to marry her an' make her happy. She's afraid she'll disgrace me, but she's a lot better than I am. She has a better education than I had, too. . . . If you can only talk a little sense into her pretty head you'll be doin' me an everlastin' favor."

"Ah! I see!" returned the minister, deeply moved, and he took Ruth's hand. "My dear child, this is a question of love and love alone. Emerson is proving his. You have told me of yours. I advise you as a father and beseech you as a minister to marry this young man. . . . I am of the West, Ruth. And I know what the foundation has been. Women are scarce on the frontier. A few pioneer women with their daughters, and the rest a horde of Indian squaws, adventuresses, prostitutes—and dance-hall girls. From these Westerners must choose their wives. And they have done so for years, are doing it now, and will continue to do so. Man must have woman. It is a hard country, this glorious West of ours. It takes big women to stand it. And bad women, if there are any bad women, have turned out big and good. They are making the West. Who shall remember in threescore years, when this broad land will be prosperous with cities and ranchers, that the grandmothers of that generation, ever were, let us say, dance-hall girls? And if it were remembered, who could bring calumny against the strong-souled mothers of the West?"

Parson Weeks married Ruth and Kalispel under the gold-leafed cottonwoods, with Jake grinning happily by. And when Kalispel bent over Ruth to watch her sign the marriage certificate, he was rather astonished to discover that he had never before known her surname.

Kalispel bought out Olsen, lock, stock, and barrel, to his own rapture and the dissatisfied rancher's great satisfaction.

A belated Indian summer fell upon the Salmon River Valley, and added its enchantment of smoky, still, golden days to the splendor of silver, black-tipped slopes, and the singing river.

While Jake scoured the Lemhi Valley for horses and cattle, Kalispel superintended the erection of a spacious addition to Olsen's log cabin. Carpenters and builders from the town peeled the lodge-pole pines that the Indians snaked down from the forests, and sawed and raised and hammered till a long living-room arose, with a large open fireplace in the center, and small, well-lighted rooms at each end. Kalispel never left the ranch, but his orders were sent out, and wagon-loads of furniture arrived. And when he had exhausted Salmon's resources he sent freighters to Boise for the luxuries he wanted for Ruth. Pictures, curtains, lamps, rugs, linen, all the things he had surreptitiously learned from Ruth were dear to the hearts of housewives, all these and many more came almost before the roof was on, to Ruth's growing consternation and rapture.

"Oh, Kal! If you are going in debt we are ruined before we start!" she wailed.

"Nary a debt," he replied, with a mysterious air.

"Kal, you couldn't have lied to me!" she implored. "You *couldn't!*"

"Wal, I don't recollect lyin' to you," he drawled. "What about?"

"You swore you have never been—oh, forgive me!—a—a bandit?"

"Shore, I swore. I never took two-bits in my life—that didn't belong to me."

"Then, Kal, you struck gold over there—struck it rich—and kept it secret!"

"Wal, there's somethin' in what you say," he replied, lazily, and then he ran out to keep from telling her of his secret, of the bags and bags of gold dust so carefully hidden by himself deep under his corner of the new house.

Kalispel planned many surprises, to Ruth's endless bewilderment. When Smoky arrived, the finest and prettiest little saddle-horse in the valley, with a Mexican silver-mounted saddle and bridle, Ruth wept and loved the horse and followed Kalispel around with eyes that made a slow, strange heat throb in his veins. What was this intense desire of his to see the light of gladness come to her blue eyes? How stern his determination to make up to her for what she had suffered, to fill the present with a joy that must obliterate the past!

However, when a young Lemhi Indian couple put in an appearance, the stalwart man to help Jake with his manifold tasks, and the comely squaw to look after the house, then Ruth arose like a roused lioness. To her wrath and her protestations and lamentations Kalispel turned a flinty, if not a deaf, ear.

"Dog-gone it! There's too much work on this big place for a little girl like you!" he ejaculated, finally.

"I'm not little. At least, if I am little, I'm strong."

"Shore. But I won't have my wife makin' a slave of herself. Not while I'm rich."

"Rich! . . . Damn you, Kal! . . . Oh, forgive me. I meant to stop swearing. . . . But I don't care if you *are* rich, you mysterious cowpuncher! I want to be worth my salt."

"Ruth, I reckon I'm findin' out you're worth gold an' rubies an' pearls."

"You are! . . . Oh, Kal, you're so careless with your speech. Remember I'm only a poor little lost waif—and if I ever thought you'd— I— Oh! . . . but let me cook and bake and sew for you!"

"Wal, I sort of think I'll like that, a little," he drawled. "But no pichin' hay or diggin' potatoes or milkin' cows or choppin' wood or scrubbin' floors, or any of a hundred jobs such as Olsen's wife had to do. You savvy, Mrs. Emerson?"

"Yes, I savvy," she replied, her eyes shining through tears.

By mid-November the leaves were off the cottonwoods and willows; the grass had grown sear and brown; the skies were mostly gray; and the wailing wind and dismal croak of ravens from the hill attested to the imminent approach of winter.

Jake had driven in a thousand head of cattle and fifty

183

horses, which were turned out in the river pastures. The freighting was all finished. Jake and the Indian cut firewood when the other farm chores left them time.

During these eventful and all-satisfying weeks Kalispel had not visited Salmon or Challis. His thoughts were absorbed by his ranch and a new something that had come into his life.

Nevertheless, he heard endless gossip from Jake, who never failed to return from town with the latest happenings. Moreover, miners and travelers, who often stopped at the ranch, brought their share of news. Only of late had the stream of miners from Thunder City diminished to a few stragglers.

Five hundred undefeated gold-diggers had remained behind to spend the winter in the ruined gold-camp. Thunder Mountain had slipped down to pile a dam a hundred feet high across the valley at the lower end. A hundred feet of water now covered the long, wide street where revelry had held sway day and night. And the lake had backed up two miles, here and there dotted by clapboard houses that had floated until they stranded in shallow places. But the gold was still there. And in the spring the hundred-ton stamp-mill would be packed in.

Of vital interest to Kalispel was the news that Masters had lingered at Thunder City long after all his friends had left. And one day, in a tent-walled gambling-den, he had clashed with two miners named Jones and Matthews and had killed them both. One of these men, while dying, had confessed to the murder of Sam Emerson, at Leavitt's instigation.

Leavitt's vigilantes had taken off their masks that last day when the landslide had saved Kalispel, and were never known by their fellow miners or heard of again.

Kalispel often inquired about Blair and his daughter, but they seemed to have vanished. Memory of the dark haired, violet-eyed girl had mellowed to something fine for Kalispel and he no longer felt any regret or remorse.

Then one day a leaden sky mantled the mountain peaks and snow began to fall. Great, feathery, white flakes floated down to cover the slopes, the ranges, the cabins, the sheds and fences, all except the dark-green, gliding river. Three feet of snow fell during that first storm of the winter, and when it cleared the mercury slipped down below zero.

Kalispel gazed out of the window that morning upon a beautiful white world.

"Gosh, how I always used to hate winter!" he ejaculated. "Blizzards on the Wyomin' range were no joke."

"I love winter," replied Ruth, gayly. "I shall wade out in the snow every day."

"Wade away, but not with me, darlin'!" he drawled. The unconscious term of endearment checked any further enthusiasm of Ruth's and again opened for Kalispel a singular train of thought, which for long had recurred, despite his perplexity and disfavor.

"Snowed in, like a couple of Missouri groundhogs! Snowed in for the winter, you an' me, Ruth! . . . Aw, it's terrible hard luck for Kalispel Emerson! Nice, cozy, bright livin'-room, big open fireplace an' stacks an' stacks of dead wood to burn!— Shore is hard luck for a down-trodden, never-understood cowboy!"

"Yes, I had observed the same thing," replied Ruth, demurely, with an expressive glance from her blue eyes.

"Shore. I'm glad you are observin'," drawled Kalispel, the mood growing on him. "An' stuff to eat! Oh, my! Two deer hangin' up in the shed an' a thousand pounds of elk meat!— Pantry full of grub! Milk an' cream an' butter all I can stuff, an' not have to lift a darn hand to get it. . . . An' then this here livin'-room. Books an' books, an' magazines galore! Nice, bright lamps an 'easy chairs! Aw, the long winter evenin's when the wind moans an' the snow blows, with all these things an' a girl no man would ever tire lookin' at!"

"Oh, so you have observed that last!" exclaimed Ruth, lightly, but she did not raise her eyes.

Kalispel had looked at her often of late, though not so keenly and realizingly as on this white morning when he accepted the fact of winter.

"November, December, January, February, March, April, May!" he exclaimed.

"Oh, the long months, eh?" she rejoined, encouragingly.

"Yep, the long months with you alone."

"Kal, isn't that prospect very—very—?" she asked, troubled of eyes, and unable to find the word she wanted.

"Shore it is," he agreed, but did not tell her what.

Ruth had greatly improved during these weeks of autumn. The hollows of her cheeks and neck had filled out, and she had gained otherwise, so that her appearance of frailty had vanished. The shadows that had once lain under her eyes were gone, and the haunting pain no longer lurked in her expression. With Kalispel's sense of relief at this transformation came his full realization of the love that had grown in him. He had long been conscious of something deeply significant for him in her presence. Every thought of her busy, happy days and evenings seemed to be for him. She lived for him. And his love, insensibly born that dusk in Sloan's cabin, had been fed by her sweetness, her shining hair and never-failing smile, her improvement in health and beauty, the day by day unfolding of her brave and loyal soul.

He kept his secret to himself for days and nights, gloating over the wonder of it, the transformation it had wrought in him. He played with this happiness and hugged it to his bosom.

But the time came when Kalispel felt that he could not keep his love secret any longer. Wherefore he reacted to his old cowboy humor and planned his capitulation.

That night he had been unusually quiet, and not responsive to Ruth's thoughtful importunities. But when bedtime came he apparently regained his cheerfulness.

"Dog-gone!— Ruth, can't you feel the cold creepin' in?" he said, as he got up to bank the red bed of embers in the fireplace. "If I don't keep pilin' on wood——"

"It was fifteen degrees below zero this morning," she declared.

"Wal, no wonder. . . . Do you sleep warm, Ruth?" he asked, solicitously, as he turned his back, raking up the coals.

"I freeze to death," she rejoined, frankly, with a laugh.

"So do I, towards mornin'," he drawled, thoughtfully. "Dog-gone it, Ruth, suppose we sleep together to keep warm."

She uttered a slight gasp, but did not reply. Kalispel went on piling the ashes over the live fire and taking pains about it. He did not want to look at her just then, because he knew that when he did there would be the end of his secret. As she did not speak, however, he began to feel that he had overstepped his bounds.

"Course I won't sleep in my chaps an' spurs, as I used to," he ventured.

"Kal! . . ." she whispered, faintly. "You—you're not—in earnest?"

"Shore, come to think of it. You see I just happened to think that married people do sleep together in winter-time. So I've been told. It's not a bad idee, Ruth."

Another long silence, which at length she broke in a strangled voice.

"Very well. . . . I—I will."

Then he let out a great exultant laugh.

"What's so—so funny about it?" she asked, resentfully.

Kalispel laid aside his poker and faced about with outward composure. He saw a very flushed and agitated girl.

"Kid, I never told you about my love-affairs, did I?"

"No. And I don't want to hear about them," she replied, achieving disdain.

"Wal, all right, then I won't bore you with details," he went on. "But I reckon I thought I was in love a lot of times. Queer thing! I had some fights, too, an' near got shot more'n once, an' shot. . . . Wal, never mind about them. . . . But when I met Sydney Blair I fell kerplunk. Gee! I was love-sick! I had luck, too, in that affair. Saved Sydney from Borden, an' again from drownin', an' along about then, after we got over to Thunder Mountain, when she got kinda sweet on me an' I kissed her that night——"

"Kal, I don't want to hear any more," cried Ruth with the red of her convulsed face changing to white. Her eyes darkened with a shade Kalispel could not endure to see there.

In one long stride he reached her, and lifting her out of her chair he kissed shut the pained eyes, and then her cheeks, and then her lips. After which he sat down in her chair and held her close and tight to his breast. About that time his secret, his humor, his tantalizing, his strange need to watch and wait and ponder the marvelous fact of his love all went into eclipse.

"Listen, Ruth. . . . I never was in love, not in those range days. That was just plain girl-hunger. I reckon I had a case on Sydney. Only that wasn't real love, either. She had me buffaloed. . . . But the night when Sloan lay dyin' an' you refused to say you'd marry me, *that* was when I lost my heart once an' forever. I didn't know till after. An' as soon as I did know, then it grew an' grew with all your sweet ways, an' your love of me, an' the fact that *you* were my girl, all the truer an' finer for the hell you'd been through. . . . An', Ruth, I wouldn't change you for Sydney Blair an' a dozen girls like her, if I could be a Mormon an' have them all. An' now that you're well an' happy, I wouldn't want it different. I don't know how to explain, but I know what I feel. . . . An' I love you just wonderful, with a savin' love that'll keep me straight an'——"

Soft lips on his ended Kalispel's revelation. Ruth threw her arms round his neck, and with closed eyes and rapt face held him tight.

"Oh, Kal! . . . Oh, Kal! How I have longed and

waited! . . . But all the time I knew it. *That* is what saved me—changed me—uplifted me—made me happy. . . . All the time I knew!"

"Wal, you wonderful girl!" he ejaculated, incredulously, and holding her as if he would never let her go, he watched the opal heart of the dying embers, his thoughts too deep and ecstatic for words.

Outside, the winter night-wind complained under the eaves; the branches of the cottonwood rustled on the roof; the river roared its melancholy song; and a wolf mourned his lonely and hungry state,—all of which sounds were of Kalispel's past; pregnant of the solitude and the wild, now gone with the hard days that were no more.